# Praise for *The Escape Game*

A fascinating read! In *The Escape Game*, ⬚⬚⬚⬚⬚⬚⬚⬚⬚ ⬚ cost of war, from harrowing conditions i⬚⬚⬚⬚⬚⬚⬚⬚ ⬚ Allied prisoner of war in Germany. The ⬚⬚⬚⬚⬚⬚⬚⬚ ⬚ methods of secretly sending escape kits ⬚⬚⬚⬚⬚⬚ ⬚⬚⬚⬚ even more interesting. Enjoy!

—Sarah Sundin, bestselling and Christy Award–winning author
of *The Sound of Light* and *Until Leaves Fall in Paris*

In *The Escape Game*, Marilyn Turk draws her readers into the perilous days of World War II, including carefully researched details that bring this fascinating era vibrantly to life. I was intrigued by the brilliant premise of this book, and I kept turning pages to see how it all unfolded for Beryl, Kenneth, and James. Turk infuses danger with hope, fear with faith, and stirs in the sweetness of a long-distance romance. Pour yourself a hot cup of tea and escape into *The Escape Game*!

—Laurel Blount, Carol Award–winning author of *Strength in the Storm*

In Turk's cleverly staged *The Escape Game*, the reader glimpses just some of the many behind-the-scenes plans to either undermine the enemy or help prisoners escape. A beautiful story of endurance and sacrificial love!

—Ruth Logan Herne, *USA Today* Bestselling author

*The Escape Game* is historical romance with characters the reader can't help but root for, Beryl and Kenneth, two brave souls thrust into war. A job well done by Marilyn Turk.

—Cynthia Hickey, author of Secrets of Misty Hollow series

Filled with spell-binding suspense, strong women, and fascinating history, *The Escape Game* will take the reader's imagination to a new level. Marilyn Turk captures tension during World War II England in a page-turning, thought-provoking, well-researched story you won't be able to put down. Cuddle up with this intriguing novel you'll not soon forget.

—Susan G Mathis, author of *Peyton's Promise*

I love stories set during WWII, I love stories built around true-life events, and I love stories with surprise endings. *The Escape Game* satisfied me on every level. With relatable characters and enough adventure to keep me turning pages, the story was a true delight from beginning to end.

—Kim Vogel Sawyer, author of *Still My Forever*

*The Escape Game* is a well-researched and fascinating look at WWII from the perspective of an American POW and a woman on the British home front. Marilyn Turk has paid special attention to the details that bring this wonderful story to life. Some of it is almost unbelievable but based in truth. The story grabbed me from the beginning and kept me on the edge of my seat all the way to the very satisfying end. Bravo to Marilyn for another wonderful book in a fantastic series.

–Liz Tolsma, *New York Times* bestselling author of
*What I Would Tell You* and *Picture of Hope*

*The Escape Game* by Marilyn Turk is a World War II story based on true events, but it is also a love story guided by faith and courage. The story centers around Beryl Clarke and her brother James, both English, and their American friend Kenneth Bordelon. While Beryl works in England trying to do her part for the war, she worries about her brother who is a pilot for the Royal Air Force. When she learns he and Kenneth are both prisoners in a German war camp, she wants to relay a secret to them that can help them escape. The story is compelling to the end. Impeccably researched and woven with a tight, gripping plot, this is a wonderful book for World War II buffs as well as romance readers everywhere. A good read!

–Lenora Worth, author of *The Memory Quilt*

If you like World War II stories with a strong dose of romance, you'll love *The Escape Game*. From the opening scene to the last turn of the page, Marilyn Turk takes her readers on a wild ride that will leave you breathless.

–Kathleen Y'barbo, *Publishers Weekly* bestselling author of
*Dog Days of Summer* and *The Black Midnight*

HEROINES OF WWII

# THE
# ESCAPE
# GAME

## MARILYN TURK

BARBOUR
PUBLISHING

*The Escape Game* ©2023 by Marilyn Turk

Print ISBN 978-1-63609-508-0
Adobe Digital Edition (.epub) 978-1-63609-509-7

All scripture quotations, unless otherwise noted, are taken from the King James Version of the Bible.

This book is a work of fiction. Names, characters, places, and incidents are either products of the author's imagination or used fictitiously. Any similarity to actual people, organizations, and/or events is purely coincidental.

Cover image © Mark Owen / Trevillion Images

Published by Barbour Publishing, Inc., 1810 Barbour Drive, Uhrichsville, Ohio 44683, www.barbourbooks.com

*Our mission is to inspire the world with the life-changing message of the Bible.*

ecpa Member of the
Evangelical Christian
Publishers Association

Printed in the United States of America.

# DEDICATION

"Then you will know the truth, and the truth will set you free."
JOHN 8:32 (NIV)

This book is dedicated to all the women and men who
have served their country both at home and on foreign soil.
Thank God for their courage and commitment to honor, protect,
and persevere, so that future generations can enjoy freedom.

# ⊵ PROLOGUE ⊴

*United States*
*Present Day*

Jillian picked up a piece of Bubble Wrap to cover the last of Grandma's treasures. Lifting the creamy ivory vase with the other hand, she admired the delicate pink roses and gilded edges. The vase was one of her favorites of her grandmother's possessions. It had come from England, just as Grandma had so many years ago after marrying Grandpa. Knowing how much Jillian loved the vase, Grandma had promised to leave it to her when she died. A pain pinched Jillian's heart at the thought. Grandma was closer to that day than ever, but Jillian couldn't bear the thought of life without her. However, Grandma Beryl would soon celebrate her one-hundredth birthday, the milestone of a lifetime. And even though she was in pretty good health for her age and her mind sharp as ever, Mother had insisted she move in with the family.

Jillian carefully wrapped the vase, securing the wrap with a piece of tape, then placed it in a box. She scanned Grandma's small apartment in the assisted living home, now stripped bare except for the bed and dresser. "I guess that's it."

Grandma's pale blue eyes followed her gaze and nodded. "All my worldly belongings are in those boxes."

Jillian sighed. "Are you sad to be leaving here, Grandma?"

Her grandmother shook her head, then smiled her sweet smile. With eyes that still twinkled, Grandma said, "Not at all. I'm looking forward to living with my family."

"We're looking forward to you being with us too, Grandma. Unfortunately, I'll be going back to college in a few weeks."

Grandma nodded. "That's important. I went to college once."

"You did? I didn't know that. Where? When?" Jillian tried to picture a younger version of her grandmother in a college setting.

"Oxford. But I didn't finish. The war interfered."

Grandma had never talked much about the war, and her mother said it was a painful subject for her, so Jillian didn't pursue the matter. As she studied her beloved grandmother's face, one that still revealed signs of her younger beauty, Jillian's attention was drawn to a necklace peeking out of her blouse. A charm hung from a strand of tiny pearls. Grandma had worn the necklace for as long as Jillian could remember and thought the race-car charm commemorated a special car her grandmother had owned.

Jillian pointed to her grandmother's neck. "Grandma, why do you always wear that necklace? Did you have a car like that?"

Grandma's translucent-skinned hand, its purple veins protruding, went to her neck and grasped the charm.

Smiling, Grandma shook her head. "Not like that one."

"It looks like an old-timey race car. Were you a racing fan?"

With a smile that made her eyes crinkle at the corners, Grandma said, "Not exactly. But this was a very special car. In fact, I think it's time I told you about it."

# ⧘ CHAPTER I ⧙

*Leeds, England*
*May 1941*

Air raid sirens wailed as Beryl jumped off her bicycle and rushed into the house. She jerked the blackout curtains closed and turned to look at her mother sitting on the couch. Mum clutched the picture of Dad with both hands, tears trickling down her cheeks. Beryl pushed aside her own grief once again. *God, please help me with her.*

"Mum! Come quickly! We must get to the shelter!"

Her mother slowly lifted her head, as if in a daze.

Beryl grabbed her by the arm and pulled. "Mum! We have to go now!"

Mum glanced at Beryl, then nodded and slowly rose from the couch, still holding the picture in one hand. Beryl grabbed her mother's knitting bag while holding on to her mother, then led her through the house toward the back garden where the Anderson shelter was.

As they hurried out of the house, Beryl's eyes searched the dark sky for planes. How far away were they? What would be hit tonight? The persistent wail of the air raid siren as it moved from a low to a high pitch every few seconds permeated the air as she helped Mum navigate the back steps and wished she could turn on the torch to guide them. They crept carefully around to the entrance of the shelter that was partially sunk into the ground and covered with earth, grass, and a few of Mum's flowers, alongside some potato and carrot plants her father had planted in their victory garden. Beryl handed her mother's knitting to her, then removed the steel shield that covered the opening. "Go ahead and step inside, Mum."

"I don't want to. I don't like it in there." Mum planted her feet.

Beryl didn't blame her mother for feeling that way. Who liked spending the night in a hole in the ground like a mole? But it was either here at home or one of the shelters under the buildings in town packed with strangers. At least they would be close to home whenever the all-clear sounded.

"Mum. Listen! Hear the siren? We must go inside the shelter before the bombs come." Beryl scanned overhead again, looking for signs of the enemy in the searchlights that roamed the sky. Mum glanced up as well, as if trying to verify Beryl's statement, then looked back at Beryl with worry.

"Remember how James and Dad worked so hard to make this shelter for us so we'd be safe?" Beryl listened for the drone of planes and the *ack-ack* of antiaircraft fire. "Now, be a dear and stoop down so you don't bump your head."

When Mum complied, Beryl gently guided her mother inside, holding on to her to keep her from falling as she stepped down into the shelter. Still wearing her air raid warden helmet and uniform, Beryl climbed in behind her mother before replacing the steel shield over the opening.

Dark and damp, the shelter smelled musty. Beryl's eyes adjusted as she and Mum crouched down to sit facing each other on the narrow cots, their knees touching. She groped for the battery-operated shelter lamp. As a precaution to keep any light from emitting from the shelter, she had placed a piece of black cloth over the door. Of all people, she was well aware of the danger, often reprimanding other people for not covering their windows at night as part of her duty. But they had to have some light in the shelter, plus it helped ease her mother's fears. She turned on the switch, then set it as far away from the door as possible in the confines of the six-foot-long shelter.

Mum placed Dad's photo beside her as she lifted the knitting and began clicking her needles, her only pastime since Dad died. At least she had something to busy herself, but Beryl worried about how isolated she'd become from her friends and neighbors.

She hoped all the people in town had made it to a shelter somewhere. Not everyone had a garden with one of these corrugated steel shelters or a Morrison shelter inside, so Beryl's job was to guide those people to the public shelters. And sadly, some people were too stubborn to go to shelters, taking their chances of being hit by a bomb. Unlike London where she served when the war started, Leeds had no tube tunnels where hundreds of people could gather. But there were some large shelters like the ones built in the town square. She might be in one of those now too, except for the fact that she had to get home to take care of Mum.

Her mother was still in the throes of depression and grief over the loss of Dad, killed only two months ago in the Nazis' biggest attack on Leeds. How unfair that Dad, a hero in the Great War, would be killed trying to help others despite his old injuries. When he volunteered to be one of the first air raid wardens in town, Beryl had been so proud of him for being so selfless in so many ways. She missed him terribly, missed hearing his jovial laugh and his praise for her, his "baby girl."

In fact, because of his example, Beryl too had become an air raid warden first in London when they allowed women to serve in that capacity, garnering praise from her father for "doing her duty." Beryl had always gone to her father for advice and support, and now that he was gone, a piece of her heart was missing as well as a piece of her whole life. The hated "nasties," as some of her friends called the Germans, had taken so much from her, and she could never forgive them for what they'd done to her family and her country.

The city was still reeling from the devastation of that Friday evening on March 14. Reports estimated forty German planes dropped bombs on Leeds, only a small percentage of the more than eight hundred that bombed the whole country that night. However, the disaster here was no less horrific. First, the planes dropped incendiary bombs, starting fires all over town. While the citizens were still putting out fires the next day, another wave of planes dropped high explosive bombs. The railway station, town hall, post office, museum, and Kirkgate Market were hit. The surrounding area of the town had also been hit, causing major damage to factories.

At least one hundred homes were destroyed, over four thousand damaged. And sixty-five people were killed, including her father.

Thankfully, Leeds had not been hit so badly since then; however, every time the sirens sounded, citizens hid in their shelters wondering when the bombs might fall next. Since that night, more people had taken the air raid warnings seriously, reinforced by the crumbled ruins that remained in town as a constant reminder of the danger. With Dad gone and her brother James off to war as a RAF pilot, Beryl was the only one left to care for Mum, a position she hadn't been prepared to take.

Every day, Beryl made sure Mum got out of bed, dressed, and ate breakfast before Beryl left for her secretarial job at the Waddingtons, a printing company that specialized in making playing cards and board games. Mum had changed so much since Dad died. Somehow, their roles had been switched as Beryl took over caring for her mum instead of her mum caring for her. The mum Beryl used to have was lively and always ready with a witty remark. But the stranger who'd taken her place was stuck in a melancholy that practically paralyzed her. Once very careful of her appearance, keeping her clothes ironed and hair styled, Mum didn't show any effort in how she looked now.

The ground shook as another bomb fell somewhere in the area. Beryl jerked her head toward the sound. She should be out there helping the other ARP wardens on duty. How many fires had started? Even though it wasn't her night for duty, she could do so much more outside than in this hole in the ground. But she couldn't abandon her mother.

How Beryl's life had changed. Just two years ago, she and James were at the university in Oxford, looking forward to bright futures. Studying had been her primary responsibility. But having fun was important too, like going to parties and meeting nice guys. One in particular stood out. A smile crossed her face at the memory of Kenneth Bordelon, the handsome American with that unique accent from Louisiana, his home in the States.

James, who shared a class with the American, had introduced them. Kenneth had a way of making her feel giddy inside, just by glancing at her with a twinkle in his eye. But when Germany attacked England, the days of flirting and parties were over as everyone scattered to perform their duties. James left university and joined the Royal Air Force, and Kenneth went back to the States. And now, here she was, working full-time, taking care of Mum, and being an air raid warden at night. During Beryl's duty shifts, Mum went to Mrs. Findlay's town house next door. The woman had been a godsend for helping out with Mum.

If only Beryl could find a way to get her mother back to her former self, independent and involved in the community, spending time with friends. But Mum wasn't the only one who suffered and grieved. All over the city, people mourned the loss of loved ones either from the bombings or in the military. The pall of death was a constant threat, and the crowded shelters and anticipated sound of sirens unnerved even the most stalwart.

In the shelter, Beryl began talking about her job at Waddingtons—anything to keep Mum from focusing on what was happening outside. She shuddered at the shadow of a spider on the wall of the shelter, trying not to dwell on how many creepy things lived alongside them. She kept up the jabbering about people she worked with, throwing in insignificant details about them, hoping to keep Mum from hearing the distant drone of planes. She wished they had the wireless radio in here with them but was afraid that whatever was on the radio would frighten Mum even more. Music would have been replaced by talk of war, either by one of the British leaders or the foreign voice of the hateful Lord Haw-Haw, the Nazi propaganda broadcaster.

"Oh, and there's a man at work who keeps asking me out." Not that Beryl was interested in dating anyone, but her mother had always been intent on her daughter finding a husband. In the past, Mum had tried to match her up with any male close to her age. Surely this topic would pique her mother's curiosity. "His name is Freddie, and he works in production. He's nice enough, I suppose."

Mum glanced up and looked at Beryl, as if she wanted to hear more. Beryl brushed dirt off the dark blue wool skirt of her warden uniform, finding a tear. "Oh dear. I wonder when that happened."

Mum glanced over. "I can mend that," she said, reminding Beryl of the government slogan to "make do and mend."

"I wish we had thread in here so you could fix it tonight. My next shift is in two days though, so you have time to mend it before then." Beryl made a mental note to bring a needle and thread to the shelter for future use.

At the sound of the *ack-ack* antiaircraft guns being fired, Mum jumped, dropping her knitting in her lap, her eyes wide with fear. She started trembling, so Beryl reached across and patted her on the knee.

"What are you making, Mum?" Beryl tried to distract her mother again. "A jumper for me?" She forced a smile to lighten the atmosphere.

Mum glanced down at the gray wool, a partially completed item between two knitting needles.

"Or maybe a nice cap for yourself?"

Mum shook her head. "Mrs. Hughes' baby."

"Mrs. Hughes? Did she have a baby?" Beryl wasn't certain if Mrs. Hughes was a neighbor or not but feigned interest to keep her mother talking.

Frowning, her mother picked up the knitting and studied it. "Not yet. It's for Mrs. Hughes' grandchild, her daughter Alice's baby."

"I see, and does Alice live with Mrs. Hughes?"

"Yes, Alice's husband is away with the army."

"So, what is it that you're making?" Talk of the army could put Mum in a funk too.

"A baby blanket." Mum held it up for Beryl to see. "It's rather drab, but I couldn't find any yarn in pretty colors."

Beryl opened her mouth to reply when a loud boom shook the ground. Mum screamed and tossed her knitting in the air. Beryl scooted over next to her and wrapped her arms around her mother. "It's all right, Mum. We're safe in here." She firmly believed what she said, having seen people in Anderson shelters survive very close bomb landings. She had to believe it for Mum's sake. "Dad built this shelter to be quite sturdy so we'd be protected." However, she couldn't vouch for anything outside the shelter.

Mum felt so weak and frail as she shuddered inside Beryl's arms. Where was the strong woman who used to be her mother? The ground shook slightly, indicating more bombs had fallen, but Beryl couldn't tell how close they were. In fact, they sounded as if they were getting farther away, or was she just hoping? Much as she wanted to get out of the shelter and go back into the house, Beryl knew she must practice what she told others, to stay sheltered until dawn or until the all-clear sounded. One never knew if the Germans were going to send another bombing attack during the same night. Not only that but the light of day would reveal the damage done. Sometimes the attacks left unexploded bombs in the ground, so it was safer just to stay in the shelter and wait until morning when the damage crews could assess the situation.

"Mum, remember what you taught me when I was a wee girl? You told me to recite a Bible verse from the Psalms, 'What time I am afraid,

I will trust in thee."

"Psalm 56:3." Mum quoted the reference automatically.

"That's right. It rhymes." Beryl took her mother's hands in hers. "Let's trust God to take care of us. Let's pray for everyone in the British Isles."

Mum looked from her hands to Beryl's face. "And James."

"Yes, and James." At the moment, they didn't know whether he was still in England or on missions over enemy country.

She and her mother held hands and prayed until there was no more noise outside. The night became quiet while they prayed first for themselves, then for James, then for their country, and then for peace in the world. At some point during the night, they both fell asleep.

# ⌘ CHAPTER 2 ⌘

*RAF Kirton in Lindsey Airfield, England*
*June 1941*

The familiar drone of aircraft engines filled the night air as Kenneth Bordelon and his squadron mates strode to their Spitfires waiting on the taxiway. He scanned the sky, disappointed to find the usual shroud of fog missing. A clear night was an open invitation for the Nazi bombers who would have better vision for their targets. Gray figures moved among the planes, tending to all the things trained ground crews do prior to flying a combat mission.

The staccato words of the briefing officers from the 71st Fighter Group raced through his mind as he adjusted the parachute harness on his back:

*"You'll be flying sweeps over northern France."*

*"German fighters have been active."*

*"You must outrun them before you run out of gas."*

*"Look for any enemy movement—trains, convoys, airfields. Hit them hard and fast and get out of there."*

*"Save some ammo in case you have to fight your way back across the channel."*

Although a veteran of dozens of sorties into German-occupied France, Kenneth's gut still clutched with fear as he paused in the shadow of his plane's wing to steel his nerves before stepping up into the cockpit. He would be leading his flight of three Spitfires on this morning's mission. The other pilots were depending on his experience and he on them for mutual support if they were to be successful. Looking up at the sky, he saw the stars, knowing they'd be gone by the time his mission was underway, a dangerous mission that required clear thinking on his part. Good thing he had quick reflexes after years of playing football and baseball. That plus his training had prepared him for the inevitable meeting with German fighter planes. And if his number was up, then he hoped he had the courage to accept his fate. Back home in Louisiana, he knew Mother would keep praying for him. She believed in that stuff, so it couldn't hurt. He needed all the luck he could get. A brief thought flickered through his mind that he had no one else, no girlfriend who would miss him if he were gone.

Only one girl had interested him enough, but when the Germans attacked England, romance went out the window as everyone left Oxford to go to war. A twinge of remorse hit him knowing he'd missed his chance to give Beryl a proper goodbye kiss. Wonder where she was now? Last he heard, her brother James was joining the RAF, and Kenneth hoped he might run into him sometime. But he hadn't yet. Wouldn't old James be surprised to learn that his American friend was also flying for the RAF? Yes, sir, a proud member of the volunteer Eagle Squadron, flying for England even though his country hadn't entered the combat yet.

Kenneth motioned to his wingmen parked on either side of him to climb into their cockpits and prepare for engine start. He checked his gear. His goggles sat on top of his leather helmet. His parachute attached to its harness was in place underneath him, his first aid kit attached, and his Mae West life preserver was on. He attached the oxygen hose to the plane's receptacle and fastened his oxygen mask to his helmet. After tugging his leather gauntlet gloves up, he gripped the stick with one hand, the other on the throttle.

Kenneth gave his wingmen the signal to start engines, and the planes whirred and sputtered to life. After a quick scan of the cockpit instruments and a check of his rudder and stick controls, Kenneth waited for his crew chief to give him a thumbs-up. He radioed "Ranger flight check" for a radio check from his flight mates and received a crisp "Toop" and "Threp" response in his headset. Hand signaling the crew chiefs to pull the chocks, they were cleared by ground control to taxi into position for takeoff.

Switching to tower control frequency, the three Spitfires in his flight taxied into position on the runway with Kenneth in the lead. Finally, the radio crackled the signal, and Kenneth released the brakes and pushed the throttle all the way forward. The engine roared to reach maximum acceleration, and gently pulling back on the stick, he lifted into the early dawn sky.

The three planes climbed. Within minutes, Ranger Two and Ranger Three had joined in formation, one on each side of him, about a hundred feet off his wingtips. Flying Ranger Two was Frank, the pilot from Texas. Ranger Three was Joe, the New Englander from Boston. They circled to the west of the airfield, then began joining in formation with other Eagle Squadron members. Kenneth swelled with pride at the sight of all twelve Americans in their RAF Spitfires lined abreast to deliver a blow to the Nazis. The four flights of three stayed together as long as they could for mutual support in case they encountered German fighters.

What seemed like only minutes after takeoff, the squadron was over the point where each flight was to split off from the group to head to their assigned destinations. Kenneth rocked his wings, signaling his wingmen that it was time to separate from the larger formation and follow him to their target area. As the sky lightened, the sun's early rays streaked across the English Channel below, exposing the brilliant white cliffs of Dover with the gleaming stone South Foreland Lighthouse perched on top while they winged their way to France. The scenery was beautiful and peaceful from up here in the sky, and war seemed far away. But the peace wouldn't last when they were spotted by the Luftwaffe, the German air force.

As they approached the coast of France, keeping radio silence, Kenneth waggled his rudder pedals, signaling Ranger Flight to spread out to about five hundred feet in a line abreast in their most offensive formation. They changed course again and headed east toward known military staging areas, flying over a patchwork of browns and greens of cultivated land and hedgerows. Straight ahead, Kenneth spotted the marshaling yard and what appeared to be a convoy of troops loading onto their trucks. Suddenly the first volley of enemy ground fire greeted them as tracers cracked past his cockpit. But he pressed the attack and squeezed the trigger to fire a salvo into the enemy convoy. Fire from Ranger Two and Ranger Three also ripped through the Nazi formation.

Pulling up to get lined up for reattack, Kenneth sighted enemy fighters. "We've got company, boys! 109s at three o'clock, slightly high."

The intercom crackled with Frank's voice. "They're turning on us!"

"I'll get them," Joe said, veering away with an enemy plane diving in on his tail.

They were still sixty miles west of their target.

The sky exploded with more weapon fire as the Spitfires dove and turned, soared, and evaded the German planes. Kenneth fired his guns while making a close pass at one of them. Another 109 swooped by, firing at him. He was pulling Gs and jinking his stick for all he was worth to avoid gunfire from the 109 on his tail. A noise like hail on a tin roof rattled the Spitfire as bullets peppered his plane. Smoke began streaming from his engine.

Kenneth scanned the sky, looking for the other two Spitfires. With horror, he watched Frank's plane take a hit and spiral downward. "Bail out! Bail out!" he shouted through the radio, his gut clenching as he searched for signs of a parachute, proving his friend made it out.

Joe was engaged with one of the remaining Messerschmitts and let go a burst that hit the enemy plane. A cloud of black smoke emerged from the plane. "Got one!" shouted Joe.

"I'm hit. Heading back," Kenneth said as his plane shuddered from the damage it had gotten.

"I'll cover you," Joe said.

Kenneth turned his plane toward the channel. Maybe if he could make it that far, he could bail out and be lucky enough to be picked up by friendly rescuers.

Time was suspended. Everything seemed to move in slow motion.

The shimmering water of the channel rippled ahead as he began to lose altitude. No time to jump now. His only choice was to ditch in the channel. He just hoped his years as a lifeguard would serve him well out there.

He pulled the throttle to idle and lowered the flaps to slow down as much as possible. Gripping the stick, he pulled back to stall the aircraft and drag the tail over the water before the nose fell as the water came closer. Kenneth braced for impact as the Spitfire hit with a tremendous splash, skidding to a halt. He only had minutes to get out before the plane sank. He jerked on the canopy hatch, but nothing happened. Maybe he should have tried to open it before the plane hit the water, but he didn't have time. The thing was supposed to slide to the rear, but it didn't, so he beat on it as hard as he could. Finally, with both hands on the latch, he pulled with all his strength, and the canopy slid back over his head.

He jerked off his oxygen mask and tossed it out of the way. Next, he hit the quick-release latch on his harness to free himself of the parachute, a sure anchor if he couldn't get rid of it. He managed to push out the pilot's door on his left-hand side just as frigid water began to rush into the cockpit. He climbed out as quickly as he could, pulling the release valves of his life vest, allowing it to inflate. He swam away from the plane before the channel water could suck him under. A growing ring of gasoline widened, and Kenneth swam farther away to avoid it, spitting out salty water. As the tail section of the plane disappeared under the water, Kenneth looked around for signs of rescue. But no one was in sight, not even a lonely fisherman. Overhead, he heard the sound of Spitfires heading home. He waved, hoping they would see him and let the base know he was still alive.

The cold water heightened his senses more than a strong cup of coffee would. He felt his body, checking for injuries. Either he didn't have any or was too numb to feel pain. How far was he from shore? Could he swim that far? The weight of his uniform and boots would make swimming difficult, but dare he take them off and put himself at greater risk of hypothermia? In the preflight briefing, the weatherman said that the channel's average temperature in June was around fifty-five degrees. Based on that fact, he would only have consciousness between two and six hours. He sure hoped he didn't have to test that prediction.

Treading water, he scanned the horizon, searching for a boat to rescue him. Good thing he could float. He thought of his childhood pal Billy who couldn't float no matter how hard he tried, sinking like a rock if he wasn't wearing a life preserver. Kenneth continued treading, watching the sun move across the sky. Pushing up his sleeve to see his watch, he saw that at least two hours had passed already since takeoff, although he didn't know exactly what time he landed in the water. His mind moved on to other things to think about—childhood memories, school, and his little brother, Kevin. *Wonder what Kevin would say now if he were still alive? Would he laugh at seeing his hero in such a predicament?* Funny what you think about when you wonder if your life is about to end.

If Dad were still alive, would he be proud of his son or think him foolhardy? A veteran of the last war, Dad had wanted nothing to do with another one. Kenneth's thoughts traveled back to his time at Oxford. What fun times he'd had there. He'd made lots of friends, but James had been his closest in recent history. It sure was nice of James to introduce Kenneth to his pretty little sister, Beryl. She was different, not your typical flirty college girl like the others he'd met on campus. No, she was a smart cookie, one he'd have liked to have known better.

Something splashed near him, bringing him back to the present. Were there sharks in the channel? If there was, he hated to find out the hard way. At least there weren't any gators like back home. However, at this point, he wasn't sure which he would prefer.

Why exactly was he here anyway, treading water between England and France? Not because he'd been forced into service. No, he had to be one of those daring adventurers who chose to fight for England because he wanted to. After living there for several years, England was like his second home, and the people were his friends. Somebody had to stop Hitler from destroying everything. And Roosevelt didn't seem to think Hitler was a threat to the United States. It still boiled his blood to think of his own country sitting on its hands while Europe was taken over by a power-hungry maniac. Besides, Kenneth had to admit his motives weren't all noble. He liked the thrill of adventure. Flying Spitfires was fun, even more exciting than riding his motorcycle. However, this kind of adventure was not the kind he'd imagined.

Kenneth's legs were numb from the cold water, and his movement slowed. How much longer could he keep this up before hypothermia took over? The sun's glare glinted off something in the distance, and as he focused on it, he saw a boat coming toward him. His pulse quickened with excitement of being rescued. But as the boat drew closer, he saw the black swastika on the boat's hull and flag. Germans. Guess it was too much to ask to be rescued by an ally. He began rehearsing the standard response he was supposed to give when captured. That is, if they gave him a chance to talk instead of shooting him on sight.

As the boat slowed to a stop near him, he recognized it as a German minesweeper. Someone shouted through a megaphone in German. Kenneth didn't know what he said but guessed. He held his hands up as if in surrender, his mind racing through air force protocol about being a prisoner of war. A ring buoy was thrown near him, and he grabbed hold as they pulled it back to the boat beside the ladder they'd tossed over the side. With his last ounce of strength, he grabbed the ladder and tried to pull himself up while rifles were trained down at him. A Nazi naval officer dressed in a blue, double-breasted wool coat with brass anchor buttons nodded to Kenneth and the men, and they leaned over to help him.

Although they'd been told not to wear the Eagle Squadron patch showing their American origins during combat, Kenneth had stubbornly refused to obey the order because he was so proud of his squadron. Now he would really be in trouble for allowing the enemy to identify him. As he tested his legs on deck, shivering from cold, his teeth chattering, he thought he might pass out. He glanced at the officer in charge.

"May I have a blanket, please?" Kenneth said, using his arms to show what he meant.

The officer nodded and spoke to one of the men in German who scurried away, then returned soon with a blanket, throwing it over Kenneth's shoulders. "Thank you," he said, making eye contact with the tall blond officer. Now, if he just had a cup of coffee, he might survive. Why not? "Coffee?" He pantomimed drinking from a cup.

"You are American," the German officer said.

"How did you guess?" Kenneth said.

"The English do not ask for coffee."

"You speak good English," Kenneth ventured.

"I lived in the United States until der Füehrer asked us to come home."

"So, what happens next?" Would they line him up against a wall and shoot him?

"You will be fine. You will go to a POW camp."

The officer made it sound like Kenneth was going to summer camp and shouldn't be concerned. Kenneth sure hoped they observed the rules of the Geneva Convention for the short time he planned to stay.

———— ≈ ————

When the boat docked, Kenneth glanced around, trying to determine where they were. His guess was the French harbor town of Boulogne, at the mouth of the Liane River. The odor of fish hit him as they neared the docks, and he glanced down the shoreline at fishing boats tied up. Poor suckers. How could they fish with all these Germans, not to mention mines, in the way? From the boat, he was escorted along the dock by gun-toting Nazis in khaki uniforms to a waiting truck and forced to climb into the canvas-covered rear.

Boy, did he want to get out of these wet clothes. Would they give him some dry ones? Surely they wouldn't give him Nazi clothes. The truck traveled to a stop in front of a tan stucco building with carved ornate pediments over the door. The building looked like it had been a former government building for the French before the Nazis took it over. Here he was forced to exit the truck before being marshaled into the place. Inside he was taken to a windowless room where barking guards ordered him to strip down to his wet long johns before they shoved him around and searched him. He frowned as his navigator's watch and black onyx ring were taken from him. But he hated it even more when they took the ivory-handled pocketknife he always carried that had belonged to his grandfather.

For the next half hour, he sat on a cold metal chair while a German officer interrogated him. At one point, the officer showed him the eagle patch on his uniform, asking about it in German. Kenneth shrugged and repeated the necessary information. "In accordance with the Geneva Convention, I am required to give only name, rank, and service number."

Would he get any of his things back? If they followed the rules of the convention, he was supposed to. Right now he wanted his clothes. Would they let him have them again? And if they did, would they still be wet? Maybe he could request the use of the laundry. He suppressed a chuckle but failed to stifle a smile. His interrogator kicked him in the shin. Kenneth grimaced. The guy had no sense of humor.

When the interrogator got tired of getting no more information, Kenneth was taken out of the room where he was handed his damp uniform. His captors gave him a minute to put it back on, then shoved him back outside and onto another truck, which contained three other prisoners. When the guard riding in back with him looked the other way, Kenneth reached into the leg pocket of his flight suit. Yep, they'd taken his compass too.

The truck bumped over an uneven road while Kenneth tried to figure out what direction he was going. Although the canvas canopy over the bed of the truck hid the sun, he guessed from the angle of the light and shadow that they were headed east. He recalled the code of conduct the RAF had drilled into him during basic training, that as a member of the air force, he was expected to escape if captured and assist others trying to escape as well. Now he had to find the opportunity to do so.

When the truck stopped again, Kenneth was able to look below the canopy and see what appeared to be a town square. Racking his brain to remember the French map they'd studied before their flights and assuming they'd started in Boulogne, this must be Calais. Nazi soldiers appeared to be the only residents. Bet the locals weren't too happy about their new neighbors.

The aroma of baking bread wafted through the air, and his stomach growled, reminding him of how long it'd been since his last meal. As he glanced outside, the guards pushed two more captives toward the truck. From the looks of these guys, their interrogation wasn't as easy as his. One had a swollen right eye and the other a cut on the lip and bruised cheek. Now would not be a good time to try to escape.

Before the truck started moving again, a black Mercedes limousine pulled up behind them. A couple of higher-ranking Nazis stepped out of the car. Another truck pulling a trailer stopped behind the Mercedes. The prisoners were ordered out and marched to the trailer. On the trailer lay the scorched remains of a Spitfire. Whose plane? Which group? One of the German officers dangled two charred dog tags in front of him. "Your friend?"

Kenneth recognized Frank's name and bit back revulsion. His gut tightened at the sight, but he wouldn't let the Nazi know he knew the owner of the tags. He owed that much to Frank. The officer snapped them in his hand and dropped them into his pocket. Kenneth wanted to punch him, but he thought instead of Frank's wife, Beth, and how devoted he was to her. Maybe someday, Kenneth could go see her and tell her what a swell guy Frank was. First, he had to get back to England somehow.

The men were ordered back into the truck, and it proceeded on its bumpy journey. Kenneth wanted to talk to the other prisoners, but the guard's presence kept all of them quiet. The other flight suits were unfamiliar, but they could have been RAF too, since there weren't many regulation uniforms among the pilots. Some wore overalls, others leather jackets over their standard military shirts and trousers. He also wouldn't know them because he was at an airfield with only Brits and Americans.

They could have been from other Commonwealth countries.

At the next stop, the truck took on more prisoners until they were wedged in tight on each side. Some of the men had visible injuries, some limped, at least one had a broken arm, and a few had burns. Kenneth hoped their captors had enough humanity to treat the injured. As the day dragged on, his hunger and thirst became almost unbearable, but he kept swallowing to keep his mouth from being dry. Since he was one of the lucky ones with no injuries, he figured he could tolerate being hungry and thirsty. He sure had no reason to feel sorry for himself. Why he had been so lucky to survive without injuries, he had no idea.

# ⫤ CHAPTER 3 ⫤

*Leeds, England*
*June 1941*

"Mum, I spoke to Mrs. Findlay. She's coming by to collect you and take you to the knitting circle at church," Beryl said as she entered the kitchen.

Stirring her porridge absentmindedly, Mum looked up. "I can knit here."

"Yes, I know you can, but Mrs. Findlay wants you to see what the other ladies are making for the war effort." Actually, the idea was all Beryl's, but she thought it would sound better if it were Mrs. Findlay's idea. Whatever it took to get Mum out of the house was more important. If only Mrs. Findlay would hurry up and get here before Beryl had to leave for work so she could be sure her plan was carried out.

"Here. Mrs. Sutton brought over some of her good raspberry jam." Beryl handed Mum a piece of toast slathered with her favorite jam, ignoring the government command to be more thrifty with food. Mum took the toast and bit into it while Beryl waited for her usual response, the moaning over its good taste like she used to, but Mum didn't respond. However, she did eat the toast, which was one thing to celebrate. Mum barely ate anything anymore, and her loose clothes looked like they belonged to someone else, someone larger like she used to be. Beryl poured more hot tea into Mum's cup, then checked the time. Where was Mrs. Findlay?

Taking her dirty dishes to the sink, Beryl washed them and put them on the drain mat to dry. *Come on!* she thought as loudly as she could, hoping she could silently hurry Mrs. Findlay.

"Hellooo," Edith Findlay's voice greeted as she came through the front door. The busty woman appeared in the kitchen, her purse over her arm and her hat pinned securely over her brownish-gray curls. She smiled at Mum. "Are you ready, Sheila?"

"I'll get her things," Beryl said, hurrying to retrieve Mum's hat, purse, and knitting bag. She handed them to her mother and helped pin on her hat.

Mrs. Findlay took Mum by the arm. "Come on, luv. The ladies are waiting, and they'll be very pleased to see you!" She turned toward Beryl. "You go on to work, dearie. We'll take good care of her, I promise!"

Beryl offered a smile. "Thank you."

Mrs. Findlay laid a hand on Beryl's shoulder. "Glad to help, Beryl. You've got too much on your shoulders already."

Beryl glanced at Mum's face. She looked resigned to comply and didn't protest as Mrs. Findlay led her out the door. Did Mrs. Findlay's comment bother her mother? After all, part of Beryl's extra work was taking care of Mum. She loved her Mum and wanted to help her, but Beryl didn't feel qualified to be a parent yet. After all, she was only twenty-two years old, for pity's sake. How she wished Mum would get back to being her old self.

Exhaling a sigh, she gathered her things for work. She closed up the house and hopped on her bike, throwing her lunch box and gas mask into the basket for the three-mile ride to Waddingtons. Much as she wanted to take a different route, that option took longer, and she didn't have time. She'd have to pass by some of the places that had been bombed, a constant reminder of the pervading tragedies they had all suffered. As she approached the dreaded area, she steeled herself, gripping the handlebars. Just ahead stood half a building. The building was a semi-attached house, which meant the missing part had housed a family. A family that had all been killed in the March bombing raids.

The adjacent house had broken windows with curtains blowing out and a flower bed in front where pretty blue forget-me-nots bloomed. The irony of the lovely flowers in such a dismal setting made her shake her head in disbelief. Just like her, those flowers continued to live as if nothing tragic had happened so close by. Those who survived had to continue, had to live despite the trauma, or the enemy would have truly won.

She rode around a large crater in the road, which men were working to refill. With a shudder, she remembered the horror of the night when a bomb blew open the road, a tragedy made even greater when an ambulance had fallen into the hole moments later, killing the driver. Near the construction area, a mobile canteen run by the Women's Voluntary Service was parked, and a line of people waited to buy tea and sandwiches. Mum had expressed interest in serving with the WVS at one point, before Dad was killed. Now, she didn't want to leave the house. At least she was helping by knitting. The Home Offense had asked all knitters to help supply socks and sweaters to the soldiers, as well as items for the refugees who had left the more heavily bombed places in Britain.

Thousands of people from the southern part of the country had streamed into Yorkshire seeking safety and a roof over their heads. Townspeople had been asked to billet the refugees. Some of the locals had sympathized with their plight while others balked at the idea of strangers in their homes. Beryl would have offered room in their home, but she didn't think it would be a good idea to bring in a stranger while Mum was in her present state of mind. If Mum were her old self, she would have readily agreed.

Most of Yorkshire had been spared the frequent bombings that cities like London, Birmingham, Coventry, and Liverpool had endured, but there was no guarantee they wouldn't still be hit. Practically every town in the country had a factory that changed its production to provide war materials. Leeds had a few as well but not as many. And although their town hadn't been hit as hard or as often, the planes could be heard passing over on their way to their targets. In fact, even a tractor factory in the Dales had been bombed. How unthinkable that someone would bomb that lovely area. When would the war end? It had already been going on close to two years. Would England ever be the same again?

Ahead, a man waved a flag. "Careful, miss. Keep your distance. Unexploded bomb over there." Every time the bombs fell, some didn't explode, waiting like wild animals ready to pounce on an unfortunate person who happened upon them. The Sappers, the Corps of Royal Engineers, stayed busy searching for these bombs, hoping to find them first and disarm them. Beryl kept a wide berth of the area, her bicycle bouncing over uneven earth and pavement.

Past the site, she glanced up at the clear blue sky dotted with big silver barrage balloons. Just how effective were those things? They looked like blimps, about sixty feet long with three fins on the back. The RAF was convinced they interfered with enemy planes, keeping the planes from flying too low, making it difficult for them to hit their targets while at the same time making it easier for the antiaircraft guns to hit them. But other folks argued that when the balloons were placed over important places like factories, they served as targets to show the enemy where to drop their bombs.

It was true that if a plane flew too low and hit one of the cables supporting the balloons, the plane would tear apart and crash. But the hydrogen-filled balloons could explode too, another danger to civilians, and required special handling. And now women in the Women's Auxiliary Air Force were being trained to operate the balloons. Beryl had considered joining the WAAF as well, like some of her school chums had done. But doing so would require her to leave Mum alone for longer periods of time while she trained. And she just couldn't do that now.

Beryl arrived at Waddingtons, three-story red brick building and parked her bike. As she entered the front door, red-haired Margaret Dewberry called out from behind her desk in the reception area. "Mr. Watson is looking for you. Better get to your desk hastily."

What now? She felt like she'd been trying to get to work all morning, but would Mr. Watson care to hear her saga? She hurriedly removed her hat and gloves, placing them on the table behind her small desk, then picked up a tablet of paper and a pencil and knocked on her employer's closed door.

"Who is it?" Mr. Watson's gruff voice demanded on the other side.

"It's Beryl Clarke, Mr. Watson."

"Come in."

She took a deep breath, then opened the door and entered. Mr. Watson, his silver hair combed straight back as usual, sat in a padded leather chair behind his wide walnut desk. Behind him was a credenza and a multipaned, arched window that overlooked the factory. He pointed to the chair in front of the desk.

"You're late."

She remained standing and glanced at the clock. Nine o'clock. Technically, she wasn't late, but since she was normally early, he apparently expected her earlier.

"Yes, sir. I'm sorry. I had to detour around bomb damage."

He huffed, peering down at his desk. "Was it bad?"

"It was old damage, sir, farther out Wakefield Drive. They're repairing the blown-up street."

A grunt. "Yes, well, we must allow for those things, mustn't we?"

She opened her mouth to answer, but he continued, his mood much more serious than normal.

"I have special guests coming today. You are not to interrupt, and make sure no one else is allowed to come in while they are here." Mr. Watson tapped the cigar lying in the ashtray before him, its smoke curling up between them.

"Yes, sir. And how will I know who they are?"

He stared at her as if he doubted her intelligence. "You will know when I tell you. Do you understand?" Why was the man acting so strangely?

"Yes, sir. You will not need me to take notes?"

"No. I will take my own notes."

He would? How unusual. She didn't know he was capable, as she wrote all his correspondence for him. What kind of guests was he expecting?

"I see, sir. And tea?"

"Right. You bring us tea, then close the door behind you." He glanced up at her. "That is all for now."

She nodded, then retreated to her own desk. As she readied her desk to work on her daily tasks, she tried to figure out who might be coming to see Mr. Watson. Was he in some type of trouble? The phone on her desk rang.

"Beryl Clarke, Mr. Watson's secretary."

"Beryl, it's Mr. Watson. I'll take some tea now."

She frowned. "Yes, sir." Sometimes the menial tasks of her job were such a bore. Would she have had to make tea if she'd been able to finish at university? She hoped not.

After delivering Mr. Watson's tea to him, she settled into her daily routine of typing and filing. For the next two hours, she became engrossed in her duties and did not notice the two men who approached her desk until one of them cleared his throat. Startled, she looked up.

The men wore long black overcoats and hats pulled low over their brows. Neither of them smiled. She felt her cheeks flush at her lack of attention.

"May I help you, gentlemen?"

The vein in one man's neck bulged as he spoke. "We're here to see Mr. Watson."

Realization hit her. These were the special guests he was expecting. She picked up her phone and dialed him. "Mr. Watson, your guests are here."

"I'll be right there."

How unusual. Normally it was her job to escort visitors into his office. She stood. "He's coming to fetch you."

The man nodded as Mr. Watson's door opened and her employer stepped out, hand extended. The men shook his hand, then walked into his office. Before closing the door, Mr. Watson glanced at Beryl. "You remember our conversation."

"Yes, sir. I'll get the tea right away."

He closed the door, and she hurried to gather the teapot from the hot plate, along with cups, saucers, spoons, sugar cubes, and milk. She put them all on the tray and balanced it carefully as she knocked on the door.

"Come in."

She carried the tray inside and placed it on the credenza behind Mr. Watson's desk, then lifted a cup and glanced at the men. The heavier man said, "Two sugars for me."

"Just cream for me," said the man with the sharp features.

She prepared their tea, then refilled Mr. Watson's cup before handing it to him.

One of the company's Monopoly games sat on the desk in front of Mr. Watson as if he was about to explain the game to his guests.

"That will be all," Mr. Watson said, his forehead pinched as he looked at her.

She nodded and hurried out.

Those men seemed far too serious to be interested in playing a board game.

At lunch Beryl took her lunch box and sat at one of the benches outside. Margaret came out of the building and hurried over to sit next to Beryl.

"So, who were those mysterious men who came to see Mr. Watson today?"

Beryl unwrapped her jam sandwich and took a bite, shrugging. "I have no idea. They didn't give any company name."

"Freddie thinks they're with the government, maybe working for Churchill."

Beryl rolled her eyes. "Freddie would. He's suspicious of everyone and everything."

"Well, how do you know they weren't?"

"What would British Intelligence want with Mr. Watson, a toy maker? If they want him to be a spy, who is he going to spy on? His employees?"

"What if they think there's a spy working here at Waddingtons?"

"But who? I mean, we're all locals." Beryl had known most of the people who worked at Waddingtons for years before she ever worked there herself.

"You know, we do have a couple of evacuees that work here."

Beryl considered a moment. "Mrs. Stout and Mr. Bridges? Why, the woman only cleans the place, and Mr. Bridges is too old to be a spy."

Margaret leaned in and lowered her voice. "What if it's just an act? Maybe they're just pretending to be who they are, but they're really Nazi spies!"

"Don't be daft, Margaret. Do you really believe that? That's sheer nonsense, and you don't need to be spreading any rumors and getting things stirred up. Poor people, they've had enough to deal with, losing their homes and everything in Birmingham."

"I guess you're right." Margaret bit off a piece of biscuit, then glanced around. "Don't look now, but Freddie's coming this way, and he's got you in his sights."

Beryl cringed. Freddie wouldn't leave her alone. Every chance he got, he sidled up to her and suggested they go on out on a date. He wasn't a bad sort, just not her cup of tea. Besides, even if he were, she didn't have time.

The pale-skinned, slight young man stopped in front of her. He sucked in a puff from his cigarette, then blew out a cloud of smoke in her direction. "Beryl! It's so good to see you today!"

She averted her face and waved the smoke away, never fond of the habit. Freddie looked ridiculous toting the thing around, puffing like a steam engine, but she had a feeling he thought it made him look mature.

"Hello, Freddie. How are you today?"

He pushed up his wire-rim glasses. "Splendid!" he replied, then drew in another drag of his cigarette.

"And how are things in the playing cards area?" she asked, referring to the section of the factory where he worked.

"Quite exciting, you know, what with all that royalty in there." He laughed in a rather snorting fashion at his effort to be humorous.

"Lots of queens and kings, I suppose," she replied with her usual response to his ongoing joke.

"And jacks. Don't forget the jacks. You know they're the princes."

"I didn't know that. I always thought of them as palace guards."

"Why, what a clever idea! You are quite the smart one, Beryl!"

Beryl checked her watch. "Better get back to work. Mr. Watson will be very unhappy if I'm late." She grabbed her lunch box and stood, then turned back toward the building. "See you later, Margaret," she said.

Margaret smiled and gave a slight wave of her hand. Freddie fell in step alongside Beryl. "I hear Mr. Watson had some secret guests today."

"He had guests, that's correct, and no, I don't know who they were. They didn't speak to me."

"I think they're with the government intelligence agency."

Beryl stopped and looked him square in the eye. "Freddie, don't go around spreading rumors. You don't have any idea who those men were, and you could imagine all kinds of things, but none of them will do you any good. You need to just let it be. Remember what Mr. Churchill said: 'Careless talk costs lives.'"

Freddie's gaze fell to the ground, and he paused. "All right, if you say so."

She proceeded to walk back to the building, thinking she'd been able to disengage herself from Freddie, when he caught up with her. "Say, Beryl, there's a new picture at the cinema. What say we go see it together?" He reminded her of a carefree puppy who never gave up following its master and wagging its tail in the process.

"Freddie, that's very sweet of you to ask, but you know I have too much to do, what with both my jobs and my mum to care for. I'm sure one of the other girls here would like to go with you, though. Have you thought of asking Helen?"

"No, maybe I will. You know I like you better." He inclined his head and winked. "So, if you should have some extra time, just let me know, all right?"

"Of course, Freddie." She pulled open the door to the building and went inside. Extra time would not be in her future anytime soon.

# ⋛ CHAPTER 4 ⋚

*Somewhere in France*
*June 1941*

As night approached, Kenneth heard the familiar drone of planes overhead. RAF bombers headed to targets in France. And where was he now? France. What if he ended up getting bombed by the good guys? Wouldn't that be ironic? Would that be the end of him? He considered jumping out of the truck but knew he'd be shot instantly. Besides, now the adrenaline he'd survived on so far had worn off and fatigue was setting in, but sleep was out of the question. The fact that he was a prisoner of war, a POW of the Third Reich, finally registered. And so were all these men in the truck with him. He'd learned that some were British, and some, based on the insignia on their uniforms, were Polish pilots that flew for the RAF. Darn good pilots, from what he'd heard, and quite motivated to join forces with England after Germany overran their country.

Kenneth didn't know exactly where he and his fellow prisoners were now, but he knew they were headed for a Nazi prison camp somewhere, probably someplace in Germany, and that was one place he had no intention of staying. His military training had taught him that there was a better chance of escaping before they reached their final destination. Chances were the other prisoners were thinking the same thing. But how could they escape? Overpower the guards? Take their weapons and run for it?

He didn't even know how many guards there were, but they were probably outnumbered. They were deep inside German-occupied France by now and miles from non-Nazi-held lines. Just yesterday he'd flown a mission over enemy territory, picked up a little flak, then returned back to a clean bunk in a warm hut with decent food. He should have appreciated that small luxury when he had it.

Hours passed before the truck stopped again, this time in front of a sprawling stone building. Other trucks stopped behind theirs, and prisoners began emptying from them. Walking toward the building, Kenneth and his fellow prisoners straightened their aching backs and stretched their legs, tolerating their injuries to march with some semblance of soldiers. Inside, the prisoners were counted and recounted before being led to a mess hall where long tables ran the length of the room. After all the prisoners shuffled in and made their way to the benches beside the tables, a Nazi officer flanked by two other uniformed men took his position in front of the room, hands behind his back in a parade rest position.

"You are at Dulag Luft. We are the reception camp for air force prisoners. I am Commandant Major Rumpel," he said in amazingly good English. "Here you will stay a short while before you reach your final camp. We will have the opportunity to speak to each of you privately and get to know each other." He scanned the group of prisoners and affected a smile. "We abide by the rules of the Geneva Convention and will treat you well." He paused, his expression darkening. "That is, as long as you behave like the gentlemen I'm sure you are." His smile returned. "Enjoy your meal and relax. We will call for you afterward." He nodded and snapped his heels together before marching away.

Finally, food appeared in the form of a bowl of thin potato soup and a small piece of black bread. It wasn't much, but after a day without anything, the food tasted like a gourmet delicacy. Just that little bit of sustenance served to restore Kenneth's strength and hope of survival. He glanced at the men sitting around him, then muttered under his breath. "Can't wait to get to know the commandant, can you?"

A low chuckle came from the other prisoners within hearing distance.

Nazi soldiers lined the room, eyeing the prisoners' every move. As soon as they were finished eating, the prisoners were marched out of that building and into one of the other two long wooden barracks in the camp. This one had plain bunk beds lined up against each wall. Most of the men found a bed and lay down on it, exhausted from their ordeal. But their hosts had no intention of letting them get much rest as, one by one, the men were taken out and interrogated. Kenneth walked throughout the barracks, looking at windows and checking to see if they could be opened. He wasn't sure where this place was, nor what the countryside was like around it, but he was willing to find out if he got an opportunity. His search gave him no clues or ideas about getting out, and guards stood beside the doors.

When they came to get him for interrogation, the commandant was waiting in a small room with two wooden chairs. "Have a seat." The commandant motioned to the chair. "So, you are American?"

Kenneth considered standing in defiance, but reluctantly obliged. He sat and responded. "Kenneth Bordelon, lieutenant, 81727."

"But that is a British number, and I can tell you are not British. You are one of the Americans called the Royal Eagle Squadron. How does America feel about you participating in a war they have not joined?"

The man was working hard to get answers, but Kenneth wasn't planning to help him.

He repeated his name, rank, and serial number.

The commandant sat in the opposite chair and crossed one leg over his knee, affecting a casual position. "Now, Lieutenant Bordelon, we are fellow officers, fellow pilots, are we not? You must be very frustrated that you cannot fly for the United States."

"The United States is not at war," Kenneth said.

Commandant Rumpel smiled. "They are not? What about the Lend-Lease measure your country passed? Are they not supplying England?"

Kenneth let that comment pass without responding.

"Those Spitfires are pretty good planes, yes? Not a match for our Messerschmitt 109s, of course."

Kenneth glanced at him and decided to use a conversation tactic of his own. "Since you're a pilot too, you must have you flown both planes, so you can tell the difference."

The commandant smiled and stroked his chin. "Ah. I must admit I have not flown the Spitfire. However, based on the number we have shot down, I can tell our planes are superior."

"I personally like the Spitfire."

"It does not float well, though, does it, Lieutenant?" the man said with a smirk.

So the man knew he had ditched in the channel. "Not very. But then, it wasn't built to be a boat."

The commandant chuckled. "Perhaps you should have joined the navy, yes?"

"No, sir. I prefer flying."

"It's too bad you won't be flying for quite some time now."

Kenneth wanted to tell the man he wasn't finished flying and that as soon as he got a chance, he'd be back up there shooting down the 109s again. He changed the subject.

"Your English is almost as good as mine, Major Rumpel. Did you ever live in the States?" Two could play the interrogation game.

Smiling, the man studied him a minute before answering. "You are very observant. Yes, I lived in New Jersey."

"I didn't notice a New Jersey accent."

"And you, Lieutenant, what state are you from?"

"Hard to say, since I've lived all over."

"I see." The commandant stood. "Our time here is finished. You will be sent to Stalag Luft I where the other captured pilots are for now. We don't have many American companions for you yet, but I'm sure there will be some more soon."

Kenneth stood. The interrogation had gone easier than he'd expected. He'd noticed that some prisoners were treated worse than others, shoved around and disrespected. However, he had heard that POWs who were airmen were treated better than other prisoners. Maybe there was some unwritten code of respect between Luftwaffe pilots and their adversary counterparts. Good thing he was a pilot.

He was sent back to the barracks and tried to sleep while other prisoners were taken out at all hours of the night. Every time the door opened and he heard the footsteps of the guard, he wondered if he might be called back again and interrogated another time less politely. But somehow he managed to get a few winks before a German voice shouted for everyone to get up and form a line. It was barely dawn as they were forced to stand outside and be counted before being marched back to the mess hall.

For breakfast they were given some kind of hot gruel and another piece of black bread before being loaded onto trucks again. Kenneth was working on a plan to escape the truck by overpowering the guard sitting in the back with the prisoners when the trucks stopped again. They were ordered to get out, and he found that they were at a railroad station. Here they were forced onto a train and crowded into small passenger compartments. The train rumbled along the tracks for at least an hour before stopping. Peering through the small window, Kenneth determined they were in a rail yard. The German soldiers locked them inside the train and left. When a few minutes had passed, Kenneth and a few other men ran to the doors and tried to open them, but it was no use.

The men exchanged questioning glances. Why would the Germans leave the train like that? Was this a test to see if anyone would try to escape so they had an excuse to shoot them? Then he heard it—the hum of planes overhead. The train was a sitting duck, a perfect target for fighters flown by the same people he was trying to help. The knowing look on the other prisoners' faces conveyed the same understanding as they waited for the bombs to fall and wipe them out. But once again luck was on his side as the planes flew on to other targets. While they waited for their captors' return, one of the prisoners, a little guy, managed to squeeze through a small bathroom window and escape. Kenneth wished him well. Too bad Kenneth was too big to fit through, or he'd try it himself. The guy must have succeeded because no shots were heard. Lucky duck.

The guards came back, and the train started again before stopping hours later. Through the window, he saw a sign hanging on the train station that read BARTH. Kenneth vaguely recollected hearing of this prison camp on the shores of the Baltic Sea. As they departed from the train, the guards forced the prisoners to line up and start marching. As prisoners before them had done, they marched in loose formation through the stone arch leading into the town while men, women, and children glared. Kenneth glanced around the small town, similar in size to his hometown back in Louisiana, and figured the townspeople weren't too happy about having these enemies in such close proximity. Some muttered comments he assumed were uncomplimentary as they passed by.

As they marched down the road, Kenneth eyed the area around them, ready to run. German soldiers marched in front, behind, and alongside the prisoners, effectively boxing them in and giving little opportunity to make a break for it. After trudging almost an hour, Kenneth spotted their destination, a series of long gray and brown wooden barracks inside a double-barbed-wire fence, an unwelcome contrast to the green forest beyond. A flag with a Nazi swastika floated in the breeze above the headquarters at the entrance. Fifteen-foot-high towers were placed some two hundred yards apart along the double-wire fences, with coiled barbed wire filling the space between. Each tower had a sentry armed with a machine gun pointed toward the camp.

The camp was divided into two areas, the West Compound and the North Compound, as he would later learn. The Germans' quarters where the guards stayed were between the two compounds.

As Kenneth and his fellow prisoners approached, the current POWs of the camp stood in the barren dirt yard on the other side of the fence, straining to see the new prisoners as they entered. Occasionally there were shouts of recognition as the "old" prisoners spotted friends in the newcomer group.

"There's Charles! Where have you been?"

"If it isn't Ronald Bristow! Hey, Ronald!"

Kenneth didn't see anyone he knew, nor did he expect to, since there were so few Americans participating in the war. But he might know some British pilots who were there. Once they were all inside the fence, the incoming prisoners were lined up and counted, then marched through another inspection where they were once again searched, frisked, and issued a blanket and a crude dog-tag-type POW identification number. Kenneth's number was 1515, a number he didn't care to remember.

At this time, they gave him back his watch and ring, but unfortunately, not his grandpa's pocketknife. He was assigned to the North Compound and entered the main camp with the others through a double-gated enclosure. As the guard padlocked the gate behind them, he said in broken English, "For you, da var is over."

Once again the other POWs lined the fences watching for a familiar face. This time he recognized a couple of Brits he had trained with and gave them a nod while they raised a hand in return. The new POWs were then divided into groups and taken to different barracks.

When he began to follow the men near him, he was pulled aside by a guard.

"Come," the guard said, and Kenneth followed him to the building at the end of the row, where they walked up the wooded steps and in the door.

Once inside, the guard turned and exited the building, leaving Kenneth in an open area where a group of at least forty men milled around, some smoking cigarettes. They stared back at him with suspicious interest.

"Hello! Anyone here speak English?" Kenneth shouted with a smile on his face. "Who's in charge of this place?"

A tall man, gray hair in a crew cut and wearing a blue RAF uniform approached. The man appeared to be in his forties and walked with a slight limp as he stepped forward.

"Colonel Herbert Gilmore." The man extended his hand. "I'm the senior ranking officer here."

Colonel Gilmore's British accent was welcoming to his ears, reminding him of his days at Oxford.

Kenneth saluted. "Lieutenant Kenneth Bordelon, sir."

"You're a Yank. Eagle Squadron?"

"Yes, sir."

"Welcome to Stalag Luft I."

"And where exactly is this place?" Kenneth looked around, trying to see outside the windows.

"Barth, Germany, near the Baltic Sea."

"Long way from Britain."

"Long way from the States too."

"Am I the only Yank here?"

"So far as I know, at least in this barracks." He motioned for Kenneth to follow. "Let's find you a bunk."

"Is everyone here British, sir?"

"No, but we're all from somewhere in the Commonwealth. We have pilots from Canada, New Zealand, Australia, and South Africa here."

And he was the only American. Imagine that. He didn't know whether to be proud of that fact or embarrassed.

The building was divided into rooms where crude bunk beds with unfinished wood frames lined the wall. Kenneth followed Colonel Gilmore inside one of the rooms. "Gentlemen, this is Lieutenant Bordelon."

The other men in the room nodded as they made eye contact. "G'day," one of them responded, obviously an Aussie.

"Do you have any injuries?" Colonel Gilmore asked, looking him over.

"Other than my pride, no sir."

"Then you'll get the top bunk. Some of the others have trouble climbing up there."

"Fine with me. I sure could use some shut-eye right now."

"Go ahead and get as comfortable as you can. You might be able to get a short nap before dinner. You men can introduce yourselves and welcome Lieutenant Bordelon." The colonel turned and left the room, closing the door behind him.

Kenneth counted fourteen other men in the twelve-by-sixteen-foot room, leaving one unoccupied bed below his. His fellow prisoners were either sitting on the edges of their beds or stretched out on them. Amazing that sixteen men were meant to inhabit the small room. A man with curly hair the color of copper approached him with an outstretched hand. "G'day, mate. Name's Angus Lawrence." He pointed to each man, going around the room. "That there is Monty, Luke, Donald, Clyde, Chester, Gerald, Stan, Lionel, Ernest, Harold, Eugene, Bart, and George." Each man nodded or offered a slight wave of the hand.

"Nice to meet y'all. Sorry if I won't remember your names right away." He looked up at his bunk. "Now if you don't mind, I'm going to get some shut-eye."

Kenneth pulled off his boots for the first time in hours. The odor would've killed a possum, but other smells in the room competed for worst. Deodorant must be in short supply. "Man, it's hot in here," he said, unzipping his flight suit and removing it to reveal his disheveled uniform. Some of the other men in the room were in their undershirts. He climbed to the top bunk, where there was barely enough clearance between his head and the bunk if he tried to sit up. He crawled across the bed, collapsing on the uncomfortable mattress, apparently filled with hay. How many critters lived in that hay? No matter, he was too tired to care and hoped they would be too.

He was flying somewhere above the earth when he was startled by a sharp rap on the back of his calves. Who was in the plane with him? Another rap and he was ready to take on whoever woke him. He turned to look at the end of the bed where two German guards stood, one holding what looked like a riding crop. Kenneth's first instinct was to jump off the bed and give the man a few choice raps with the stick to return the favor, but on second thought, he decided against that course of action.

"You! You will come with us!" the shorter guard spat out.

"Do I have to?" he said, just for fun, but got no reaction from the straight-faced guards. Somehow, he didn't think this was a dinner invitation.

Kenneth had to back down to the end of the bed and down the ladder before his feet hit the floor. He faced the men in their pressed khaki uniforms with shiny buttons. Kenneth felt a little underdressed in his wrinkled uniform.

"You are Lieutenant Bordelon?" the unsmiling guard said, close enough for Kenneth to smell his rancid breath.

"I am. According to the rules of the Geneva Convention. . ."

"Enough! Come." The German pointed toward the door.

Kenneth motioned to his boots by the bed. "Will you let me put my boots back on first?"

The soldier nodded and crossed his arms, his lips a thin line as he waited.

With some effort, he worked his damp boots back on over his nasty socks, then straightened. As he followed the Nazis out of the room, the Aussie called out, "Good luck, Yank."

Kenneth was gonna get along well with that guy.

# ≡ CHAPTER 5 ≡

*Leeds, England*
*June 1941*

On Saturday Beryl stood in the queue outside the bakery, shopping bag on her arm as she waited for her turn to buy bread or rolls. She glanced around her at the storefronts with all their windows crisscrossed with strips of paper to keep the windows from shattering if bombs exploded nearby. She had moved closer to the door when a familiar voice rang out.

"Beryl!"

Beryl's head spun toward the voice of her best friend, Veronica. Her raven black hair was styled in perfect victory rolls, accented by the red lipstick she wore better than any movie star. Veronica waved with one hand, the other holding her grocery sack, then ran toward Beryl.

With a cheeky kiss, Veronica greeted her friend. "I was wondering when I'd see you again! You have been so busy!"

Beryl smiled and nodded. "As have you too, I hear."

"Ambulance driving is sporadic, never knowing when or if the bombs will fall, but when they do, it's challenging."

Veronica had always been the brave one, always ready to step up to the task, no matter how frightening it might be, managing to look beautiful in the thick of it.

"Can you come by for a spot of tea this afternoon?" Veronica lived just a few blocks away from Beryl with her father, mother, and little sister.

"I'd love to, actually, after I get our week's rations."

It had been weeks since Beryl had seen her friend, and she was eager to spend time with someone besides Mum or her workmates.

"Wonderful! See you about three?"

The queue moved forward, so it was Beryl's turn to go inside the store. "Yes! I'll see you then."

After leaving the bakery, Beryl joined another queue, this one in front of the grocery store, just a few doors down. She studied the ration book in her hand, hoping she would be able to get her allotment of sugar, tea, and flour before the store ran out. At the grocer's, the clerk weighed out the cheese, margarine, and butter into small, pitiful pieces and wrapped them in brown paper.

"Have you any eggs today?" she asked, doubting an affirmative answer.

The clerk pursed her lips as if the question was foolish and pointed to a sign Beryl had overlooked: NO EGGS TODAY.

Just as well, since their ration was only one per person for the whole week, and baking was practically impossible. Maybe Mr. Cuthbert would bring some back from his brother's farm. These days it seemed only the farmers had enough food.

The butcher shop was her next stop. Once again she waited in a queue like everyone else in town. While she waited, she listened to the conversations of others standing in line. "I heard Hitler isn't going to bomb England anymore."

Beryl's ears perked up.

"Fed up, is he? It's over, then?"

"The wireless says he's set his sights on invading Russia now."

"So, we can do away with all these blackout curtains and these infernal masks?"

"I suppose the government will let us know."

Beryl was tired of all the precautions as well, but she didn't believe they were finished with Hitler yet, even though the attacks seemed to have lessened, thank God.

The butcher lifted his hands in defeat as he told her he had nothing for her besides a soup bone.

"I'll take it," she said. At least they could have a good broth instead of the powdery mix they had to use without any real meat.

At home Beryl laid out the groceries she'd gotten and tried to figure out a meal plan. Frustrated, she needed her mother to be more involved.

"Mum? Can you please come here?"

A few moments later, her mother came into the kitchen.

"Mum, I need you to help me figure out what our meals will be. Can you get creative with these ingredients? I've run out of ideas, and all I can think of is bread and jam!"

Mum nodded. She eyed the items on the table—flour, a tiny bit of sugar, tea, potatoes, the meager amount of butter, margarine, and cheese, and the soup bone.

"Tell you what. I'm going over to Veronica's this afternoon for tea, and while I'm gone, I want you to make up a list of meals we can make with what we have. And if you feel like it, you can prepare one for our dinner tonight. After all, you are a superior cook, much better than I am." Beryl picked up a booklet called *Food Facts for the Kitchen Front* sent from the Ministry of Food. "Why don't you sit down here and take a look at this and see what kind of ideas the government suggests?"

Mum took a seat at the table and flipped through the pages of the booklet.

"I'll be back in a couple of hours. If you need me, I'll be at Veronica's house."

The day was lovely for a bike ride, but most of the people she saw had that same tired look on their faces that revealed the toll the war had taken on them. A brooding, unsmiling countenance was the result of life that was too serious to smile anymore. Days of potential enemy invasion and sleepless nights due to sirens and firing of antiaircraft guns would do that to people. Strung somewhere between "We'll win" to "What will we do when Germany invades us?" people didn't know whether to run or stand and fight. Gone were the days of Prime Minister Chamberlain's attempts at negotiations with Hitler. Mr. Churchill was now in charge and sending messages of encouragement over the radio. But after Dunkirk, and the relentless bombing for the past eight months, the people of England wondered how long they could hang on against such a powerful enemy that was sweeping through Europe. Was it true what she'd heard in town, that the bombing had ended?

As Beryl turned down Veronica's street, a Spitfire flew overhead, apparently from the nearby airfield. She paused to watch it, thinking of her brother, James. Why hadn't he responded to her last letter? She pulled her bike up in front of Veronica's flat and knocked on the door. Veronica's eight-year-old sister, Nancy, who could have been Veronica's miniature twin, opened the door. "Hello, Beryl. Where's your warden hat?"

"Hello, Nancy. It's over there." Beryl pointed to her bike where her black steel warden hat with the white *W* on the front rested in the basket. "But I'm not on duty now, so I don't need to wear it."

Veronica appeared behind Nancy. "Go on with you, Nancy, and let Beryl in."

Nancy's lips pouted as she stepped aside. Beryl followed her friend past the parlor where Mr. and Mrs. Holmes sat, he in an armchair, reading the newspaper, and she on the sofa, reading a book.

Mrs. Holmes looked up from her book while Mr. Holmes peered over his glasses.

"Hello, Beryl," Mrs. Holmes said. "How's your mother?"

"She's fine," Beryl fibbed, giving the expected answer and not interested in discussing Mum's state with anyone. "Thank you for asking."

Before Mrs. Holmes could ask anything else, Veronica pulled Beryl away toward the kitchen. She poured tea for them both and put a plate of biscuits on the table. Beryl sat down at the table, and Veronica joined her, picking up a biscuit and taking a bite. Beryl followed suit, tasting the blandness that was evident from sugar and egg rationing.

"Have you gotten any word from James?" Veronica asked.

"Not lately. He was writing regularly when he was at the base here in England, but I think they shipped him off. We haven't heard from him in three weeks. Mum hasn't asked about him, so I don't bring it up. What about you? Have you heard from Rodney?" Rodney was Veronica's fiancé, and they'd hoped to be married this year, but he was called up and they didn't have time for a proper wedding, the kind Veronica wanted.

Veronica's eyes filled with tears. Beryl leaned in toward her, lowering her voice.

"Is something wrong? Is he all right? What have you heard?"

Veronica grabbed a serviette from the table and pressed it to her nose. "I haven't heard anything from him in over a month, not since he was sent to North Africa." She sniffed and wiped her eyes with her sleeve. "I don't know if he's hurt or. . ."

Beryl grabbed her friend's hand. "Have you checked with Rodney's parents? Maybe they've heard from him."

Shaking her head, Veronica said, "They haven't heard from him either. Oh, Beryl, I'm so worried."

"I know you are, but worrying won't help. It just gets you all tied up in knots." Beryl had never seen Veronica so vulnerable. "You just carry on. We must, you and I. We have our parts to do here."

Veronica sniffed, then straightened in her chair. She took a sip from her cup. "Jolly right, Beryl! What am I going on about? Our men have more important things to do, like fighting a war. We must be strong here at home too, not some blithering weaklings. Thank you, Beryl. You're always so mature and know just what to say."

Mature? Beryl didn't think that was the appropriate description for her. She just had to keep her head about her, for Mum's sake, if not for her own. Stiff upper lip and all that.

"Oh, Veronica, stop. You know what they say. 'Just soldier on.' That's what we do while we're waiting to hear from them. That, and pray. Anything that's outside of my control, I hand over to God. He sees the whole picture, and I only see a little piece of it. Besides, He cares about James and Rodney as much as we do." Beryl's words were not just for Veronica; they were to convince herself as well.

"You're right. I should have more faith."

"Sometimes we need to pray for that too, especially when all those bothersome thoughts slam into our heads."

Veronica sighed, then smiled. "So, how's Freddie?"

Beryl gave her friend's arm a slight shove. "He's Freddie."

"Still asking you out?" Veronica poured more tea from the teapot into their cups.

Beryl rolled her eyes. "Yes, I'm afraid so. I don't know why, because I keep turning him down. There are other women at work he could bother besides me."

"But none are as pretty as you, luv. He's got good taste."

Beryl laughed. "You might not say that if you were around him very long."

"Well, he's got good taste in women anyway."

Beryl spent another hour at her friend's house, enjoying the time they had together. Laughing and talking with her childhood friend was relaxing and freeing. For the first time in a very long while, she started to feel normal again, instead of having to be so responsible all the time. Too soon it was time to go home. Veronica walked her to the door.

"Beryl, I'm so glad you came over."

"I am too. Next time you must come to my house."

"All right, I will." Veronica gave Beryl a big hug. "You take care, friend."

Beryl pedaled home, smiling all the way as she remembered her afternoon with Veronica. She sucked in a deep breath of air, relieved from the load she'd been carrying, even if temporarily.

As she reached her home, the telegram carrier with his navy-blue uniform with red stripes down the side was riding toward her on his bike.

"Are you Mrs. Clarke?" the young man said. "I have something here for you." He held a manila envelope out to her.

"Actually, Mrs. Clarke is my mum, but I'll take it for her."

The lad looked a bit uncertain, then said, "All right."

"Thank you." She took the dispatch as he tipped his cap and rode off.

Beryl stared at the official-looking envelope, her heart pounding. *Dear God, what could this be?* Even though it was indeed addressed to Mum, Beryl was afraid to let her mother see it unless Beryl knew what it said first. She glanced around, then ran her fingernail under the seal. She pulled out the single piece of paper and scanned the words.

> *The Royal Air Force has reported Lieutenant James Clarke to be Missing in Action as of May 31, 1941.*

# ⟁ CHAPTER 6 ⟁

*Stalag Luft I, Barth, Germany*
*June 1941*

Kenneth assembled with close to one hundred other newly arrived POWs in the prison yard in the chilly predawn air. He recognized a few of the men who had arrived the night before at the same time he did. They all looked as tired as he was.

"*Aufmerksamkeit!*"

He didn't know German, but from the tone, it sounded similar to the command to stand at attention. The others responded in like manner.

An older German officer in full uniform with medals on his breast pocket and a swastika hanging on his neck strode in front of the group, then stopped and faced them.

"I am Major Burkhardt, the commandant here at Stalag Luft I. You are prisoners of the Third Reich, and you are all airmen." He paced back and forth in front of the prisoners, shouting. "You will be treated well if you are good prisoners. We observe the rules of the Geneva Convention, so you are allowed to send and receive mail and also receive packages from your families, the Red Cross, and other charitable organizations. Keep the rules and keep your quarters clean, and there will be no trouble." He stopped and pointed at the guard towers. "Do not try to escape. If you do, you will be shot." Scanning the row of men once more, he harrumphed, then stalked away. When he left, the guards nudged them back to their assigned barracks.

Kenneth returned to his room and found the other prisoners awake and in various stages of dress. "What are you men up to? What's on the day's agenda?"

The Aussie grinned and walked over. "G'day!"

Kenneth smiled. "And good morning to you."

"How'd you get here? What were you flying?" the Aussie asked.

"Spitfire. Ditched in the channel after the engine got shot up. You?"

Angus pulled his undershirt on. "I was flying a Sunderland escorting some Allied convoys, sinking U-boats along the way. Took some enemy fire and had to land in a field in France. Germans found me hiding in a barn."

"So, have you been here long?"

"'Bout eight months. Long enough to show you the ropes and the fun things we do here."

"Fun, huh? Y'all don't look like you're having fun."

"Y'all? You from the deep South?"

"'Bout as deep as you can git—Louisiana."

Angus smiled. "Went to New Orleans once. Good food."

"Speaking of food. . . Do they serve us breakfast?"

Angus laughed and patted Kenneth on the shoulder. "They are not very good waiters. We feed ourselves, mate. Come, I'll show you."

They walked out into the hallway of the barracks and down to the far end where a coal-burning stove sat in the corner. One of the men standing in front of it stirred a strange-looking pot.

"We cook our own food and make do the best we can. They give us some coal, we have to go get our one pitcher of water per room, and the food is rationed out like that." He pointed to a chart on the wall. Kenneth studied the chart while Angus continued. "They don't give us much, so we celebrate when we get Red Cross packages with more foodstuffs in them. We also have a little garden out back where we grow some vegetables. We get more to eat during the summer because we can grow more then. But the winter was tough. It was miserable cold, the parcels didn't arrive as usual, and we barely had enough food to stay alive."

"We take our turns here at the stove, one room at a time. We also alternate through the room, taking turns to do the cooking." He faced Kenneth. "Can you cook, mate? We need a decent cook in our room."

"I can cook an egg," Kenneth said.

"Well, that'll do you no good here because we haven't got any eggs, not real ones anyway. Sometimes we get some of them powdered eggs." Angus stuck his finger in his mouth as if to gag.

Kenneth looked back at the list.

*Bread—8.3 oz. per day*
*Potatoes—16 oz. per day*
*Margarine—⅔ oz. per day*
*Meat—4⅓ oz. per week*
*Barley—1.3 oz. per week*
*Rolled oats—1.3 oz. per week*
*Dried vegetables—5 oz. per week*
*Sugar—4.3 oz. per week*
*Cheese—⅔ oz. per week*
*Ersatz coffee—⅔ oz. per week*

"That's not much," he said.

"No, it's not, especially if they don't give us the specified allotment, so we pool our rations together and add what we can to make it stretch."

"What is ersatz coffee?"

Angus made a face. "Awful stuff. It's the German substitute for the real thing—made from acorns, they tell me."

"No tea?"

"Not a bit unless some arrives in a package from home. Then there's a lot of bartering going on. We parlay all our packages together and keep the goods in our pantry. Come, I'll show you while we're waiting to eat."

Down the hall, Angus stopped at a door and opened it. They went inside, and Kenneth marveled at the variety of goods they had. Arranged on shelves along the wall were vitamin pills, cakes of soap, cigarettes, a couple cans of Spam, cans of vegetable stew, salmon, sardines, and corned beef. On another shelf, there were jars of peanut butter, margarine, instant coffee, and powdered milk. And above that shelf were rows of packages of prunes, raisins, cheese, crackers, and chocolate, which were called D-bars.

Kenneth whistled low. "You got all this food from the Red Cross?"

"And packages sent from relatives. It might look like a lot, but there's a lot of us here, so it doesn't last long. Some of this stuff arrived just this week, and it'll be gone before you know it. That's why we take our time using it. You never know when the next package will get here."

"This Spam would be good for breakfast," Kenneth said, picking up a can.

"Go ahead and take it, and we'll add it to today's breakfast."

They went back out to the kitchen area. By this time, other men had gathered in the room, waiting their turn to cook or eat. Angus introduced Kenneth to the others. Most of them were surprised to discover he was an American, although a couple had heard of the Eagle Squadron.

"Are you crazy?" one man asked. "Your country isn't even in the war, but you are."

Kenneth smiled. "Guess I am crazy. I went to college in England a couple of years and have many friends there. I couldn't sit back and do nothing or wait until Roosevelt decides to get his hands dirty."

A Brit stepped toward him, hand extended. "We thank you for helping us."

Kenneth clasped his hand but laughed. "I'm not helping you much now, am I?"

"But I trust you did some damage to the Krauts before you got here."

Kenneth nodded. "I did my fair share." He looked around at the others in the room. "So, what else do you do here? How do you pass the time? Do they make you do hard labor?"

Angus shook his head. "Not us officers. They treat us like we're something special. They make the noncommissioned officers do most of the manual labor, but we help out here to stay strong and productive. Besides, it's not fair for the NCOs to carry the workload. We have other ways to stay occupied as well. We keep fit by walking around the yard, lifting weights we made, and doing pull-ups on the doorframes. And for fun, we play cricket or football in the athletic field." He glanced at Kenneth. "That's real football, you know, not the kind the Americans play."

Kenneth laughed. "We call your football *soccer*." He received some head wagging in response. "However, I played that with some college chums, so I'm willing. Anything to stay busy and strong."

"When the weather's bad, we stay inside and do a lot of reading. We're accumulating a library here. Sometimes we get a book or two in our charitable packages, as well as some playing cards and maybe a board game. In fact, some blokes have asked for certain books from their families and have received them. Some of these guys are even using this time to learn a new skill. We're starting to accumulate quite a library."

"I'm not too keen on reading unless it's a magazine about motorbikes or a manual about how to do something. However, I can play some mean poker. But what do you use for gambling money?"

"Cigarettes. Actually, cigarettes are pretty much our currency." Angus lowered his voice and leaned into Kenneth's ear. "The guards are particularly fond of cigarettes, especially American ones, if you need a special favor."

Kenneth raised his eyebrows. "What kind of favor?"

Angus smirked. "You'll find out. But keep it quiet in case there's a ferret lurking about."

"A ferret?"

Angus kept his voice low. "Sometimes the Germans plant security guards in the camp who pretend to be workers, usually dressed in overalls, but who are really spies, listening for us to reveal something. Or listen for talk of escaping. They carry torches and steel spikes to probe for tunnels. That's why some of the other prisoners don't seem to be very friendly. They don't want to let our secrets out. And others have learned to keep to themselves. Those who have been here since Dunkirk have settled into the environment and don't want to be bothered."

Angus handed the Spam to the room's appointed cook, George, who cut it into chunks and added chopped potatoes and onions in a pan and heated it all together. As the men from Room 3 stepped up, George served it in each bowl along with a piece of bread. "Sorry, bloke, it's not your mum's bangers and mash."

Kenneth's mom hadn't made the British sausage and mashed potato dish, but he enjoyed the other ways she cooked sausage.

"Back in Louisiana, we would call that jambalaya if it had rice instead of potatoes." Kenneth took a sip of the coffee, agreeing with Angus' opinion of the stuff.

He made a face and shook his head. "Definitely not like our chicory coffee back home."

Eggs would have been a great addition to this meal as well, but in his current state of hunger, he was happy for the food he had. He examined the unique utensils and cookware, as well as the dishes they ate from.

Kenneth lifted his bowl. "Did you make this?" he said to Angus.

"No, but we have a couple of other chaps who are good with metal, and the camp has a place where we can make things we need."

In addition to the bowl, each man was given a mug made from pottery, a metal spoon, and a crudely made fork.

"We get quite creative here. See that pot? It was made from powdered milk cans flattened with a mallet, then rolled into shape and fastened with a metal strip over the bent edges. Works pretty well too."

"Great improvising," Kenneth said.

"We use those pots for cooking as well as for hot water, if you want some for a hand bath or shave."

Angus offered to take Kenneth on a walkabout through the camp, to which Kenneth readily agreed. He needed to see how much of a stronghold the place was while he looked for places and ways to escape. Had Angus ever considered escaping?

The camp had two compounds separated by German quarters. The barracks were long, rough, wooden structures standing on small foundation posts about a foot off the ground. Some of the barracks looked brand-new, and some looked unoccupied.

"They must be expecting a large population here."

Nodding, Angus said, "Hitler plans to capture lots of men from the Commonwealth."

"Let's hope he never fills them up."

"At least we got the double bunks. I heard some of the POW camps have triple bunks."

They walked past a crudely constructed smaller building. "What's that little house for?"

"It's a church. Well, actually a chapel. They let us build it ourselves. We have a combination Catholic/Protestant service here."

"That sounds interesting." Kenneth wasn't a churchgoer, but he'd be willing to try one if only to break the monotony of the place. Mom would be proud to hear he went to church once he could write her. That might ease her pain and worry somewhat.

"Where do you find the ministers?"

"We have a couple of men here who were in seminary, believe it or not."

"*Kriegie* chaplains," Kenneth said, using the German word for POWs.

"That's right, mate. Welcome to the kriegie life."

At one end of the prison yard, some POWs looked like they

were playing cricket with a board and a ball. Kenneth and Angus paused to watch.

"I never have played that game," Kenneth said. "Maybe now's my chance to learn how."

"You played baseball in the States?"

Kenneth straightened and puffed out his chest. "Two point five ERA."

Angus rubbed his chin. "Let's see. So you were a pitcher. Right, mate?"

"That's right. A good batter too."

"Well, you might make a good cricket player after all."

Kenneth nodded toward some German guards standing in a small group, also watching the game. "Do they ever play with y'all?"

"Ha! I bet they wish they could! Poor chaps are on duty, you know."

"What if the ball goes over the fence? Could you go get it?"

Angus smirked. "I'm afraid not, chap. The guards are more than happy to retrieve them for us and show off their throwing skills."

After observing for a while, Angus said, "Let's show you the rest of the place."

They turned down another side of the yard and saw about a dozen gardens being tilled by the POWs.

"This is how we supplement our meals." Angus pointed to the small garden plots. "What vegetables the Germans give us are barely enough, so we grow what we can. We have onions, potatoes, carrots."

"Where do you get the seeds?"

"We ask our relatives to send them."

"So, you really do get mail then?"

"Yes. Every man gets four postcards and three letter pages a month. You can ask for anything from home you want, and most of the time, you'll get it. The Brits get theirs back in about a month."

"I'm sure it'll take much longer from the States."

"Right. Takes a while from Australia too. Oh, and you can expect the censors to cut parts of your letters out, going and coming. Sometimes they look like paper dolls when you get them."

Kenneth nodded. "Of course." He couldn't wait to get a letter off to Mom. No telling what she was thinking or even if she knew he was a prisoner. "Seems like you have made yourselves pretty comfortable here."

Angus cut him a glare. "Don't be fooled. Those guards are harmless most of the time, but they can get mean if provoked. The last time we had an air raid, one of the POWs didn't go inside his barracks and was standing in the doorway looking up to see what planes might be flying over, and the blasted guard shot him!"

"But I thought they weren't supposed to shoot the prisoners, according to the Geneva Convention."

"Unless they have a reason to, like getting too close to the fence." Angus pointed. There was a row of barbed wire low enough to step over, then a space of ten feet, then the tall, barbed-wire fence. "That's why they put that low fence there, to warn you not to go past it, plus I think it's to tempt you to try too."

"So, it's not all fun and games."

"Not hardly." Angus' expression darkened. "A couple of chaps made the mistake of testing the boundaries. They didn't live to regret it."

Kenneth's stomach tightened at the fate of those prisoners. His escape would be more creative and not as obvious. They walked in silence a few moments as Angus' words sank in.

Angus changed the subject. "We do what we can for entertainment. We even have a theater they let us build so we can put on shows. Do you like the theater?"

"Sure. I like Jimmy Stewart, Clark Gable movies."

"I don't mean that kind of theater. I mean classical, like Shakespeare, that type."

"Oh sure. I like that too. I was in a play in college."

"You were? What part did you play?"

Kenneth chuckled. "A gravedigger!"

"In *Hamlet*?"

"Yeah, that's the one."

"I'm familiar with it. Perhaps you'd like to be in one of the plays here."

"Nah, I don't think so." They walked on some more. "It's almost like being at summer camp, with all the activities the men have."

"They're good actors. And I'm not referring to their performance on stage." Angus shook his head. "I believe what you're hinting at is whether anyone has plans to escape."

"Yeah, I guess that's what I want to know. I don't plan to stay here long myself."

Angus cocked a brow. "That right? We should talk about it, perhaps have a little meeting with some of the others. We can tell you what works and what doesn't. A few men have tried to escape, but they didn't get far."

"What happened to them? Did they get shot?"

"The ones that made it outside the fence were recaptured and brought back. The penalty for escaping is supposed to be ten days in the cooler, but sometimes they make them stay longer."

"What's the cooler?"

Angus pointed to a small building that had little windows spaced apart and about seven feet above the ground. "Solitary confinement. Anyone caught breaking the rules is put there for a mandatory two weeks. The rooms are so narrow, you can hardly turn around in them. You can barely breathe in the summer, and it's very cold in the winter."

They had gotten back to their barracks when "Roll call!" echoed down the hall. Hundreds of prisoners casually strolled to the athletic field to fall in where Kenneth's roommates told him they'd be counted. He'd also been told this happened twice a day, one time very early in the morning. During roll calls, the ferrets took advantage of the empty barracks to inspect them for contraband or hidden escape items, probing mattresses and other items with long screwdrivers, sometimes leaving a mess behind.

Kenneth stood at attention and looked up and down the long lines of oddly dressed men. The assortment of uniforms consisted of bits and pieces of nonmatching air corps uniforms and helmet liner caps, with rank insignia he learned later that was made from tin cans polished with tooth powder. The Red Cross donated sweaters, and assorted footwear completed the attire. Far from a dress parade back at base, there was still order in the motley ranks.

The commanding officer, Colonel Gilmore, stood with his executive officer, Major Fisher, facing the lines of prisoners as they waited for the officers of the Luftwaffe to ceremoniously enter the area and begin the long count. The Germans walked up and down in the front and rear of the ranks and counted heads. They never seemed to agree on the same number, but finally, after meeting to go over their counts, they decided no one had escaped. As the German staff exited through the gate, Colonel Gilmore dismissed the prisoners.

As Kenneth walked back to his barracks, he glanced at the guard towers where the guards were watching. There sure were a lot of prisoners to keep their eyes on. Would they really notice if one just "disappeared"?

The rumble of a truck caught his attention, and he looked over his shoulder to see the vehicle stop at the gate, waiting for it to be opened. The truck was piled with crates that appeared to be empty. A garbage truck? He studied the scene, noticing how long the truck had to wait before it was allowed through. Kenneth tried to look nonchalant as he strolled back in the direction of the truck. As he did, another truck pulled up behind it. Perfect. This could be an easy way out.

He strolled behind the second truck and glanced around. Not seeing anyone watching him, he slid under the truck and grabbed hold of the axle. When the truck began moving, he tucked his feet up under the carriage, lifted his head, and held on. The second truck followed the first one out, and Kenneth held on with all his strength until the vehicle cleared the fence and passed the German headquarters. As soon as he saw trees on either side, he let go and the truck moved on ahead.

He rolled to the side of the road, then stood and ran to the woods. When he reached the tree line, he stopped behind a large tree to catch his breath. Now what? He had no choice but to follow the road, not knowing the area. When the two trucks had gone around a curve, he took off down the road, running. The road snaked between fields on either side, with an occasional farmhouse and barn positioned between them. At the rumble of an approaching vehicle, he ran toward the closest building. His heart pounded as he watched the tractor-drawn wagon pass by. Boy, was he thirsty. He eyed the animals' trough. Hurrying to it, he bent over, cupped his hands, and began drinking the water. The cow standing nearby watched him with curiosity.

As he straightened, a prickly sensation of being watched by something besides the cow made him freeze. He slowly turned around and faced a farmer, pitchfork in hand, tines pointed out toward him. The farmer said something in German that Kenneth didn't understand, but when the man acted as though he was going to spear Kenneth with the pitchfork, Kenneth slowly raised his hands in surrender. The German nodded his head toward the road. *"Marsch! Schnell!"*

Kenneth got the idea and turned toward the road, the farmer walking behind. They headed back to the camp while Kenneth considered making a run for it.

But as they rounded the curve, an open car full of German guards headed in their direction.

The farmer called out to them, and they stopped, aiming guns at Kenneth and then motioning for him to climb into the vehicle with them.

"Did you miss me?" Kenneth said to the stoic guards who apparently had only recently realized his escape.

They drove back to the camp and marched him into the commandant's office. The officer sat with his hands clasped on the desk in front of him, a frown on his face. "Lieutenant Bordelon. What a foolish thing to do, trying to escape our camp," he said, his lips forming a straight line. "How did you get out?"

"I jumped over the fence." Kenneth had no intention of letting them know how easily he got out of the camp in case he wanted to try that method again. Couldn't have guards looking under the trucks.

The commandant lifted his eyebrows. "You must be very athletic to jump that fence."

He grinned. "I was a pole vaulter in school." Not really, but he had tried it once without success.

"Then you must be tired. You will have a chance to get rest in the cooler for ten days. Perhaps you will think better of doing that again. You are very lucky, you know. If a guard had seen you jump over, you would have been shot."

"Good thing they didn't see me."

The commandant nodded to the guards standing by the door. "Take him to the cooler."

# ⟩ CHAPTER 7 ⟨

*Leeds, England*
*June 1941*

How was Beryl going to tell her mother? It was imperative for her to find the right time when she thought Mum would be able to take the news without crumbling. She sucked in a deep breath and opened the door. Inside, the aroma of food greeted her, and she rushed to the kitchen.

"Mum! You've cooked dinner!"

Mum turned around from the stove with her apron on, holding a spoon aloft. "I made stew."

"Stew? We have meat?"

"With the bone you brought home from the butcher."

Beryl walked over and looked in the pot full of vegetables. She would call it "soup," but it didn't matter what her mother called it. This was the first time she had cooked something since Dad died. Thank God, maybe Mum was finally coming around. Even still, there was no way she could tell her about the telegram right now and set her back again.

Beryl took two bowls from the cupboard, and Mum dipped the stew into each one. Beryl tasted her mother's concoction. "Mum, this is delicious! Thank you for preparing such a good supper!"

Mum nodded. "How are the Holmeses?"

"They're doing well, and they asked about you."

Before they could finish their food, the air raid sirens went off.

Beryl grabbed her torch. "We'd better get in the shelter."

"I need my knitting," Mum said, glancing around.

"Where is it, Mum?" The fear and confusion on Mum's face told Beryl not to wait for an answer. "Never mind, I'll find it. You wait here."

Beryl raced through the dark house, briefly using the torch to illuminate the rooms. Not seeing the knitting downstairs, she raced up the stairs to Mum's bedroom and found the knitting on the bed. Listening for the sound of planes, bombs, or gunfire, she ran back downstairs.

"Here it is." She handed the bag to her mum. "Let's go."

Once they got into the shelter, the air filled with noise. Planes and gunfire erupted all around as if a battle was going on in the air. A couple of times the ground shook as a bomb landed. Didn't the folks in town say the bombing was over? The Germans hadn't gotten the message. The cacophony continued through the night, making it impossible for Beryl to sleep. Her mother finally lay down and closed her eyes, but Beryl's mind raced. Where was James? Had he been shot down? Was he hurt? Or. . .no, she couldn't let herself think of that option.

Maybe he had been rescued. Maybe he just wasn't able to let anyone know where he was yet. Beryl racked her brain trying to remember if he had said anything in his last letter about where he was going. At least Veronica knew Rodney went to North Africa. Is that where James went too? *Dear God, wherever James or Rodney are, please keep them safe.*

Sometime during the night, the all-clear siren rang out, and Beryl hadn't slept a bit. She decided not to wake her mother and tried to rest. When the first rays of sunlight peeked through their shelter, Beryl woke up. It was the wee hours of the morning, but she had to get some fresh air.

She gently shook her mum's shoulder. "Mum, are you awake? It's safe to get out now, so let's go in the house and clean up."

Mum opened her eyes, then sat up. "Where are we?"

"The Anderson shelter in our yard. We stayed overnight. I don't know about you, but I could use a good bath. What do you say, Mum?"

Mum looked around the shelter, as if she were seeing it for the first time. Actually, it had been a while since they had seen the inside of the shelter in the daylight. It didn't look nearly as spooky as it did in the dark. As Beryl stepped from the shelter, the sky was hazy with ash, and the acrid stench of smoke filled the air. "Quick, Mum! Put your gas mask on!" Beryl hastily donned hers and helped her mother do the same before she went outside the shelter.

Dread filled her with a heaviness because something or someone had suffered destruction and loss from the bombing. And based on how dense the air was, a bomb had landed nearby. Who was hit this time? Anyone she knew?

As they reached the back door of their house, she saw it—a giant crater where just yesterday a house had stood only halfway down the block. Relief that her home hadn't been hit was reduced to guilt that someone else's had. Beryl ran around inside her house to assess any damage. She threw open the blackout curtains to discover the glass in the bay window had been blown out by the explosion. All the other windows had cracks running through them. Plaster from the ceiling lay on the floor, but the house was still intact. She went out the front door and looked at the exterior, finding debris in the yard that had been blown from other places.

Inside, Mum sat at the kitchen table, that faraway look in her eyes again.

"Just a little bit of damage, thank God. Let's have some tea, Mum."

While making the tea, Beryl fought against her own feelings of doom to pretend a chipper mood and hopefully lift her mother's spirits.

"Just a few broken windows is all, nothing we can't live with." Beryl hoped the brown tape would hold the pieces back together. If not, perhaps Mr. Findlay could find a way to board them up.

She poured Mum's tea and sat down beside her.

A knock on the door brought Beryl to her feet again. Mrs. Findlay hurried in when Beryl opened the door.

"Are you all right? Your mum?" Mrs. Findlay said in a lowered voice.

"We're fine." Beryl glanced at Mum, remembering how she'd almost been normal last night. But had this last air raid set her back? "How about you? Your house?"

"Well enough. Looks like yours. But the Harris family down the row. . ." She shook her head.

"No! They weren't in their shelter?"

Shaking her head, Mrs. Findlay said, "Mr. Harris was stubborn and wanted to sleep in his own bed on the second floor of the house. So he and his wife were killed. We hope they were asleep when the bomb got them."

Beryl felt sick to her stomach. Why didn't people know the danger of not seeking shelter? "What about their daughter Millie?"

"Thank God, they had sent her out to the Dales to spend time with her Gran. But poor dear, she'll be without her parents now."

Beryl pitied the poor child, knowing full well what it felt like to lose a parent—but thankfully not both.

"Forgive my manners keeping you standing here. Won't you come in and have a cuppa with us?"

"Tea is just what I need. And how is your mother taking this?"

"Taking what?"

Beryl and Mrs. Findlay jerked their heads toward the voice of Beryl's mother standing outside the kitchen door. Exchanging glances conveying their mutual uncertainty about what to say, they moved toward the woman and changed their conversation.

"We were just discussing the latest visit of the unwanted guests," Mrs. Findlay said as she took Mum's arm and turned her back around to the kitchen. "Let's have some tea. It's been a long night, hasn't it?"

Beryl took out some bread and jam. "Would you like some?" she asked their guest.

"If you can spare it, that would be lovely."

Beryl poured tea for everyone, then set down the food and plates. Her nose tickled, probably from the smoky haze sneaking in through the broken windows, and she sneezed. Reaching into her pocket to retrieve a handkerchief, her hand settled on the government telegram, the one she hadn't told her mother about yet. How could she broach the subject now? Mum needed to know, and there would never be a good time to tell her. Yet maybe now would be as good a time as any with the support of Mrs. Findlay and her ever-positive attitude.

She pulled the envelope out and laid it on the table. "I forgot that the postmaster gave me this yesterday just as I arrived home."

The other ladies eyed the envelope.

"Well, what is it, luv?" Mrs. Findlay said.

Mum reached for the envelope and withdrew the telegram while Beryl held her breath. Mum's eyes scanned the document, then she looked up at Beryl. "James is missing."

Beryl nodded, her eyes misting. But she mustn't fall apart. She needed to keep her chin up and hope for the best.

Mrs. Findlay glanced between the two. "Now that's good news, isn't it? I mean, it didn't say he was dead, did it?"

Beryl shook her head while Mum stared.

"He might have been found by a kind farmer and hasn't been able to let us know yet," Mrs. Findlay continued.

Why hadn't she thought of that? "Yes, maybe he's safe somewhere and trying to get back."

"But he could be a prisoner of war, and the Nazis won't tell us who is in their prisons," Mum said.

"Oh, I think they do notify our government if they've captured one of our men," Beryl said.

"And if he has been captured, that's all the more reason we need to volunteer with the Red Cross. We can help put together packages that are sent to the prisoners," Mrs. Findlay said.

"I'd like to do that," Mum said. "For James. If he's in a German's prison, I pray he'll get the Red Cross package we put together."

"Brilliant! You've always taken care of your family, and you can still do it." She glanced at Beryl, sending a silent message of encouragement. It had been several months since Mum had taken care of anyone, even her daughter. "I'll come get you soon as I freshen up. I'm sure you should do the same, what with staying in that hole in the ground all night. You and I will get ourselves down to the Red Cross store and volunteer."

Mrs. Findlay finished her tea, stood, and rushed out.

"I should get cleaned up for work," Beryl said. She laid her hand over her mother's. "James will be fine, Mum," she said more to convince herself. "He's steady and will get home as soon as this war is over."

Mum nodded, staring into her cup of tea. "He's a good lad."

"He is. You and Dad raised us right."

Mum looked up at Beryl and smiled. "We tried."

# ⌇ CHAPTER 8 ⌇

*Stalag Luft I, Barth, Germany*
*June 1941*

As Kenneth was marched into the POW camp, his fellow prisoners nodded their hellos. He shrugged and smiled. So he got caught. At least he tried.

The guards escorted him to the stucco building that stood a distance from the barracks, then ushered him inside. There were five doors lining each side of the hallway. After opening one of the doors, the guards shoved him into it, slammed the door, and locked it behind him. Kenneth found himself in a small room, about four feet wide by four feet long and eight feet high. One small window with vertical bars emitted the only light and air, and it was placed high on the wall. He walked to the wall and jumped, grabbing hold of the window ledge and pulling himself up to peer out. All he could see was the dirt prison yard and the fence beyond it. As he let go of his grip, pieces of stucco came loose.

Hmm. Maybe he could dig through the stuff. But not through the floor. It was concrete, so a tunnel wouldn't work. He paced the small room awhile, then sat down on the hard floor with his back against the wall, staring at the window. Noticing a pointed piece of stucco that had fallen on the floor, he grabbed it and returned to the window, using it to knock more pieces loose. When it broke, he found other pieces to use, working the stucco down to the base of the bars.

Working on the window kept him busy the next five days until he found the base of the bars. He grabbed hold of them and shook them until they came loose. He could remove the bars! He used his hands to measure the width of the window. About eighteen inches. Even with his thirty-two-inch waist, he couldn't get through there. Besides, where would he go if he did? He didn't know how close the sentry tower was to the cooler. He stood on his tiptoes to watch the activities outside, hoping another prisoner would walk near so he could talk to him. But the other prisoners stayed clear of the cooler, understandably.

He put the bars back in and tried to make the window look normal, scattering the stucco crumbs around the cell so no guard would notice if he looked in. They didn't, only opening the door enough to slide in a meager piece of brown bread and cup of thin cabbage soup three times a day. For now, he would stay put but do some reconnaissance around the building so that the next time he was sent to the cooler, he would have a plan to get out. In the meantime, he needed to stay as fit as he could by doing push-ups and sit-ups and running in place.

After ten days, the guards unlocked his cell and released him, ordering him to return to his barracks. Boy, did it feel great to stretch out and walk after being confined so long in the small space. As he walked past other kriegies, he received some pats on the back and "attaboys." Kenneth smiled but didn't think he had earned celebrity status. Hadn't he just tried to do what they were all supposed to do? Try to escape? At least he had gotten out, although he had been recaptured. So he'd accomplished part one of his plan. It was obvious he needed to prepare more for the next parts of an escape. A map and a compass would be most helpful.

The guys in the barracks glad-handed him when he returned. They all wanted to know what it was like beyond the fence. Angus pulled him aside and said, "Colonel Gilmore wants a debriefing about your escape. He'll meet you near the gardens."

Kenneth reported to the colonel, and they took a walk as Kenneth detailed his escape, what went right and what went wrong.

"Good information. Glad you stayed safe."

"Sir, I have some ideas."

"Fine. We'll get some of the other men in on the conversation another time. From the looks of you, you could use something to eat."

"Yes, sir, I sure could."

"Then go take care of yourself. We'll talk later."

Kenneth went back inside and found some crackers in the pantry, then returned to his room. He climbed up on his bed and stretched out, thankful for the uncomfortable mattress instead of the concrete floor in the cooler. A nap would be welcome, but it dawned on him he hadn't written his mother yet. He couldn't waste any more time contacting her. Who knew how long it would take for him to get a letter anyway?

He sat up and found the stationery he'd been given when he arrived. Hunching over the edge of his bunk with his legs hanging over the end, he paused, the pencil stub in his hand, ready to compose his first one-page letter to Mom. He would tell her he hoped to be home before the letter arrived, knowing the chance of that happening was slim. He focused to see in the diminishing light of day. Writing as small as he could yet legible, he tried to fit his words in each of the twenty-four lines of the single, five-inch-wide piece of paper. He'd list everything he wanted her to send, even though he had no idea how long it would take to get them.

> *Dear Mom,*
>     *I haven't written in a while, but I wanted to let you know my adventures have led me to Germany, where I'm a guest of the Third Reich. Don't worry, I'm fine and have met some new friends. Would you mind sending me a few things I'm short on over here?*

He continued with a list of items—No. 2 pencils, paper, pencil leads, scissors, pocketknife, and chewing gum. He paused a minute, knowing the impossibility of getting anything with a point. But why not ask anyway? He added vitamins, baking powder, cinnamon, cream of wheat, dried fruit, and razor blades. Should he ask for cigarettes to use for money? No, Mom didn't like smoking. Besides, if he had his way, he wouldn't be here when the package arrived. His stomach growled as he thought of Mom's food back home. Boy, wouldn't he like to get some of her good gumbo now. He pictured her cooking over the stove, stirring a roux to make the gumbo, a pile of shrimp and sausage sitting on a plate nearby. He could almost smell the delicious concoction. Chuckling to himself, he realized how impossible that menu item would be here.

He hoped he'd get a parcel from someplace soon that contained food. Apparently the Germans were supposed to provide one per man per week that contained German-issued meat, fresh vegetables, and bread. However, he was told the parcels didn't arrive on schedule, and sometimes there weren't enough for every man in the barracks to receive one. No wonder the men looked thin. You could tell who had been there the longest by how skinny they were.

Angus' copper hair poked in the door. "Hey, Yank. Got a poker game waiting for you."

"Be there soon. I've got to finish this letter first."

"All right. You do that." Angus backed out and closed the door.

Kenneth finished the letter, folded it to fit the envelope he'd been given, and addressed it to his mother. Had anyone told her he was a prisoner yet? Or did they think he was dead? His heart wrenched. He hated for her to be sad or worry herself sick over him. If only he could communicate with her more quickly.

He climbed down from the bunk and went out to the community area where a card game was in progress. The light was dim, thanks to one lonely low-wattage bulb hung on a twisted cord from the corner of the room.

"Looks like you've already got enough people to play," he said.

Angus held up another deck of playing cards. "We can get two games going."

The Australian pulled up some makeshift stools made from logs to a crude wood table balanced over a couple of barrels. Two other men sat down at the table, and Kenneth joined them.

Kenneth glanced at the other men. "Who's shuffling?" he asked.

Angus handed him the deck. "You can do the honors. This here is Jan, that's Milo, and this is Pop. He flew in the last war."

Kenneth nodded a greeting and dealt the cards. A pack of cigarettes lay on the table, which Pop, an older guy with thinning hair, divided four ways to each man to use for money or chips.

"You guys fly together?" Kenneth asked, noticing a foreign accent from Jan and Milo.

"We did," Angus said. "Jan and Milo flew with the Polish Air Force before Hitler invaded Poland, then they joined the RAF. We're lucky to have them on our side."

Kenneth smiled at the two men. "Good for you."

Studying his hand of cards, Kenneth hummed.

"What tune is that, Yank?" Angus asked.

"'Thanks for the Memory.' Bob Hope sang it in a movie."

"Do you like to sing?"

"Sure, I've always enjoyed singing."

"Then you should join the glee club."

"You have a glee club here?" What these guys wouldn't do to pass the time.

"Sure do. One of the guys in the other barracks leads it. Think he used to be a choir director."

"You don't say." Kenneth enjoyed singing. Why not, as long as he was there? "Sounds like something I'd like to do. Do you know when they practice?"

"About ten in the morning, over by Barracks 9."

"I'll look into it."

"So, what are the words to this song you're humming? Why don't you sing it for us?"

"Sorry, I don't know the words. But I like the music. Too bad we don't have a radio."

The other men at the table exchanged glances.

Kenneth raised his brows. "Hmm. Something tells me you know something I don't know."

Footsteps outside warned them they were about to be interrupted. Two guards walked in and went to each window, closing the wooden shutters over the windows and sliding a board in place to hold them.

"Blackout," Angus said to Kenneth in a low voice.

The POWs waited until the guards left to resume their conversation.

"So, what's this secret you guys are keeping?" Kenneth leaned toward the other men, keeping his voice soft.

Angus grinned. "We have a fella here quite talented with electronics."

"Yeah? He made a radio? With what?"

Angus used his hands to describe. "Scraps of metal, bits and pieces of wire."

"Where'd he get the stuff?"

Angus winked. "Remember I told you the guards like American cigarettes?" He glanced at the others. "They come in handy sometimes."

"I see. I'll remember that. So where is this radio?" Kenneth gazed around the room.

"I'll show you later. We only use it to get the BBC broadcasts and find out what's really happening outside instead of the Nazi propaganda they tell us."

"Clever."

"We don't keep it put together all the time. If there's a goon around, we dismantle it and stuff the parts in a wall."

"Even more clever." Kenneth had discovered that *goons* was the name the POWs had given the guards, of course not to their faces.

After a couple of hours, the guys were ready to call it quits. Kenneth was the big winner, having accumulated a pile of cigarettes. Good thing he didn't smoke, or he'd use up all his currency. And he might want to use some to befriend a guard. He swept them into one hand with the other, smiling.

"Thank you, gents. It's been fun."

The men scattered to their rooms where each man tried to make his quarters as livable as possible, using some ingenuity to arrange his corner with its stark furnishings to his own tastes.

"Think I'll brush my teeth." RAF protocol required the airmen to continue personal hygiene habits and show professionalism in their dress if possible. "And wash my socks too." Kenneth had gotten a toothbrush from the barracks trading post and was happy to use it, even though he had to use baking soda instead of toothpaste. He walked to the end of the barracks where the latrine with only the bare necessities could be found. There was a gang lavatory, a center water column with eight spigots surrounded by a concrete wash bowl. Kenneth never thought he'd enjoy brushing his teeth so much. He had a sliver of soap someone shared with him and used that to wash his face and wash his socks, rinsing the latter as much as possible, then wringing them out. He'd hang them on the rungs of the ladder to his bunk and hope they dried overnight.

The building was dark and eerily quiet, with no lights on inside and any outside light closed out by the shutters. Groping his way back to his room, he discovered a couple of his roommates already snoring. He strode to the boarded-up window and peered through the cracks, watching the systematic beam of the searchlights as they roamed the camp from the guard towers. The distant sound of a train whistle broke the silence between snores. How long could he tolerate this place? He had to find a way to get out and stay alive.

During roll call the next morning, Kenneth focused on the way the sun lit up the sky as it started the day and lifted over the trees. How eager he used to be to witness that sight, expecting the day to be filled with excitement and activity. He sure did miss that feeling, even though he'd only been at the camp a few days. But he wouldn't give in to the hopelessness that doomed so many and sapped their strength. He'd concentrate on getting out and how he could make that happen.

Without a compass, he had to assume that if the sun was coming up over the forest, then that must be east. And England must be. . . northwest? Too bad the tree line wasn't in the west, since that's the direction he wanted to go when he escaped. But he had no idea of the territory or surrounding towns. If he had to get out on the wrong side of the camp, then he'd have to circle back around somehow. Boy, wouldn't he like to fly over the camp and see the area. Kenneth, you idiot. If you could fly over the camp, you wouldn't be stuck in it! Sure would be nice to at least have a map.

While they stood in formation, the gates opened, and two trucks entered the camp. The guards waved them on, and they drove to the other side. Kenneth lifted his eyebrows and glanced at Angus standing beside him.

"Workers," Angus said under his breath. "They're here to pick up an NCO work party."

After roll call, the men broke ranks, and a short time later, the trucks came back filled with men in the truck beds. When the guards opened the gates and waved them through, Kenneth determined he would join one of the work parties as soon as he could.

When the counting charade finally ended and the men went back to the barracks, the men lined up for breakfast as usual. Angus pulled him aside. "I know what you're thinking."

"Yeah? What's that?"

"I saw how you watched those work trucks. You're going to try to get on one, aren't you?"

Kenneth shrugged. "Why not?"

"It's been tried before."

"Not by me."

"Let's talk about it outside."

Once they were outside, Angus said, "This is the safest place to talk, just in case any Germans are listening. They stand by the windows and try to overhear what's said. Several escape plans have been foiled by a guard hearing about it."

"So, how do I get in a work detail?" Kenneth's mind raced to think of everything he'd need to do to succeed this time.

"You need to be an NCO."

"Or take an NCO's place."

"Or that. You'd have to change the insignia."

"That shouldn't be a problem. At least the rest of the uniform is the same color."

"And it's hot, so jackets would be removed while on the job anyway."

Why was Angus being so negative? Or maybe he was just cautious. Whatever, Kenneth was anxious to make it happen. "Good point. Think I can get an NCO to trade places with me?"

"For the right price, probably. They go out every day and get pretty tired. I'm sure someone would appreciate a day's rest."

"What kind of price do you suggest? Cigarettes?"

"Unless you've got some prime beef."

"Ha. Do you know any of the NCOs, someone you can introduce me to?"

Angus paused and studied the ground. "Yes, I do. If you really want to do this, I'll take you over to meet him when the work detail comes back tonight."

"I really want to do this, Angus. I'll take all the necessary precautions to be successful."

"Meanwhile, stay busy and don't talk to anyone else about it."

"Not a problem. Thanks for your help. In the meantime, I'm going to find the glee club."

Angus nodded. "Good idea. See you later."

Kenneth followed the directions Angus had given him for the glee club and found a group of around a dozen men standing outside one of the barracks with another man facing them.

"Is this the glee club?" Kenneth asked, scanning the group.

"It is," the man in front said. "Richard Brown. I'm the director of this group."

"Kenneth Bordelon. I'm new here."

"American. You're our first. What do you sing?"

"Tenor mostly, but I can sing bass if you need me to."

"Excellent. Glad to have you. We were just about to practice 'We'll Meet Again.' Do you know the song?"

"I know the melody. Not sure I remember all the words."

"We've written them down. I'm sure you'll know them after a couple of times through." Mr. Brown motioned to the group. "The tenors are there, on the right side."

Kenneth stepped in place by a dark-skinned man who nodded hello. From his accent, Kenneth deduced he was from one of the British Commonwealth countries like Jamaica or Bermuda. The group was oddly mixed like the camp itself, with fair-skinned men from Ireland to tanned New Zealanders. Together the accents and tones combined to make a unique melody.

While they were singing, the melancholy words of the song drew his thoughts away from his escape plans. "We'll meet again, don't know where, don't know when. . ." An image of Beryl Clarke appeared in his mind. Would they ever meet again? Maybe when the war was over he could go see her. But perhaps she was married now. After all, he hadn't seen her in two years. So much had changed. Was she the same girl he knew at Oxford? He sure hoped so. Maybe he didn't have a girl to go home to, but seeing Beryl again was an extra incentive to get out of this place.

If things worked out right, he'd be on his way back to England tomorrow.

# ⣿ CHAPTER 9 ⣿

*Leeds, England*
*June 1941*

During lunch break the next week, Freddie asked Beryl to attend a dance being held the coming weekend.

"No, Freddie, I can't. I'll be on duty." Actually, she wouldn't be, since she had already served her three days of the week, but the excuse was convenient and avoided giving him a flat "No."

His face crestfallen, Freddie shrugged and walked away.

"Beryl, you really should do something fun once in a while." Margaret put her hands on her hips. "I know you're not on duty every night," she said.

Beryl reached out her arms, pleading. "How can I have fun when my brother is missing?"

"Do you think James would want you to stop living?" Margaret pursed her lips. "No, he wouldn't."

Beryl's chest tightened. "It just feels wrong."

"For Pete's sake, they're even having parties in London, and God knows they've had it a lot worse than we have."

Beryl knew what Margaret said was true, but it still felt wrong.

"Remember, Hitler wants you to live in fear. You don't want him to win that battle, do you?"

Anger rose in Beryl. "No, of course not. I promise I'll think about it. But do I have to go with Freddie?"

Margaret laughed. "No, you don't. In fact, some of us girls are going together, so you can join us."

"Maybe I will." Beryl's thoughts drifted to Veronica. Perhaps she could convince her friend to go too. Veronica sure needed to spend some time in a social atmosphere and take her mind off worrying about Rodney, but would she go to a dance? On the other hand, Mum needed company too, and Beryl couldn't keep imposing upon Mrs. Findlay. Their sweet neighbor was with her every day anyway, either in their knitting group or at the Red Cross store.

After work that day, Beryl considered going by Veronica's but decided to take the road around town that passed through some of the countryside instead. The rolling dales and green fields dappled in sunlight gave her a feeling of peace, taking her mind off the war temporarily. She paused near the intersection of a road that led down the valley to take in the view of a distant grass-covered hill dotted with grazing sheep, and the words to the twenty-third Psalm came to her. *"The Lord is my shepherd; I shall not want. He maketh me to lie down in green pastures: he leadeth me beside the still waters. He restoreth my soul: he leadeth me in the paths of righteousness for his name's sake. Yea, though I walk through the valley of the shadow of death, I will fear no evil: for thou art with me; thy rod and thy staff they comfort me."*

A plane from the nearby airfield flew overhead, and she looked up, shielding her eyes to follow its path through the clear blue sky. She was thankful for the sight of a Royal Air Force plane, a Spitfire, reminding her of James and how he was trying to keep her and England safe. *Lord, what can I do? I'm just one person, and I'm stuck here at home. I want to make a difference, but I don't know how. All I can do is pray and do my meager part here. Please keep James safe and show me what else I can do to help our cause.*

A sense of calm came over her. Maybe God did listen. Maybe this peace was His way of letting her know James was all right. She grabbed her handlebars and continued her ride but couldn't avoid seeing the bombed-out neighborhood ahead. Her temporary peace diminished, faced by the harsh reality of the war. She slowed to walk her bike around a hole in the road caused by the bombing from the week before. Everything around her was unnervingly quiet with no one else around, but a faint sound came from the area of the damaged houses. She stopped to listen.

Did she hear a cat? No one lived here anymore, so how could a cat?

The pitiful cry was weak, and Beryl's heart pinched. Had it been injured or just abandoned? So many animals had been euthanized two years ago because the government thought it was the best thing to do in wartimes to keep the animals from starving when food was scarce for humans. Few people besides farmers had pets anymore.

Beryl climbed off her bike and leaned it against the stone wall that lined the road. She stepped cautiously toward the direction she thought the sound had come from.

"Meow."

Beryl looked around and said, "Kitty, kitty. Here, kitty, kitty."

"Meow." The sound was closer. Beryl kept calling softly and crept toward the noise. Finally, she saw it, a small black and white kitten standing in the crevice between two rocks in what was left of a garden wall. The kitten eyed her warily, opened his mouth, showing his pink tongue, and gave a feeble hiss.

"There you are." Beryl knelt down and extended her hand, but the kitten hissed again. A thought struck her. She had not eaten all of her sandwich at lunch, tiring of the same sandwich every day. She walked back to her bike, opened her lunch box, and retrieved the leftover food. Going back to where the kitten was, she pinched off a bit of the sandwich, knelt down again, and offered it to the kitten. The little thing hissed again, then sniffed the air and moved cautiously toward Beryl's hand. When he got within an inch of Beryl, he stopped and hissed again. The poor thing was afraid to trust her. No wonder, after what he had been through. Yet he was thin and must be starving. Beryl tossed the food to the kitten, who leaned down to lick it, then quickly ate the morsel.

"Good kitty. Would you like some more?" She pinched off another bite and repeated the process. The next time, she kept the food in her hand, and the kitten mustered enough bravery to come all the way forward and eat it from Beryl's hand. As he ate, Beryl gently stroked his little body. After some time, he relaxed and looked at her with searching eyes. Beryl gently reached out and picked up the furry bundle, which was light as a feather. As she stroked the animal again, he began purring.

"Bless you, little one. You need a home, and I know someone who needs something to take care of."

She buttoned her sweater and put the kitten inside, holding it in place with one hand as she climbed on her bike and pedaled home.

Hopefully her surprise would garner the response she envisioned.

When she arrived at the house, she called out, "Mum?"

"In here," Mum replied from the sitting room. Beryl found her knitting as usual.

"I brought you a surprise." Beryl held her breath, waiting for her mum's response.

Mum looked up, a frown between her eyes. "A surprise? What kind of surprise?"

Beryl opened her sweater, revealing the kitten. She took him with both hands and held him up. "Isn't he the sweetest?"

Mum lay her knitting aside and reached for the kitten. The animal hissed as Beryl released it to Mum's hands, but Mum smiled anyway, the biggest smile Beryl had seen in a long time. "Well, now, you have a bit of an attitude, I see." The cat, however, allowed her mother to hold him against her chest and stroke his fur. She glanced up at Beryl, her eyes misting over. "Where did you get this little dear?"

Beryl told her about finding the animal near the ruins of a neighborhood. "I wonder if the poor thing has been there since the bombing. He was terribly shy, but starving. I only managed to make him come to me by feeding him some of my leftover sandwich from lunch."

Mum continued petting the kitten, whose purrs were loud enough to hear several feet away. "We must get him some milk."

"We have a can of evaporated milk we can dilute."

"What do you want to name him?" Mum asked.

"I thought you might want to name him, Mum."

Mum shook her head. "It reminds me of a cat I had a long time ago, but mine was completely black, so I named it Midnight. But this one, with the white streak down his nose and white feet, doesn't suit that name."

Beryl's mind sparked with an idea. "I know just what to name him. Spitfire, like the planes. You know, with all his hissing and such. Don't you think that's appropriate?"

"Isn't that the type of plane James flies?" Mum asked.

"Yes, I believe so." At least that's the plane he used to fly. Was he still? *God, please let us know if James is safe.*

"Then Spitfire it is." Mum held the kitten in front of her face. "Come, Spitfire. Let's get you some milk." Mum stood and went to the kitchen and took a can of milk out of the pantry. Once she found the can opener, she pierced the can and poured some of the milk into a cup, mixed it with an equal amount of water, and then poured it into a saucer and set it on the floor. Mum put the kitten down beside the saucer and crossed her arms, watching as the animal drank hungrily. "I'll have to make a bed for our little Spitfire." Mum hurried out of the room while Beryl stood with her mouth agape. When was the last time Mum had hurried with such a purposeful attitude?

The kitten finished drinking, then sat back and began licking his paws and washing his face. Mum returned to the kitchen, holding a basket with a piece of soft gray blanket folded inside. "That blanket was old anyway. I was going to cut it up and make some shopping bags from it." She gently lifted the kitten and set him inside the basket. Spitfire sniffed the blanket and stretched, his pink tongue sticking out as he yawned, then curled up in a ball and closed his eyes.

"Poor little thing. It's probably been a long time since he's had a comfortable place to sleep," Beryl said.

"Well, he has a nice comfy place now, and he won't have to go hungry anymore either," Mum said.

Mum's pleased expression as she considered the sleeping kitten warmed Beryl's heart. She hugged her Mum. "I knew you'd be a good mum for the kitty."

"Spitfire is part of our family now. It's my job, taking care of my family."

The kitten purred his agreement.

# ▦ CHAPTER 10 ▦

*Stalag Luft I, Barth, Germany*
*June 1941*

As the men broke up after roll call, Kenneth eased over to the NCO section and found the man he was going to switch places with that day. Jimmy Blackstock had already been a prisoner for two years and was willing to make the swap, saying he welcomed the rest from manual labor. Jimmy gave Kenneth his cap, a nondescript regulation cap minus the officers' insignia. Kenneth joined ranks with the other men going out that day and kept his head down as they formed a queue to get on the trucks.

None of the guards noticed the difference as he climbed onto the back of the truck. The NCOs didn't say anything either, even though they exchanged glances with each other. A guard climbed into the truck with them, further encouraging silence. Kenneth's palms were wet with sweat, and he wiped them on his pants. The truck rumbled on for at least half an hour, shaking the men as it bumped over potholes before it finally stopped and the guard hopped out, then ordered the men to climb out as well.

In front of them was a dense forest, and each man was handed a saw or hatchet and pointed to an area where they were to begin cutting down trees. Kenneth scanned the area, noting stumps where the previous day's work had ended. As he followed the group up a rise to the assigned area, two other NCOs joined him on either side.

"If you're going to make a break for it, we're going too," the gaunt-faced man on his left said in a low Irish brogue.

"I don't need company," Kenneth responded.

"We know which way to go. We've been here before," said the muscular man on his right, also sounding Irish.

What choice did he have? Maybe they could help. "All right," he said.

"First, we get busy while the guards are watching us," one of the guys said.

Kenneth noticed that most of the guards stayed near the trucks with their eyes on the work party.

The man continued. "When they start talking and relaxing, they quit watching us so much. Then we go farther and farther into the woods until they can't see us anymore. From there, we run."

"Have you tried this before?" Kenneth asked.

"We haven't yet, but others have."

"And did they make it?"

"For a while, yes. But then they were recaptured."

"And returned to camp?"

"Yes, then spent some days in the cooler."

"And you think it will work this time, for you? Why?" Kenneth asked.

"We're faster and smarter."

"I see." Kenneth hoped their assessment of themselves was correct. "Do you have names?"

"I'm Bryce Pearson," the man on the right said.

"Scott McIntosh," said the other one.

"I'm Kenneth—"

"We know who you are. You're the Yank," Pearson said.

"Guess that covers it," Kenneth said with a sense of pride.

They walked on until they reached the edge of the work area and began chopping at the base of one of the trees, all the while watching the guards' behavior. Kenneth's heart raced with excitement, but he tried to act calm and not arouse suspicion. After a couple of hours, the guards began talking and laughing among themselves, smoking cigarettes. The time was right, and the three men glanced at each other and nodded. Kenneth and the other two slipped into the woods and hid behind some trees. When no one called out, they took off running as fast as they could. The other side of the forest was downhill and ended in a valley near a farm. They kept running, but now they were out in the open, a dangerous place to be. His heart pounding, Kenneth kept looking over his shoulder for signs of the Germans in pursuit.

Pearson tripped and rolled down the hill. Thank goodness he didn't cry out. Kenneth glanced over and saw McIntosh stop, run over, and help his friend up. Unharmed, the two started running again.

As they neared the farm, they ran behind a haystack, then beside a wagon, then edged along a barn, keeping their eyes and ears open to the sound of Germans on the road. The town of Barth was in sight, so they moved cautiously across the land toward the red brick clock tower that held prominence over the town. Once they neared town, they skirted the perimeter to get to the train station without being seen. They found the station, then hid in the woods nearby and waited.

"What are we going to do now? Board the train in these clothes?" Kenneth asked.

"We could remove our jackets," one of the men said.

"But do you speak German?" Kenneth asked.

"Just a few words that mean hurry up, stop, thank you."

"You'll need to know more than that," Kenneth said.

"What will you do for train tickets?"

The other two men shrugged their shoulders. "We thought we'd hop in a baggage car."

"Good luck," Kenneth said. "I think I'll just follow these tracks and see where they lead."

The whistle of an oncoming train sounded, and the men waited until the passengers disembarked when it stopped. From their vantage point in the woods, Kenneth watched Nazi guards scout the passengers, occasionally asking for identification papers. How could he get his hands on some of those? He needed a change of clothes as well because there was no way he could disguise his RAF attire.

"Are you going with us?" Scott asked Kenneth.

"No, I'm going to try another way, but good luck to you two."

They nodded, and then as the train began to slowly move away from the station, they ran along the side, grabbed hold of a baggage car, slid the door open, and disappeared inside. Kenneth hoped they wouldn't get caught.

He considered his options and decided to follow the tracks, keeping to the edge of the woods in case anyone saw him. As he walked, he thought of things he should have done or wished he had, like a map and a compass. He had no idea what direction he was headed, just that it was away from the prison camp.

No doubt by now the guards knew they had escaped, so a full-on search would be in force. Kenneth hoped there would be no negative repercussions for the others left behind. Every time he heard a noise, he ducked behind a tree or a bush and listened, his pulse racing. Often the noise was made by an animal moving through the woods. He sighed in relief, then continued on his way. Once he heard voices and ducked for cover again. Two men were walking through the forest, speaking in relaxed German and not shouting like soldiers would. Yet even though the voices weren't threatening, would German civilians want to help an escaped prisoner, or would they turn him back in like the farmer had? The probability rested with the latter, unfortunately.

His stomach growled as he continued down the tracks, and he chuckled. Boy, that was loud enough to get someone else's attention. Where could he find food? He didn't dare venture too far in case he'd get lost. He scanned the area as he walked and spotted some black-berry bushes. He hurried over and grabbed a few, popping them in his mouth and savoring the burst of flavor. A vision of Mom's blackberry pie taunted him. He ate until he didn't feel hungry anymore, wanting to take some with him but knowing what would happen if he put them in his pocket. He glanced at his hands—purple from the fruit. Hopefully his face didn't look like that too.

The tracks left the forest and traveled across the countryside. The view was beautiful and tranquil, but he had to remind himself that this was war. He had to lay low and find things to hide behind as he traveled across the land. What was the next town anyway? Too bad he couldn't stop and ask directions. Too bad he couldn't speak German either. But soon he would be back in England and wouldn't need that skill anymore.

He skirted the edge of a farm, scaring up a flock of quail, reminding him of the last time he and his father had gone hunting. Mom had roasted some for dinner afterward. There he was, thinking of food again. Why hadn't he brought some with him? Spotting some clothes hanging behind the farmhouse, he realized he needed to change his own. He crept over to the back of the house. Not seeing anyone, he made a quick dash, grabbed a shirt, and ran, then put the shirt on over his own.

The ground continued to slope downward, and as the tracks took a turn, he saw the red roofs of a small town and a church steeple tow-ering over it. Beyond the town was a large body of water. Was that the Baltic Sea? His heart thrummed with new energy as he considered the possibilities. Maybe he didn't need to take a train after all. He could just stowaway on a boat until he reached another town or perhaps country.

At a house just outside of the town, he snagged a hat sitting on a fence post and put it on, then slipped through the streets until he reached the train station. Had the other guys made it this far or even farther? The sign on the station said Stralsund. So that's where he was. With the hat covering his face and his new shirt, he was more confident to stroll through town. Spotting a couple of soldiers, he took a deep breath and tried to act nonchalant so he wouldn't attract attention.

Stralsund was a pretty town, a medieval-looking place with colorful buildings built side by side with high-pitched roofs. The cathedral appeared to be in the gothic design. The place would be nice for sightseeing if one didn't have the constant fear of being caught. The aroma of fresh bread drew him to a bakery. If only he had some money. There was an outdoor café near the bakery, so he drifted toward it. Two men got up from their table, leaving an appetizing chunk of bread and some beer in a stein. Kenneth made a pass by the table, snatching the bread and the stein, and consumed them both by the time he made it to the next street corner, setting the empty stein on a windowsill.

Kenneth inhaled the sea air as he walked down to the waterfront. Freedom smelled great. At the harbor, he strolled past the docked boats, scouting each one to see how tight the security was and how he could get onboard without being noticed. He paused beside a building and watched the activity at the docks. When two Nazi soldiers walked onto one, he sucked in a breath and slinked around the corner, hoping he hadn't been noticed. As he turned, he heard shouts as two other soldiers joined the first two. Glancing over his shoulder, he saw them point to him.

He took off running, hearing shouts and footsteps behind. Adrenaline coursed through his veins, pushing him harder and faster than he would have thought possible on only a piece of bread and a few sips of beer. Turning the next corner, he hid inside a recessed doorway and waited. For a few moments, all he could hear was the blood pounding in his ears. But as his heart rate slowed, he heard nothing. He stepped out and headed down the street, stopping at the next corner to look both ways.

At the sound of a rifle click behind him, he froze. In broken English, a voice said, "Stop or ve shoot."

Kenneth raised his hands in surrender.

# ⧉ CHAPTER II ⧉

*Leeds, England*
*July 1941*

When Mum came home from the Red Cross, she went straight to Spitfire's bed and picked up the kitten, holding him close to her face. "How's my little bundle of fur?"

Spitfire meowed and purred in response. Beryl smiled at the way her mother and the animal had bonded. Thank God she'd found the kitten. In fact, she was certain God put her in the area at just the right time to find Spitfire so she could give him to her mum. Now Mum had something good to focus on, and her entire demeanor reflected the change.

"What shall we have for dinner tonight?" Beryl asked, looking in the cupboard.

"I'm going to make Woolton pie!" Mum put the cat down on the floor and washed her hands, then tied her apron around her waist. Taking out some carrots, turnips, swedes, and a couple of potatoes, she put them on the counter beside a chopping block.

"Here, you cut these up, and I'll make the pastry."

Woolton pie was one of the recipes that supposedly came from the chef at the Savoy Hotel and was promoted by the Ministry of Food's head, the Earl of Woolton. The vegetable pie was meatless and easy to prepare from garden vegetables when meat was so rationed. Beryl liked it fairly well, since the brown sauce gave it some flavor. Even better, she was truly thankful her mum wanted to make it. Besides, Beryl hadn't yet mastered making pastry crusts.

When the pie was ready, Spitfire turned up his nose at the portion Mum gave him.

"Well, what are you, royalty? Too good for Woolton pie, are you?" Mum picked up the bowl and scraped it off. "Well, you must have more than milk." She opened the cupboard and took out a tin of sardines. "I bet you'll like this!"

"Mum! You're going to give the cat all that?" The Minister of Food certainly wouldn't approve of that waste of food.

"No, not all of it. I'll mix it with some of the Woolton pie and give him a little at a time."

She took out a couple of sardines and cut them into little pieces, mixed them with the pie, then transferred the mixture to the cat bowl. Spitfire wasted no time digging into the food, showing great satisfaction with his meal.

"You'll spoil that cat." Not that Beryl minded her mum's attention to the cat.

"He needs spoiling after what he's been through." She sat back down at the table to eat her dinner while Spitfire ate his.

"Mum, some of the girls at work want me to go with them to a dance at the social club this weekend." Beryl took a spoonful of her pie, appreciating the variety of flavors.

Mum looked up from her plate and eyed Beryl curiously. "Are you going?"

"I don't know. Freddie asked me, and I turned him down."

"That doesn't mean you can't go. I think you should. When was the last time you did something entertaining?"

Beryl gave her mum an incredulous look. "You really don't mind if I go?"

"No, of course not. Spitfire and I will keep each other company."

Was she hearing right?

"All right. I think I will. I wish I could get Veronica to go too, but she thinks she'd be betraying Rodney if she went."

"Any word about him?"

Beryl shook her head. "Nothing." Wanting to keep Mum from thinking about James and getting despondent again, she changed the subject. "What should I wear to the dance? It's been so long since I've been to one."

Mum squinted as if in thought. "You always look pretty in that pale blue dress. And the white one with the little red flowers, I like that one too."

"I think I'll go with the blue one. I'll have to get it out of the closet and freshen it up. I might need to iron it too."

"I can do that for you." Mum finished her meal, then pushed her plate away. She glanced up suddenly. "Guess what I found out today?"

"What, Mum?" Had she heard from James?

"Did you know that your company, Waddingtons, donates playing cards to the Red Cross?"

"No, I didn't know that," Beryl said. Why didn't she know about the cards?

"Yes, isn't it wonderful of Mr. Watson to do such a thing?"

"It is. I'll thank him for the gesture at work tomorrow."

"You do that, and tell him I thank him too. Those cards go in the Red Cross boxes that are sent to the prisoner of war camps. Just think, the cards that are made right here in Leeds go to our very own soldiers! I am so proud of that fact."

"Yoo-hoo!" Mrs. Findlay's voice rang out.

"We're in the kitchen, Edith," Mum said. "Come on back."

Edith Findlay bustled into the room and eyed Spitfire sitting by his bowl, washing his face.

"So, that's the little love. I just had to meet this darling Sheila was talking about all day."

"That's my Spitfire," Mum said, smiling. "Would you like to have some of our Woolton pie, Edith?"

"No, thank you. I just had dinner with William," Mrs. Findlay said, not taking her eyes off the cat. "May I hold it?"

"Certainly, but be careful. He has a bellyful and might need to go to the loo."

"I'll be careful." Mrs. Findlay leaned over and gently picked up the cat. "Aren't you a dear? Ooh, you're soft as a baby's bum! And what a pretty little thing you are!" She sat down at the table with the cat in her lap and stroked it. Right away, the room was filled with loud purring. "Now, that's the sound of a contented cat."

"I was just telling Beryl about Waddingtons donating playing cards to the Red Cross."

Mrs. Findlay looked up at Beryl. "You didn't know?"

"No, I didn't. But I'm glad to hear about it."

"And it went on right under your nose."

Beryl's face flushed, and she felt a bit ignorant for not knowing about the playing cards. Did Margaret know? Or Freddie?

"Obviously, Mr. Watson didn't communicate with me about that gesture."

"Hmm. Perhaps he's humble about his part in the war effort," Mrs. Findlay said. "There's so many things going on in this war that we don't know about. We have to get our information from the BBC and trust they're telling us the truth."

"Why wouldn't they tell us the truth?" Mum said. "We're not the enemy."

"No, but they want us to stay positive, 'keep a stiff upper lip,' you know, and not give us bad news. I heard that since the Nazis listen to our radio, our government doesn't want them to hear that we've had any losses and give them more confidence."

More war talk. Beryl was so sick of it. Everyone had an opinion about what information was truthful and what wasn't, whether England was winning or not, what the government should do, and so on, while none of them could do anything about those problems. All they could do was help in whatever way they could, praying it was to some good for the war effort.

"Mrs. Findlay, maybe you could help me decide what to wear Saturday night," Beryl said, steering the conversation away to a more pleasant subject.

"What's going on Saturday night? Do you have a date?" Mrs. Findlay smiled, glancing at Beryl's mum.

"Beryl's going to a dance at the social club!" Mum clapped her hands together, her eyes bright.

"And no, I don't have a date. I'm going with some of the girls from work."

"Why, good for you! It's about time you got out and mingled with your friends. So let's see what kind of pretty dresses you have."

"I'll go get them." Beryl stood and put the dirty dishes in the sink, then hurried upstairs to her room. Opening her wardrobe, she found the two dresses she was considering. She liked them both, but what difference did it make how she looked? There was no one she was trying to impress. The other girls were excited that they might have a chance to dance with some airmen from the nearby base. But Beryl didn't share their excitement and wasn't expecting to find her "dream" man, as Veronica called Rodney.

She took the dresses back downstairs, where the older women made her hold each one up in front of her. The decision for the blue dress was unanimous.

"Who's going to help you do your hair?" Mrs. Findlay asked.

"My hair?" Beryl combed her fingers through the ends of her straight blond hair. "I thought I'd just wear a headband."

"Nonsense! You should do some victory rolls."

"My hair doesn't do that well."

"Tell you what. I'll come over before you go and help you. I know how to make them look perfect," Mrs. Findlay said.

Beryl was tempted to roll her eyes. Looking at Mrs. Findlay's frizzled hair, one wouldn't expect her to be a hair expert. But what could it hurt?

"Beryl, isn't it nice of Mrs. Findlay to offer?" Mum patted Beryl's shoulder like she was a wee girl needing to be reminded of her manners. "Yes, Edith, you come on over on Saturday, and we can get Beryl all fixed up."

---

Saturday night, June, Margaret, Louise, and Beryl entered the social club and scanned the room. A small orchestra of older gentlemen sat on a stage at the far end warming up.

"Shall we find a seat?" Beryl said, eyeing the tables.

June glanced around, her gaze resting on a group of servicemen on the other side of the room. "Hmm. I like the scenery!" She offered a wide grin to the men and gave a little wave, receiving some smiles and nods in return.

Beryl headed for a table, and the others followed, taking their seats so they could face the stage.

"Why don't I go get us some punch?" Margaret said. "Louise, would you like to come with me?"

Louise nodded, and the two women walked toward the refreshment table. While they were gone, the band struck up the melody to "In the Mood."

"Now, that's more like it," June said, smiling at one of the servicemen. He smiled back and walked toward the table.

"Care to dance?" he said.

"Absolutely!" June got up and went out on the dance floor with him.

When Louise and Margaret returned with the drinks, they eyed the dancing couple. "What a lucky duck!" Margaret said. "She's always the first one to get asked to dance!"

June had no problem being noticed, her platinum-blonde hair, red lipstick, and form-fitting cherry-red dress demanding attention. In addition, she was a master at flirting, a skill Beryl hadn't perfected, not that she wanted to.

Moments later three more men arrived at the table, each asking one of them to dance. The women accepted and joined June and her companion.

Out on the dance floor, Beryl overlooked the unconventional movements of her dance partner. She just wanted to dance, and any partner would suffice. Once she glanced across the room and spotted a tall serviceman with black hair, and her heart leaped. Kenneth?

What had prompted that thought? Kenneth was an American who was far away from England now. How ludicrous to think he'd be in an RAF uniform. A ripple of disappointment touched her heart, regardless of the impossibility. At Oxford she'd attended a dance and had danced with Kenneth every dance. She smiled at the memory of the handsome man who kept her laughing the whole evening—and recalled that his dancing style and movement were far beyond that of her present partner.

At the end of the song, Beryl said she needed to catch her breath, so she went back to the table. She wasn't really tired of dancing, just tired of her partner and tired of wishing he was someone else. If only she could go back to that time in her life.

"Would you like to dance?" A man's voice broke her reverie.

She glanced up at the attractive, light-haired soldier and smiled. "Sure." Life had to go on, and she'd have to find a way to enjoy it.

# ﹥ CHAPTER 12 ﹤

*Stalag Luft I, Barth, Germany*
*July 1941*

"To the cooler!" the commandant shouted, pointing toward the window. This time his nostrils flared when he gave the command. "Lieutenant, you are testing my patience and my generous hospitality. You will be in the cooler two weeks. Perhaps you will see the futility of your efforts."

Two guards grabbed Kenneth's arms and led him out of the commandant's office. As they entered the POW camp, the gate guard gave his rote greeting. "For you, da var is over."

"That's what you think," Kenneth muttered under his breath.

Kenneth's prisoners nodded their hello when he was marched by them. He shrugged and forced a smile. His stomach tightened from the frustration of not succeeding again, even after more planning. Two weeks in solitary confinement was no picnic, but at least he wasn't going to be shot.

Once again he was escorted to the cooler. The guards ushered him inside and shoved him through one of the doors, slamming it behind him. Why did it sound so loud this time? He heard the bolt sliding into place and the door being locked. He shuddered, feeling like a trapped wild animal. He went to the window but was disappointed when he realized he was in a different cell than before. Looked like he'd better start work on this window now. At least he had something to occupy his time.

A sound from the adjoining room piqued his curiosity. He pounded on the wall.

"Hey! Who's in there?"

"Yank? That you? It's me, Pearson!"

"Pearson! When did you get caught?"

"They got us coming off the train at Stralsund."

"McIntosh is in here too?"

"Yes, he's next door to me. Where'd they get you?"

"Same town. I was going to get on one of the boats there at the harbor, but they found me before I could."

"Well, we tried."

"Next time we'll succeed," Kenneth said.

"Next time?"

"Sure. Now I know what I need to do better."

For the next two weeks, Kenneth planned another escape. Occasionally an accusing voice echoed through his head, telling him what a failure he was. After all, he'd ditched his plane, become a prisoner, then failed at two escapes. What made him think he'd get out the next time? But he shoved those thoughts away. He had to get out, get back to England, and finish this war. He didn't tell the men next door about the windows because he hadn't surveyed the area outside the cooler yet, and he didn't want one of them to try to get out before he had a plan. When the guards unlocked his door at the end of his solitary confinement, he was ready to go back to the barracks and discuss with Colonel Gilmore what he'd figured out about escapes.

After meeting with the colonel, Kenneth returned to his room where Harold sat with some pencils and drawing paper.

"Hey, Harold. You get that from home?"

Harold nodded. "Yes. Mum knows how I like to draw, so she keeps me supplied with material."

Kenneth snapped his fingers. "I should've asked my mom to send me some too."

"I can afford to share some of mine with you until you get some supplies of your own."

"Gee, thanks, pal." Kenneth took the sketch paper Harold handed him and one of the pencils, in much better condition than the stub he'd used to write his letter. He began drawing the compound layout showing the arrangement of the barracks and other buildings. Visualizing it as he thought it would look from above, he pretended he was flying over it. He drew the woods to the east and the commandant's office in the west. He drew the guard towers, which Angus called goon boxes, the warning wire in front of the barbed-wire fence, the playing field, and the gardening area.

He was so engrossed in his drawing, he didn't even notice the door open.

Colonel Gilmore's voice drew his attention.

"Gentlemen, you have a new roommate. This is Lieutenant James Clarke."

Kenneth bolted upright on his bed, hitting his head on the ceiling. Putting his drawing aside, he hopped off the bed.

"James!"

James' eyes lit up when he saw Kenneth, and a smile worked its way across his face.

"You two know each other, I assume," Colonel Gilmore said. "Well, carry on then." He saluted and left the room.

"James, of all people!" Kenneth threw his arms open to give his friend a hug, but James backed away.

"Careful." He pointed to his arm, which Kenneth hadn't noticed was in a sling. "I just got released from the hospital."

Kenneth looked at the sling, then back at James. "Were you hurt very badly?"

"Some cracked ribs, broken arm, concussion. Not as bad as some poor blokes though. At least I survived. When our plane was hit, I was able to parachute out. But I hit a tree on the way down when my chute got hung up, then I landed on the ground."

"How long have you been here? Do you know?"

James shrugged. "Not very sure, but maybe three, four weeks. I'm actually not sure what today is."

Kenneth noticed Angus and the others watching them. "Hey, guys, I want you to meet my good friend, James. We were in college together at Oxford until the war ended all that."

"Nice to meet ya," Angus said, and the other men murmured greetings as well. He pointed to the last empty bunk below Kenneth's. "How convenient that you two ended up together. Make yourself comfortable."

"Thank you," James said, going to the bunk and sitting down. Kenneth sat beside him.

"But what are *you* doing here, Kenneth? Last I heard, the United States hadn't entered the war, unless that changed while I was in the hospital."

"No, it didn't change. Long story, but I went to Canada where some guys were hiring pilots for the RAF. They hired me and shipped me to England where I trained and flew for the 71st Squadron."

"The Eagle Squadron. I've heard of them. Thanks for joining the fight," James said, offering his hand.

Kenneth shook it. "Sorry, I wasn't in it very long, but I intend to make up for it when I get out of here."

"You mean before the war ends?"

"Of course, but we'll talk about that later. Do you know if your parents are aware that you're a prisoner?" Kenneth asked James.

James shook his head. "No, I don't. But there's only Mum now. Dad was killed in a bombing back in March. He was an air raid warden and was trying to usher people into the shelter when the bomb hit. Unfortunately, he didn't get inside himself."

"I'm so sorry, James." Kenneth paused, reflecting on the unfairness of the attack. "And your sister, Beryl? Is she okay?"

"She's well. She moved back home to Leeds to be with Mum after Dad died."

"That's good of her. She's a nice gal. I enjoyed being around her back in Oxford."

James nodded. "Yes, she is. Mum was devastated by Dad's death, and Beryl thought she shouldn't be alone. She was in London during the Blitz, helping out as much as she could. Leeds hasn't been hit nearly as much, but then it's a smaller city. As soon as the government allowed women to join the ARP, she became an air raid warden as well."

Kenneth's brows lifted. "That so? Well, somehow that doesn't surprise me. She strikes me as a pretty brave gal."

"She is. She'd probably do more if she didn't have to stay with Mum."

"I hate all the devastation Hitler has done to England. I wanted to give him what for, but I didn't get finished before I was hit. Had to ditch in the channel before a Nazi minesweeper fished me out," Kenneth said.

"I know what you mean. I thought I was helping to bring a swift end to this war too." James stroked his face where blond stubble was showing. "I could use a shave, but I'm not too good with my left hand."

Kenneth scrutinized his friend's face. "Yep, you don't have much of a beard, but it's pretty scruffy. Would you like me to shave for you?" He grinned. "I promise not to cut your throat."

Chuckling, James said, "I'm pretty desperate, so I might let you have a go at it."

"Well, come on, then!" Kenneth grabbed his razor and a piece of soap, and they walked down to the latrine. The other guys in the latrine laughed as Kenneth worked up a lather with the soap and applied it to James' face. As Kenneth poised over James with the razor in hand, Angus called out, "We have a new barber, fellas! Who wants to be next?"

"Don't make me laugh, Angus," Kenneth said. "I really don't want to hurt my good friend here."

Guffaws and laughter followed as Kenneth focused on keeping a steady hand, thankful James' beard wasn't coarse. Soon he was finished. James rinsed off his face and rubbed it. "Pretty good. Thanks, Kenneth."

"All right. All done." He looked at the others. "Barbershop closed. James, what say we go for a stroll?"

"Would love to stretch my legs," James said. "Lead the way."

Outside, Kenneth followed the path Angus had taken him when Kenneth was new to the camp. "So, this is our temporary home."

James lifted an eyebrow. "What do you mean by 'temporary'?"

"As temporary as I can make it." Kenneth spoke in low tones, keeping an eye on whoever was near them.

"You're planning to escape, then?"

"You mean, escape again. I just did my time in the cooler for the second time."

James' eyebrows raised. "You got out? Truly? Tell me how."

Kenneth told James all about his first two attempts.

"But we have to keep trying. You know they warned us in training that if you don't escape early on, you get comfortable and complacent. I'm working on how to make the next time successful. Don't worry. I'm doing my homework."

"Are any others involved?" James glanced around.

"Not with me. Not yet anyway. But I think they might have something going on too."

"Then perhaps we should work together."

"Yeah, maybe so. But I don't want anybody to slow me down."

James gave Kenneth a sidelong glance. "You always have been an impatient one, haven't you?"

Kenneth chuckled. "You noticed."

"I remember you wheeling around on that motorbike at college. Couldn't walk like the rest of us. Beryl said you wouldn't give up before she let you take her for a ride."

Shrugging, Kenneth said, "I can't help it. I like speed. Maybe that's why I like flying so much. Besides, Beryl loved it."

Come to think of it, he loved it too. She was such a joy to be with as she giggled and screamed in the sidecar when he took sharp turns. He sure liked being with her. And when she climbed out of the sidecar, her blond hair in stunning disarray, held back by a headband, and her cheeks flushed—wow. The image still stunned him and made his heart thump. He sure wished he could see her again.

"She did. She's a bit of a daredevil herself. In fact, if it weren't for staying with Mum, I would expect her to join the WAAF."

"Just imagine that. Beryl in the Woman's Auxiliary Air Force." Kenneth pictured the slim blond in a uniform. She'd make even the dull blue military suit look good.

As they passed the recreation field, they paused to watch some POWs playing cricket. "I'm surprised the prisoners have so many activities," James said. "I thought it would be worse."

"As long as you look busy and stay out of trouble, they'll leave you alone. We airmen are treated better than some of the other POWs, from what I understand. Seems that Reichsmarschall Goering was a fighter pilot in the last war and has the highest regard for airmen. Rumor has it he's having a special prison built for airmen, and when it's finished, they'll move some of us to it."

"I suppose that's something to be thankful for," James said. "It could be worse."

Kenneth lifted his eyebrows at James' remark. "I want you to know I don't intend to be here long enough to get moved to another camp."

James gave him a questioning look. "I'd like to hear more about that."

"You will, just as soon as I get things figured out."

They walked past the chapel, and James nodded at the cross over the door. "A chapel?"

"Sure is. They have two here, built by the prisoners."

"Have you been to a service?"

"Nope, not my cup o' tea, as they say, but hey, if you want to go, I'll go with you, just to keep you company."

James cocked his head at Kenneth. "All right. I'll take you up on that."

"Say, James, you like to sing, don't you? Didn't you tell me you were a tenor back in Oxford?"

"Yes, that's right. Why? They have a choir?"

Kenneth laughed. "No, not in the chapel. But there is a glee club. I just joined it. Why don't you join too?"

"Sounds like a smashing idea. Sign me up."

"Just come with me at ten this morning. They could use another good voice. They can't rely on just mine." Kenneth grinned.

"You never did lack for ego, did you, Kenneth?"

"Why should I?"

They both laughed.

"Can we write letters home? I'd love to tell Mum and Beryl that I'm here and so are you, but. . ." He pointed to his arm in the sling. "I'm right-handed."

"Why don't I write it for you? You just tell me what to say."

"Splendid. Let's get to it."

Back in the barracks, Kenneth took a piece of writing paper and a pencil and sat down on the edge of James' bed. "I don't know what will make it past the censors, but you can ask for things. Go ahead, shoot."

"All right."

*Dear Mum and Beryl, Greetings from a prisoner of war camp in Germany. I want you to know I am all right. Got a little banged up on the way here but am fine now. However, my right arm is in a cast, so a mutual friend of ours, Kenneth Bordelon from university, is here as well, so he is doing the writing for me. I certainly was surprised to see him here. We have been catching up and discussing his favorite bird, bald eagles. We should be getting some Red Cross parcels, but if you would not mind, please send me some biscuits, jam, tea, Spam, sardines, and fine chocolates, if you can spare them. Kenneth and I are joining a glee club here because we both enjoy singing. You may be surprised to*

*know there is a small chapel here as well. Kenneth said he*
*would attend with me! Much love from James.*

"Perfect! Let's get this one sealed up and ready to go out," Kenneth said, folding the paper.

Angus poked his head in the door. "Barracks meeting in five. Colonel Gilmore needs to speak with all of us."

# ⬛ CHAPTER 13 ⬛

*Leeds, England*
*July 1941*

Beryl lifted one end of the sheet, and Mum took the other end to hang it over the clothesline that stretched between their town house and the row of other town houses across the garden behind them. The kitten entertained himself as well by jumping in and out of the clothes basket on the ground. When Beryl went inside to get more clothespins, there was a knock at the front door.

She hurried to answer it and opened the door to find a young telegraph courier.

"Mrs. Clarke?"

Beryl nodded, not bothering to explain she wasn't her mother. The courier handed her an official-looking manila envelope, which looked just like the last one they'd received. As she studied the envelope, her heart sank. *Oh God, please don't let this say that James is dead.* But no, it couldn't be that. When someone was killed in the line of duty, military personnel delivered the news in person.

The envelope was heavy in her hand as she returned to the garden.

"What is it, Beryl?" Mum eyed the envelope, and the color drained from her face.

"This." She held out the envelope. "Would you like me to open it?"

Mum appeared to be in shock. Then, as if reaching out to touch a venomous snake, she took the envelope. "No, I'll do it myself."

She opened the envelope and withdrew the telegram. Tears filled her eyes as she read it. She covered her mouth with her hand while Beryl's stomach twisted in knots. Mum handed the missive to Beryl. The message was short. "The Air Ministry wishes to inform you your son Lieutenant James Clarke is a prisoner of war in Germany."

"Oh no," Beryl said, her heart sinking at the look of despair on Mum's face. She reached for Mum's hand. "Let's go inside and I'll put the kettle on. It's getting a bit breezy out here. I'll get Spitfire." Beryl picked up the basket with the cat in it, and they walked toward the back door, moving as if their shoes were made of lead.

Mrs. Findlay's voice called out from the front door. "Sheila? Beryl?"

"In the kitchen. Come on back."

Beryl put the teakettle on as Mrs. Findlay came in, her expression worried.

"I just saw a courier leave your house. Any news?" she said, her eyes glancing from Beryl to her mother.

Beryl pulled the telegram from her pocket and set it down on the table. She glanced at Mrs. Findlay. "James is a prisoner of Germany."

"Oh dear."

The three women sat in silence for a few minutes before Beryl spoke.

"That's good news. I mean, we know he's alive now." She had to find a way to keep her mother from sinking back into despair.

Mrs. Findlay nodded. "You're right." She and Beryl looked at Mum for her reaction.

Mum's shoulders sagged, and she sighed. "I suppose we can be thankful for that. We must pray that he's treated well."

Mrs. Findlay reached across the table and patted Mum's hand. "We will certainly do that, luv."

Mum's head popped up. "Maybe James will get one of the Red Cross boxes we are packing. Wouldn't it be something if he got a pack of cards from Waddingtons, from Leeds, his hometown!"

"That's the spirit," Mrs. Findlay said.

"From now on, I'm taking extra care to make sure those boxes have special treats, just in case James gets one."

"I wish we knew exactly where he was so we could mail a package directly to him," Beryl said.

"Can you do that? Will the Germans allow it?" Mrs. Findlay asked.

"Yes, I heard that Karen Ross' brother Andrew is a prisoner too, and she said they can send him packages."

"But how can we get the address?" Mum asked. "Can we ask someone in the government?"

"From what I've been told, the Ross family got a letter from Andrew with some kind of instructions about how to send him parcels."

"So we wait for James to write us?" Mum said. "I hope he can."

"If he can, I know he will," Beryl said, praying he would be able to.

———————— ≋ ————————

As Beryl buttoned the jacket of her ARP uniform later that afternoon, James was still on her mind. How was he being treated? What was the prison like? She shuddered at some of the pictures that ran through her mind. *God, please protect him.* Downstairs, she said good night to Mum and Mrs. Findlay. Mum would go to the Findlay town house while Beryl was on duty, a practice that had started after Dad was killed. Her mother was doing better lately, but Beryl still didn't want her to be alone at night, especially if the sirens went off. She'd even dealt with the news of James becoming a prisoner better than expected. No doubt the kitten had helped. Naturally, Spitfire would go to Mrs. Findlay's with Mum.

Beryl reported to her ARP post downtown and greeted the others on duty that night. Mr. Browning, a stout gentleman in his fifties, was her partner in their sector of town.

"Good evening, Miss Clarke," he said, his bushy white mustache moving up and down as he spoke. "Let's hope it'll be a good one, eh?"

She smiled at the older man as they donned their helmets, buckled the leather straps under their chins, and went out together. They headed toward their designated sector and began walking the streets. Although it was barely past six o'clock, the night sky was overcast and dark, and with no streetlights, they had to be careful where they walked. They flicked on the beams of their torches, pointing them downward to keep as little light as possible from showing while their eyes got accustomed to darkness. At least they didn't have the danger of as many cars on the road as she had dealt with when she lived in London. Accidents happened, and pedestrians were hit on a regular basis there due to blackout conditions.

Beryl and Mr. Browning took opposite sides of the street to patrol. Beryl would take the right side and Mr. Browning would take the left, searching the houses for any sign of visible light.

Ahead, light shone from windows on either side of the street.

"Buggers!" Mr. Browning said, as he headed toward the home on the left. "I've told these people over and over again to keep their curtains drawn!" He banged on the door, and when a young man opened it, he said, "Your blackout curtains are not closed again. You must keep them closed at night or you endanger yourself and your whole neighborhood. Please comply with the rules. I'll have to write you a citation this time because this is your third warning." He whipped out a pad of paper from his pocket, wrote something on it, tore it off, and handed it to the man. "You can pay this at the police station tomorrow."

The sound of a baby crying inside the house made Beryl pity the young man. It was hard enough to manage a young family at times like this. The man took the paper and went back inside. Soon each of the curtains in the house had been pulled together.

The house emitting light on Beryl's side of the street was farther down, but she too approached the door and rapped the brass knocker several times before a diminutive snow-white-haired woman opened it a crack, peering out with wide-eyed worry.

"Ma'am, I must ask you to close your blackout curtains. There is light coming from your windows."

The woman appeared confused. "What did you say?"

Beryl raised her voice. "You need to close your blackout curtains!"

"I'm sorry, I can't hear you."

This time Beryl yelled, and the woman nodded. "There is?" She looked around.

Beryl glanced over her shoulder where Mr. Browning waited. "I'm going to help her," she said. "She can't hear."

He nodded and crossed his arms.

"May I assist you to close your curtains?" Beryl asked in a loud voice.

The woman gave a nod and stepped back, opening the door for Beryl to enter. Beryl noted the woman's bent stature as she shuffled into the parlor, following Beryl. Beryl crossed the room to the front window and pulled the tall curtains closed.

"Thank you. I forgot to close them. And they're rather heavy."

"Are you here alone?" Beryl yelled, glancing around.

"No. My husband is here, but he's sleeping upstairs."

"Do you have a shelter?"

The woman pointed to a box on the floor of the kitchen. "There."

They had a Morrison shelter, an indoor oblong cage-like box that doubled as a kitchen table for many people.

"Good. Then in an air raid, you and your husband will get inside it and be safe. Do you understand?"

The woman fingered the strand of pearls around her neck and shrugged. "At our age, it's rather difficult to climb into that uncomfortable thing. And it's almost impossible to wake Harry up."

"You must try. Do you understand?"

Getting a nod, Beryl turned to go. Outside she met Mr. Browning and shook her head. "That poor old couple has a Morrison shelter, but I don't think they ever use it for a shelter. And the woman is so hard of hearing, I don't know that she would even hear the air raid siren."

"That's Mr. and Mrs. Dowd. Have lived there since I was a wee one. People like that should go to the city shelters, but that's even harder unless someone helps them get there. I just pray there won't be any bombs dropped here." He scanned the area outside the door. "At least they have a water bucket and a sand bucket."

Everyone had been encouraged to have the two buckets in case a bomb landed near their homes. The sand would be used to snuff out incendiary bombs, while the water would be used to put out fires. Most of the time the buckets were used by the fire departments when they were needed.

Beryl and Mr. Browning continued their patrol, talking about the war as they walked.

"We've heard from the government that my brother James has been taken prisoner," she told him. "So that explains why we haven't heard from him for a while."

"Oh, that's too bad. But now you know where he is. He should be safer now than in combat."

Beryl hadn't considered that possibility. "Do you think they'll treat him poorly?"

"I don't know. I guess it depends on where he is. Did you say he was a pilot?"

"Yes, he is."

"Then I hear he may be treated better than some of the other prisoners." He patted her on the back. "Don't worry. This war will be over soon, and he'll be back home."

"Do you really believe that?" she asked.

"Yes, of course. Why, look how they've let up on bombing us. I hear Hitler's diverted his attention to Russia. Guess he didn't count on our Royal Air Force to put up such a fight. We scared them away!" He chuckled.

"I hope you're right."

They had just turned a corner when the air raid siren sounded, startling Beryl. The last week had passed with no air raids, plus these sounded much earlier in the evening than usual. She and Mr. Browning looked at each other briefly, then turned toward the nearest public shelter downtown and began walking briskly, shepherding people who didn't have home shelters to the public ones.

"They're early tonight," Mr. Browning said to her. He turned to the people rushing beside him on the street. "Come along. Be careful, mind you. No pushing or shoving, please."

The dreaded drone of approaching airplanes further frightened the crowd, and they began to run. There was no point in trying to stop them. The only thing Beryl and Mr. Browning could do was try to keep anyone from being knocked down. When they reached the four brick shelters in the center of town, ARP wardens who stood at each entrance waved the crowd in.

"We've got room in here," one said.

Beryl and Mr. Browning waited until everyone had gotten inside a shelter before they too squeezed inside. When the raids were more frequent, more people automatically went to the shelters at night. But some people had become convinced the raids had ended and stayed home. And still a few had decided to live in the shelters, having nowhere else to go since losing their homes in a bombing. The authorities frowned on that habit and encouraged them to go to families or billet with someone else in town, but there were still the "sitters."

Beryl listened to the droning vibration of passing planes, feeling the movement through her feet. The image of the elderly Mrs. Dowd came to her mind, and she shuddered. Had the woman heard the sirens? Did they try to get into the shelter this time? Beryl struggled with regret as the din of "ack-ack" guns responded to the intruders with heavy firing. Should she have gone back and made sure they were sheltering? Soon the sound of dull thuds signified bombs landing, tearing apart their targets. A swish and a whistle meant firebombs or incendiaries had been dropped as well. She and Mr. Browning exchanged glances. They needed to get outside and help extinguish the devices before they started fires. How long would they be stuck inside before the long, steady blast of the all-clear sounded? What would they find when they got out?

# ⚏ CHAPTER 14 ⚏

*Stalag Luft I, Barth, Germany*
*July 1941*

"Wonder what happened," Kenneth said.

"We'd better go find out," James said.

The gathering area was crowded as the men crammed in to hear the colonel. Some guys squatted on the floor so others could see over their heads. A haze of cigarette smoke hovered over the room. When they were all there, the colonel stood in the middle of them. He looked back at one of the men who was looking through the window near the door watching for ferrets. The man gave him a thumbs-up.

Scanning the group, the colonel began. "Gentlemen, as you know, one of our men recently escaped." He looked at Kenneth. "Unfortunately, he was caught. However, I'm sure you've all spoken among yourselves about escaping. I want you to know that as members of the Royal Air Force, it is our duty to try to escape. There have, in fact, been several escapes from here, but all the men have been recaptured. Although we would prefer not to get caught, those efforts are still worthwhile.

"Why? Because for one thing, it ties up a lot of German soldiers to look for the escapees. That means fewer soldiers who are fighting against the Commonwealth, and it unsettles them. Secondly, anyone who gets out can provide us with information about what worked and what didn't. They can also give us important observations about what lies beyond the perimeter, depending on how far they get. Remember, we are still at war, and this is how we can fight the enemy here.

"The important thing is to keep trying. However, we need to work together and come up with some more organized plans than the previous attempts. For those of you who are new to the camp, we will let you in on what we have done so far. If you plan to escape, you need to come talk to me about it because we will have to make plans to cover your absence as long as we can and to give you a head start. If you have any ideas, run them by me. We may have tried them before, and they didn't work. But if your idea is worth trying, we'll support you."

James cut a glance at Kenneth, who stood with his arms crossed.

"Even if you don't plan to be one of the men who escape, you can help the cause. The fact is, the longer you stay here, the less you'll want to escape, and that means you are shirking your duty to fight. Which is just what the enemy wants you to do. And should you escape and be found, just surrender, and if you don't resist, you'll be fortunate enough to be brought back here and spend some time in the cooler. After that, you'll be reunited with your fellow kriegies and can start working on a better plan. Of course, if you're foolish enough to run or resist, you'll get shot."

Several of the guys standing around turned toward their neighbors and muttered something under their breath.

"Men in other barracks are planning escapes too, so we'll form a committee in order to coordinate with the leaders of those barracks to make the escapes as successful as possible. Remember, you are still members of the RAF, and we are still at war with our captors. What I need to know now is what you are particularly good at, what kind of skills you have that would be useful. Perhaps your job before the war can assist our future plans. We will each be assigned specific duties to help the effort, but we will keep that information as private as possible. The less you know, the less you can be interrogated about, should that happen.

"Whatever you do, don't talk about any ideas inside. You never know when a ferret might be listening." He stomped the floor. "In fact, there may be one listening right now!" He lowered his voice. "We'll talk outside, individually. Is that understood?"

The men responded with a crisp "Yes, sir!"

"Very well then. You're dismissed."

The men ambled out of the building and formed groups of two or three, then proceeded to stroll the grounds, walking by guards who eyed them suspiciously.

Angus caught up with Kenneth and James and walked alongside them. "So, mates, what are your special skills?"

"I flew a crop duster," Kenneth said, grinning. "I can fly away."

Angus snorted. "We could all do that, mate."

"You're a pretty good artist too from what I remember," James said to Kenneth. He looked at Angus. "What about you?"

"Me? I was in the theater, an actor, you know."

Kenneth and James stared at him, mouths agape. "You don't say! What sort of theater—comedy?"

Angus laughed. "You may find this hard to believe, but mainly Shakespeare."

"Well, isn't that a surprise? I'd never have pegged you for a Hamlet."

"To be or not to be, that is the question." Angus assumed a pose, then flourished a bow. He turned to James. "And you, sir, do you have a special skill?"

James shrugged. "I've dabbled with electronics."

"Now, that does indeed sound promising."

Kenneth, James, and Angus met with Colonel Gilmore, who used a crude walking stick as he tried to mask his limp. As they walked around the prison yard, Kenneth eyed the cooler and what it was close to. He didn't relish spending more time inside the building, especially now that it was August and the heat inside was miserable, even with the window, because no air circulated. The next time, he'd have to make sure he could get out quickly.

"Lieutenant Bordelon, I'd like to see your sketches of the prison yard. What we'll do is start measuring the distances between buildings, fences, and so forth."

"May I suggest we should also measure the distance from the cooler to everything else as well?"

Gilmore looked at Kenneth. "Are you planning an escape from the cooler, Lieutenant?"

Kenneth grinned. "We have to be prepared for any scenario, in my opinion."

"Then, fine. We'll measure that too. And anything else you think of, then note that on the sketches. Do any of you know how many inches your foot is?"

"Yes, sir. I can walk off the distances and add the figures to my sketches," Kenneth said.

"Actually, you need to measure your stride, not just your foot. It would look fairly obvious that you were measuring if you put each foot toe to heel when you walked."

Kenneth chuckled. "Good thinking, Colonel."

The colonel responded with a wry smile, then turned his attention to James. "Electrical?"

"Yes, sir. I can install circuits, wiring, and such."

"Good. We'll need that in the next tunnels we're going to dig." The colonel glanced around. "Do you have a problem with claustrophobia?"

"I don't think so, sir." James pointed to his arm. "It might be difficult going underground at this time, though."

"Of course. We'll find some work for you above ground. Besides, not everyone will be assigned to digging. Your job will be to coordinate with the other electricians who are underground."

The colonel glanced at Angus. "An actor?"

"Yes, sir. I can improvise any kind of character you need."

"First, you need to know how to speak German."

"Working on it, sir. I know several languages, including French and Italian."

"Good. In fact, I'm going to request that we all learn to speak German. Once we get out, we need to not only communicate but know what they're saying around us."

"*Jawohl!*" Angus said, saluting.

The others glanced around to see if any guards had noticed, but none were close by.

"Careful, Lieutenant. We mustn't let them know we understand their language."

"Right, sir. One of the guards is rather friendly. He's one of the good Germans, so I ask him about words sometimes. His name is Klaus, and he's fairly naive and enjoys teaching me."

"I see. Well, keep it up and make a list to share with the others." The colonel stopped walking and stood with his hands clasped behind his back. He glanced at each one. "So, is that it, or can you think of anything else you might be able to do to help the cause?"

Angus nodded. "Yes, sir. Since I've been involved in many aspects of theater, I've learned to make costumes too. Perhaps I can assist by making any improvisations in uniforms, in case we need to assume other identities."

"Excellent idea. In fact, why don't all of you request needle and thread in your letters to your families? Sometimes we get those items in the Red Cross packages, but we can use more, much more."

"Yes, sir," they all responded.

"Fine. I'll meet with the tunnel diggers next and see what they need. Lieutenant Clarke, I need to introduce you to the other electricians. Come with me."

"Yes, sir." James glanced at Kenneth and nodded before walking away with the colonel.

"What happened to his leg?" Kenneth asked as he and Angus watched the colonel walk away.

"Bad break when he landed. His parachute didn't open properly. The German doctors put a cast on it at first, but I don't think they could get it fixed back to normal. I think it still bothers him."

"No doubt."

# ═ CHAPTER 15 ═

*Leeds, England*
*July 1941*

"I can't stay in here any longer," Beryl said. "They need our help out there."

Mr. Browning nodded. "Right. I'll go with you. Just be careful."

He pushed open the door, then took Beryl's arm as they walked outside the shelter.

All around them, the sky was aglow from fires in various parts of the city. Firemen called out to each other as they battled the blazes. A plane flew over, dropping metal canisters that clinked when they hit the pavement.

"Incendiaries!" Beryl yelled as one of the containers bounced only feet away from her. She ran to grab the nearest sandbag, then carried it back and dumped its contents over the explosive device, the only way to put it out before it exploded. Water only made them burst into flame. Satisfied she had doused it, she spotted another and ran to put it out too. As she did so, she gazed around at the chaotic scene. She looked toward their assigned area, and alarm shocked her body. The area was on fire.

She started running toward it as Mr. Browning called out behind her. "Miss Clarke! Wait for me!"

She couldn't though. All she could think of was Mrs. Dowd and her husband. She ran as fast as she could toward their street. When she reached the end of their row of town houses, she paused and stared. The scene was horrific. Partially destroyed homes stood beside piles of rubble that only moments before had been someone's home. Flames rose from several houses as firemen fought to put them out. Mr. Browning grabbed the nearest stirrup pumps and began attacking the fires near him. In the meantime, Beryl searched the street for the Dowd town house and spotted it. *Oh no.* She ran toward the building.

"Ma'am, look out there!" a fireman shouted. She ignored him and kept running until she reached the home of the elderly couple. The top half of the structure was gone, having fallen into the first floor. Her heart sank, seeing the hopeless situation. There was no way the couple could have survived. Despite her doubts, she ran up the stairs to the door, now standing slightly ajar, pushed it all the way open, and stepped inside.

"Mrs. Dowd!" She yelled as loudly as she could above the din of noise outside, hoping the partially deaf woman could hear her if she was alive. "Dear Lord," she muttered as she scanned the debris, trying to recognize anything that looked familiar. Heading to the kitchen area, she saw the Morrison shelter—empty. "Mrs. Dowd!"

Beryl stepped over pieces of fallen ceiling, carefully picking her way through the house. Near the back door she saw what looked like a curio cabinet lying on the floor. What was that underneath it? Was that a hand? Trembling with dread, she moved to the cabinet and lifted it as much as she could to see underneath. Pieces of glass and broken figurines were scattered about the small form of a pale figure lying beneath. Mrs. Dowd.

Beryl felt the lady's wrist, then her neck, not expecting to feel a pulse. But there it was, faint, yet there. She had to get the woman help, but she was wedged under the debris. "Help!" Beryl called, not thinking anyone would hear her.

"I'm here." Mr. Browning's voice sounded behind her. "Let me help." He leaned over and moved the cabinet all the way off the woman while Beryl moved other debris. "Is she alive?"

"Yes, I feel a pulse." She glanced around. "But where is her husband?"

Mr. Browning looked up at the open sky showing through and shook his head. "If he was upstairs, I don't expect we'll find him alive." As his eyes searched the house, he grimaced, then pointed. Beryl's gaze followed. In a section of the upstairs that remained was a bed with a figure in it that was obviously dead. A lump formed in Beryl's throat. She glanced back down at Mrs. Dowd. "Can you lift her?"

"Yes, I'm sure I can. She weighs practically nothing—less than a sandbag, I'd guess."

He bent over and picked up the woman, carrying her out the front door and down the steps. "See if you can flag an ambulance."

Beryl ran down the street, waving her arms at the ambulance moving slowly near the end of the road. Recognizing the driver, she said, "Veronica!"

Her friend stopped the vehicle and got out. "Bad night," she said, her dark uniform showing stains, probably blood. She looked behind Beryl and saw Mr. Browning coming with Mrs. Dowd in his arms. "Someone you know?"

Beryl shook her head. "We just met tonight. Her name is Mrs. Dowd."

Walking to the rear of the ambulance, Veronica opened the door and retrieved a stretcher, laying it on the ground. Mr. Browning put the tiny pale figure on the stretcher, and then all three of them lifted it and put it into the ambulance. Closing the door, Veronica turned to Beryl.

"Do you want to ride along?"

Beryl glanced at Mr. Browning, who nodded. "Go ahead."

Beryl climbed into the ambulance just as the all-clear siren sounded. The threat of more bombers was over now, but the destruction they'd left behind would last a long time.

"Does she have family?" Veronica asked, keeping her eyes on the road as she drove carefully, avoiding impassable areas. She swerved out of the way of firemen rushing across the street to a flaming building.

Beryl glanced at the figure lying behind them, then lowered her voice. "She had a husband. . ." She shook her head.

"Oh."

"I don't know if there's any other family. If there is, it seems like they would be watching out for them."

"Surely someone knows, maybe neighbors."

"Perhaps."

After the night's bombing, how many of those neighbors were still alive? Beryl shuddered at the thought. No matter how many times she had seen the destruction created by the Nazi onslaught, she never forgot the cost of lives and families devastated. In London the citizens seemed to adapt to the routine, recuperating and repairing on a regular basis so their daily lifestyles continued. But here in Leeds where the bombings were less frequent, the shock was more difficult to absorb. She stared out the window in the direction of home. Had her neighborhood been hit as well? If not, did Mum have any idea how terrible the other parts of the city had suffered?

"And we thought it was over," Veronica said. "Wishful thinking."

"Sometimes it seems like it will never be over," Beryl said.

"I know, but we can't give up hope, can we?"

"No. Mr. Churchill keeps reminding us. We can't give up hope that Germany will stop bombing us. And we can't give up hope for our soldiers. I haven't had the chance to tell you that we learned James was taken prisoner."

Veronica jerked her focus away from the road to look at Beryl. "He has? Dear God." She returned her gaze to the road. "So now you know where he is. How's your mum taking the news?"

"Better than I thought. I believe she's more motivated to help at the Red Cross, now that she thinks she's helping James."

"We've still no news about Rodney," Veronica said.

"That must be good, though," Beryl said. "I mean, if he had been captured or anything else"—she refused to say 'killed'—"surely you would have been notified by now."

"I keep hoping that's the case."

Veronica pulled in front of St. James Hospital and stopped. They both got out of the car and walked around to the back of the vehicle. As Veronica opened the door, a hospital attendant in blood-soaked clothes approached. "What have you got?"

"Elderly woman. Alive but unconscious. No sign of injuries other than some scratches."

"I'll help you take her inside."

Beryl felt Mrs. Dowd's pulse again, reassuring herself that the woman was still alive. She helped the others lift the stretcher and carry it into the hospital. The situation inside was chaotic. The hallway was filled with injured people either lying on stretchers or sitting with wounds that needed attention. They found a place to set the stretcher down while doctors and nurses ran back and forth checking on people and calling out orders.

"She'll have to wait awhile before the doctor can get to her and she can be put in a room," the attendant said.

Beryl looked at her friend. "I'll stay with her. I don't want her waking up alone in the midst of strangers. At least she has seen me before, if she remembers." She glanced down at Mrs. Dowd. "But would you please go by my house on your way home and tell my mum where I am so she won't be worried?"

"Of course. Take care."

"You do the same."

Watching Veronica leave, Beryl considered what would happen to the elderly woman. How was she going to tell her that her husband had been killed? If she survived, where would she live now that her home was destroyed?

The doctor rushed up to check on Mrs. Dowd. Beryl filled him in on what she knew. He felt her pulse, then touched the scratches.

"Those are probably from the knickknacks that fell out of her curio cabinet when it landed on her."

"They don't look too deep. That cabinet might have saved her life," he said.

"Do you think anything is broken?"

"Not that I can tell. But she could have internal injuries." He gently pressed on the stomach, legs, and arms but got no response. "I think she just got knocked unconscious, so we'll have to wait and see."

"I'll wait with her for a while."

"All right, we can move her to a ward now." He signaled an attendant, who ran over. "Take her to the third-floor ward."

The attendant nodded, then pushed the gurney down the hall. Beryl followed, trying to avert her eyes from the other injured people they passed. They took the elevator to the third floor, where a nurse on the floor helped them move Mrs. Dowd to a bed.

"Is she your relative?" The nurse looked at Beryl.

"No, but I'd like to stay with her, if you don't mind."

"Suit yourself. But you can't stay past noon."

Beryl had no idea why she felt compelled to stay with the older woman, but she just couldn't leave Mrs. Dowd alone yet, not until the woman knew where she was. If it had been her mother or gran, she would have behaved the same way. This lady had no one, as far as Beryl knew. Perhaps she could tell Beryl where her family was once she was alert.

Beryl looked around the room at the number of patients, many who had just arrived. Some of the other patients had family with them, and many people had bandaged heads or arms in slings. She didn't want to stare, nor did she want Mrs. Dowd to be concerned if she saw the others, so she reached up and pulled the curtains that separated the beds and gave the woman more privacy. A single metal chair sat beside the bed, so Beryl settled into it. Fatigue overcame her as her body relaxed after the long night of activity, and she closed her eyes, allowing sleep to take over.

Rustling sheets woke her, and Beryl slowly opened her eyes. She took a moment to reorient herself. Drab gray walls, white curtain, metal bed—a hospital.

"Where am I?" a weak, trembling voice said.

Alerted, Beryl stood, moving beside the woman in the bed. She took Mrs. Dowd's hand.

Mrs. Dowd's eyes darted to look at Beryl.

"Who are you?" she said.

"I'm Beryl Clarke, Mrs. Dowd. A bomb hit your neighborhood and you were injured, so we brought you here." Beryl pulled the chair closer so she could be heard without disturbing the others in the room.

Mrs. Dowd seemed confused as she tried to take in the information. "A bomb? We should get in the shelter."

"No, dear, the danger is past now. You are safe now."

Mrs. Dowd's gaze moved from one side of the bed to the other.

"Harry? Where is Harry?"

# ⫸ CHAPTER 16 ⫷

*Stalag Luft I, Barth, Germany*
*July 1941*

"Let's go to the theater," Angus said, and Kenneth followed him. The building consisted of a stage with a back room where the actors prepared to go onstage. A curtain made of bedsheets hung between them, separating the areas. In front of the stage were crude benches the prisoners had made.

"Not bad. I look forward to your next performance," Kenneth said.

"Sometimes the guards watch too and enjoy the diversion."

"Too bad we can't get them all in here and keep them until we can get away."

"Good idea, but we can't have a building that big." Angus grabbed hold of the curtain, looking it up and down. "Hmm. I believe the Germans can help us with our costumes."

A smile eased over his face as Kenneth understood what Angus was saying. "You're not talking about for the plays, are you?"

"Yes and no. In the interest of better-looking performances, some of the guards might help us find more material, old clothes, and even dye. Wouldn't that be helpful?" Angus grinned.

"Indeed. Surely they have some cast-offs they don't need anymore."

"All right. You tell me what kind of clothes people outside are wearing, and we'll recreate them for our 'special' costumes."

"I like the way you think," Kenneth said. "And I have a new appreciation for the theater."

"A little culture never hurt anyone," Angus said.

As they walked back toward the barracks, excited voices came from the front of the compound. Soon they saw the reason why when POWs passed them toting large corrugated cardboard boxes on their shoulders.

"Ah. The Red Cross parcels have arrived," Angus said. "Let's go collect ours."

Just inside the gate a truck was parked, and the POWs lined up behind it waiting to get their packages. Kenneth and Angus joined the queue.

"Gee, you'd think this was Christmas," Kenneth said, observing the smiling faces.

"To a kriegie, it is. Thank God for the Red Cross and other charitable organizations like it."

Kenneth hoped they wouldn't run out of packages before they got to him. With the increasing population of the camp, it wouldn't be a surprise if there wasn't enough packages to go around. But he did receive one, and a little thrill raced through him too, as if Santa Claus had just come and brought him a new toy. The box was stamped with the words PRISONERS' PARCELS, BRITISH RED CROSS AND ORDER OF ST. JOHN, WAR ORGANISATION. A large red cross was prominent on the front of the box as well as the words COMITE INTERNATIONAL, CROIX ROUGE, GENEVE TRANSIT.

Returning to the barracks with the parcel, he joined the others who were opening theirs and sorting through the contents. As he scanned the items inside, he was surprised at the variety.

There was a package of tea, a can of cocoa powder, and a can of pudding. There were also cans of sardines, preserves, margarine, and sugar. In addition, there were cans of meat, cheese, condensed milk, dried eggs, and cookies, which the British called biscuits, Kenneth recalled with a chuckle and a longing for the fluffy buttermilk biscuits his mother made. He also had a box of cigarettes, which for his use would be money. And perhaps the most exciting things he found were a bar of soap and a Cadbury Dairy Milk Fruit and Nut chocolate bar. He was about to unwrap it and wolf it down when Angus said, "Remember, we take all our goods to the pantry to share."

"You mean I can't eat any myself?"

"You can, but those chocolate bars come in handy for bribes. The guards love chocolate, and they don't get it often with their meals."

Kenneth's mood plummeted as he stared down at the chocolate bar in his hand. He hadn't had anything that good in months.

Angus must have noticed his reluctance because he patted Kenneth on the back. "But I think you ought to eat that one so you know how good it is. Then you can show what a sacrifice it is to give one up when you need to use one for a bribe."

"Thanks, pal. I will savor every bite."

Angus laughed. "You do that, Yank."

"Do you think it's okay if I take a bar of soap too? Mine has been used up for weeks."

Angus waved his hand in front of his nose. "Please do!"

Kenneth grinned. "We must keep up our daily regimes, mustn't we?" He looked across the room at Lieutenant Habersham from Britain. The man always looked impeccable—every hair perfectly combed, clean shaven, shoes polished, uniform pressed. "What's with that guy? How does he manage to stay so neat and tidy when the rest of us are scruffy and our clothes sloppy?"

"Habersham? He's always been that way. His father was a tailor, so he was brought up to be well dressed. The military helped reinforce his standards."

Kenneth rubbed the stubble on his chin. "But here? In a prisoner of war camp? Couldn't he be a bit lax?" He rubbed his chin. "I thought there was a shortage of razors, seeing as how most of us are scruffy with either stubble or beards."

"Ha. Habersham makes shaving as much a priority as his clothes. Do you know how his uniform stays pressed?"

Kenneth shook his head. "He has an iron?"

"He lays it out under his bed so he presses it when he sleeps."

"Really? Guess he doesn't toss and turn much."

"Never."

They both laughed as they watched Thomas, the lanky guy in charge of the larder, arrange the Red Cross items in order on the shelves.

"However, his looks might deceive you," Angus said.

"Habersham?" Kenneth said with a mouthful of chocolate. "How so?"

"Would you expect someone who looks like that to escape?"

Kenneth studied the man. "No, not really. He looks too perfect to get dirty, like someone who never got in trouble at school or anything, just always followed the rules, unlike yours truly, who was quite the opposite."

"See? Because he looks so respectable, the commandant likes him, and the guards respect him. He's the kind of chap who you'd like to have tea with."

"So, he's friendly with the folks in charge?"

"Quite. He engages them in conversation so they trust him enough to share information."

"I can see how that might get a better response from them than I do. I'm afraid I've already been branded as a troublemaker."

"Unfortunately, yes. So they'll watch you more."

"But they won't suspect Habersham. Is he in on the escape plans?"

"Absolutely. He can provide good distraction as well as good information."

"Interesting. You know, even his name sounds respectable."

James walked up. Eying Kenneth's partially eaten candy bar, he smiled. "Looks like you got some good stuff."

"Yum. I sure did. But it might be my last taste of good stuff for a while. Angus says we need to save it because it comes in handy when you need something from a guard."

"So I heard." James clasped Kenneth's arm. "No worries, though. When we get back to England, you can have all the Cadbury you want."

"Sounds good. Maybe you can get your mum to send us some. What did you get?"

"Food, such as everyone else, plus a deck of cards."

"Good. We could use a new deck," Angus said. "I heard a chap in another barracks had a Monopoly game in his box. Lucky guy. We could use something besides cards here too."

"Maybe he would trade with us," James said. "You know, my sister works for the company that makes those in England."

"You don't say!" Kenneth said, surprised at the connection as the image of Beryl came to mind. "Why, it would be like a taste of home if you could get your hands on one, wouldn't it?"

James nodded. "I wonder if they've received my letter yet."

"*Our* letter, don't you mean?" Kenneth grinned. "You could say we co-wrote it."

"As long as I have to wear this"—James pointed to his sling—"looks like that'll be the status quo."

Later on during roll call, Kenneth's mind raced as he observed another truckful of garbage boxes being let through the gates.

James, standing beside him, followed his gaze. "You're not thinking about doing that again, are you?"

Under his breath, Kenneth said, "Not the same way as before. But I do have another idea that might work."

# ≡ CHAPTER 17 ≡

*Leeds, England*
*July 1941*

Beryl silently prayed. *Lord, please give me the words to say to this dear lady.*

"He was badly injured," she said, leaning forward so the woman could hear.

"Is he here, in the hospital?"

Beryl shook her head, her eyes filling with tears.

The woman's bright blue eyes widened with understanding. "He's dead? My Harry is dead?"

Beryl clasped the woman's hand in hers and nodded. "I'm so sorry, Mrs. Dowd."

The woman looked up at the ceiling, a tear trickling down her cheek. "Sixty-five years we've been married."

Beryl tried to comprehend how long that was. Her own parents had celebrated their twenty-fifth anniversary shortly before Dad was killed. This woman would be the age of her grandmother, even great-grandmother, if they were still alive.

Mrs. Dowd looked back at Beryl. "Are you married, dear?"

"No, ma'am. Not yet."

"Well, I pray you'll find a man as fine as my Harry."

"My dad was a fine man too. He was killed by a bomb several months ago."

Mrs. Dowd squeezed her hand. "I'm sorry, dear. Your mum? How is she?"

"She's coping."

"I thought we would both die when the bombs fell because we didn't use the shelter. But I thought we would die together. We've always been together, you know."

"Mrs. Dowd, do you have any family here?"

She shook her head. "Not here. My daughter, Helen, died of cancer ten years ago, and her husband was killed in the last war."

Poor woman. She had no one to take care of her now.

"I do have a granddaughter, but she lives in the States. She married an American." Her voice trailed off as if she had run out of energy.

Beryl wanted to ask more questions about the granddaughter but could see Mrs. Dowd was falling asleep.

"I'll be back to check on you later," she said and kissed the woman on the forehead.

When she returned home, Beryl's mum ran to greet her, encircling her with her arms.

"Beryl! Dear Lord, I've been so worried about you. I heard the bombing was terrible. The ground shook all night."

"Didn't Veronica tell you where I was?"

"Yes, but when you didn't come home, I got worried. And look at you." Mum held her at arm's length and scanned her up and down.

Beryl looked down at herself, noticing how dirty and disheveled her clothes were. "I'm fine. I just need to clean up a bit and go to work."

"Work? Why, you haven't even gone to bed!"

"I napped at the hospital." Although that was true, Beryl still felt like she couldn't stand up much longer.

"You need some tea and toast. Sit your bum down in the kitchen, and I'll fix you some. Then you can get a bath. Mr. Watson will just have to wait."

"Meow." Spitfire rubbed against Beryl's legs.

"See, Spitfire was worried about you too." Mum leaned over and picked up the kitten while its purrs rumbled loudly.

Beryl touched the kitten's head. "How did he do during the raid?"

"He was a little nervous, but we kept each other company and made it through."

Beryl nodded, thankful the two had each other. As she plopped down in the kitchen chair, her thoughts returned to Mrs. Dowd. Who did she have now?

After she'd freshened up and had two cups of tea, Beryl headed to work, thankful she was off duty tonight. Why had they been bombed again? During the Blitz, they'd expected the raids every night, but the persistent attacks had ended months ago. Now the surprise raids were so unpredictable that no one knew if they were over or not. After last night, they were certainly not over. But when would the next one be? Leeds was not a large industrial center like Birmingham nor a Navy station on the coast. Why couldn't they be left alone?

Beryl was ashamed to have such thoughts. Everyone in the country wanted to be left alone from Hitler's irrational decisions. She pedaled to the factory and set her bike in the rack outside, grabbing her lunch and mask from the basket. When she entered the reception area, Margaret glanced up from the telephone.

"Long night, wasn't it? Are you all right?"

Beryl nodded. "I'm fine. Is he looking for me?"

"He asked where you were, but when I told him your mother called to say you'd been up all night on duty, he didn't say anything. Just nodded and went into his office."

"So I guess he's not angry with me."

"No, I think not. He was rather calm."

As Beryl turned to go down the hall to Mr. Watson's office, Margaret called out behind her. "Freddie's been looking for you."

Beryl stopped and turned around. "Did he say why?"

"No, but he had a sparkle in his eye as if he were up to something."

Beryl shrugged and continued to her desk. Right now Freddie was the least of her concerns. At her desk, she took off her hat and put the teapot on the single electric burner. Mr. Watson was no doubt waiting for his tea. She picked up her steno pad and pencil and knocked on his door.

"Come in," he said.

He glanced up as she entered, but his expression showed no emotion.

"I set the teapot on. Did you need me to take dictation?"

"Thank you, Beryl. No, I don't need any letters written right now. And truth be told, Margaret poured some tea for me earlier." He pointed to his cup on the desk. "However, I'll take a refill when you have more ready."

"Yes, sir." Why was he being so nice? "Is everything all right, sir?"

"With me, yes. But we lost one of our best workers, Richard Davies, in the attack."

"Dear God, I'm so sorry. He was a nice man."

"The nicest. His son is off somewhere in the army, and his daughter is a military nurse."

Beryl shook her head. So much loss.

"I understand you were on duty last night," Mr. Watson asked.

"Yes, I was. It was a bad hit," Beryl said, using words that understated the enormity of the event the way most Britishers did lately.

"Thank you for your bravery, Miss Clarke. I don't know that I would have been as brave."

Beryl flushed, not prepared to take such commendation from her employer.

"Just doing my duty, sir." If only she could explain that she wasn't brave, she just felt the need to be responsible. James was the brave one. He was the one who fought the enemy, and now he was paying the price for it. The teapot whistled, so she excused herself to get the tea.

At lunch later, the employees were subdued, still reeling from the previous night's bombing. Several people knew someone who had suffered either the loss of their home or their life, plus now everyone at Waddingtons knew about Richard Davies. She was definitely not in the mood to speak to Freddie. But he appeared in front of her anyway, smoking his infernal cigarette. She glanced at Margaret and rolled her eyes.

"Hello, Beryl," he said.

"Hello, Freddie."

"Guess you heard about what happened to Richard Davies."

"Yes, I did. It's very tragic."

"It is." He looked over at Margaret as if he didn't want her to hear what he had to say. "Can I speak to you alone for a moment?"

If he asked her out again now, she would lose her temper. But the hesitancy in his voice was different than his usual eagerness, so she decided to find out what he had to say.

Beryl started to stand, but Margaret jumped up instead. "I have to visit the ladies' room. You go ahead and sit down, Freddie."

He tossed his cigarette on the ground and rubbed it out with his shoe, then sat on the bench beside her.

"I hope you aren't offended by what I have to tell you, but I'm just bursting with what I found out, and I wanted you to be the first to know."

"Good grief, Freddie. What on earth is it?" She was too tired for Freddie right now.

"Well, it turns out that the company needs to replace Richard's position."

"So soon?"

"Yes, well, Mr. Watson doesn't want to hire someone from outside to fill it."

"Go on."

"So I've been asked to fill the spot."

Was he gloating over the man's demise because it gave him a new position? Her ire began to rise, but she was too tired for a scene.

"Congratulations."

"Oh, I don't mean for you to congratulate me. It's not just the new position, but where it is that's so important."

"Where? He worked here, at Waddingtons."

He leaned in closer, his cigarette breath making her hold hers. "Promise you won't tell anyone? It's top secret."

"Freddie, please. Enough of your fantasies. I'm really not in the mood."

He laid his hand on her arm. "No, really, Beryl. I'm telling the truth." He lowered his voice. "There's a secret room here."

She raised her eyebrows and studied him. "A secret room? Where?"

"I can't tell you."

She started to stand. "All right. Well, I need to get back to work."

"Wait. I promise. There really is, and I'll be working in it."

She sat back down. "What will you be doing in this top-secret room? Making bombs out of playing cards?"

"I'm not sure yet. They're supposed to show me this afternoon."

"Will you tell me what you're doing when you find out?" She hadn't known about the cards donated to the Red Cross, so she needed to find out what else was going on at her company.

"Of course I will. But maybe I shouldn't tell you here. Maybe we should meet somewhere else."

So that was his motive after all, to get her to go out with him. "Freddie, so this is your new way of asking me out? I should've known."

His face fell. "I was afraid you'd think that way. But please believe me. I want to tell you, but I don't want to lose my job. So after I find out, I'll tell you. You can choose the place and time. All right?"

"All right, Freddie. I believe you, and I'll think of someplace and some time you can meet me."

A smile broke across his face. "Good, then. Wish me luck."

Why would he need luck? But the bigger question was, why did Waddingtons have a secret room?

# ⧱ CHAPTER 18 ⧱

*Stalag Luft I, Barth, Germany*
*July 1941*

"So, tell me about this idea of yours, Lieutenant Bordelon." The colonel focused on the ground as he placed his cane down with each step.

"Well, you know the boxes the food parcels come in?"

The colonel nodded.

"Well, each day we fill them with the empty cans and pile them on a cart that the NCOs push out of the camp. What I was thinking is there might be some way to hide a man in the box. Of course, it couldn't be a very tall man like myself. But we examined one of the boxes and think it could be enlarged a little. With a false bottom that doesn't attract attention, a man could hide underneath and be carried out on the cart. A man would only need to stay in it a couple of hours until he was clear from the compound."

The colonel paused and lifted his gaze to scan the prison yard. "We couldn't get more than one man out at a time, but it could be effective to distract the guards for a while. And someone might succeed in getting free," he said. "Go ahead and build one, and we'll test it out."

"Yes, sir!"

Kenneth hurried back to find Angus and James and tell them what the colonel said.

Soon the three were working on the box. Angus nabbed two from the trash pile. Taking the sturdiest box, they took it apart to enlarge one and make the false bottom. Kenneth borrowed a mallet from the kitchen for a hammer and reused the nails that were already in the boxes. Once the box was ready, it needed to be tested.

"Who wants to try it out?" Kenneth asked the other two.

Angus and James eyed the box.

"We're all too big to get in," Angus said.

James shook his head. "I'm afraid I can't lie on my arm or have anything lying on it just yet."

"I'll see if I can fit," Kenneth said. He squeezed in, lying on his side with his head and neck bent in one corner and his knees drawn up to his chin. After they placed the false bottom over him, he was stuck in place and wouldn't be able to move until the bottom was removed. But he fit, even just barely, and he was ready to take a chance. Hopefully he wouldn't get a cramp.

The guys removed the false bottom and helped him out. "I better go get Shorty," James said.

"Actually, I'll do it," Kenneth said. His adrenaline pumped at another opportunity to escape, overriding any discomfort he'd have to endure. Besides, even if Shorty could fit better, Kenneth doubted Shorty's confidence and ability. "I can tolerate the position a short time."

"You *are* a crazy man," James said.

Kenneth smiled. "I take that as a compliment." He pointed to the bottom. "But there needs to be a hinge of some type that I can open so I can get out by myself. The guys that carry me out can't take the chance to be seen opening the box."

They removed a hinge from one of the closet doors and fixed it to the bottom so that it wasn't visible from the top. Kenneth had to get into the box just right so he could get his hand on the latch.

Before the actual escape could take place, he needed to observe the way the boxes were handled and loaded onto the cart. The men who loaded the box would have to be told, because not only would the box be heavy, but they would need to coordinate a signal to let him know when he could get out of the box. Noticing the way empty cans were thrown into the box, Kenneth realized the juices would likely seep through and onto him. Besides getting greasy, he would be even more uncomfortable. When he told the NCOs his idea, they agreed, amused and eager to see if it worked. They also decided to line the bottom with more absorbent paper to absorb the juices.

The colonel's reaction to his decision to get into the box himself was predictable.

"You are putting yourself in danger unnecessarily."

"But I prefer to put myself in danger instead of someone else."

The colonel blew out a deep sigh. "You have a point. When are you going to do it?"

"Tomorrow."

"All right, then we'll have to cover your absence at roll call. We will tell them someone is in the john, then one of the guys can slip out and return as if he's returning from there. They have a hard enough time counting us even when there's no movement."

"Thank you, sir."

"Good luck, Lieutenant."

The next day, Angus delivered the special box to the kitchen area, and later Kenneth strolled over and climbed into it when the other boxes were being loaded. The bottom was placed on top of him, and he tried to focus on hearing instead of on how uncomfortable he was. The position was almost unbearable after a while, and he suffered cramped muscles, but he amused himself by thinking of the German guard who would be standing alongside completely unaware of Kenneth's presence.

As the cart was being pushed, he hoped he had thought of everything to make the plan successful. Kenneth listened to the muffled voices when the cart stopped and assumed the NCOs were speaking to the guards at the gate. Sure enough, it started rolling again until it stopped another time, apparently beyond the gate. The box was lifted off the cart and placed on the ground. His heart pounded as he listened for the next signal. While the NCOs distracted the guards, he opened the hinge, and when he heard the prearranged whistle from one of the NCOs, he crawled into a small wooden hut and hid under some timber. He watched and waited, as the daylight slowly disappeared and it became dark outside. Finally, he stood and stretched, his limbs stiff from hiding so long. After an hour passed, he slipped out of the hut and into the surrounding woods.

The taste of freedom was exhilarating, so with new enthusiasm he decided to head back to Stralsund where he'd seen the harbor, planning to stow away on one of the ships. This time he was dressed as a day laborer so he wouldn't attract attention. He walked for two days before he saw the harbor. The seafront was swarming with sentries, so he went farther down the shore from the boats and observed the process by which the ships were loaded. He spotted a Swedish ferry and decided to stay where he was so he could determine the ferry's schedule. He took an invigorating bath in the sea, then sunned himself on the beach, away from anyone's sight. That night, he lay under the dark sky and watched a shooting star. *God, if you're up there, tell Mom not to worry about me.* Peace settled over him like a warm blanket, so he closed his eyes and slept, waking the next morning prepared to get on the ferry and head to real freedom.

The ferry was surrounded by barbed wire, and the only way onboard was either through the passenger entrance or through the well-guarded entrance that trucks used. The latter was his best option. As the trucks were being loaded, he went around to the opposite side of the traffic, found a mail van, and crawled underneath, grabbing hold of the axle, since that had worked on his previous escape. The truck pulled onto the ferry, and when the boat was at sea, he climbed into the empty cab of the truck.

Kenneth could see the shore ahead, and assuming it was Sweden, a neutral county, he anticipated finally being free from the Germans. Scanning the interior of the truck, he found a wrench lying on the floor, picked it up, and stuffed it in his shirt. You never knew when any kind of tool would come in handy.

A sentry walked by and spotted him in the truck. Kenneth sucked in a breath, and his pulse raced at the prospect of being caught. *Stay cool, Kenneth*, he said to himself. He tried to act nonchalant, like he was supposed to be there, and nodded, exhaling a sigh of relief as the sentry walked past. However, a few moments later, the man returned with another sentry who leveled his gun at Kenneth and demanded him to get out. He slowly climbed out of the truck and froze while they searched him.

He'd stuck the wrench inside his jacket sleeve underneath his arm, and somehow they missed it. Well, that was a small victory. What would they do now that they were away from shore? His question was answered when the ferry turned around and headed back to Stralsund, where Kenneth was released back to waiting German guards and returned to the camp. This time he'd been away five days. He'd gotten so far and yet not far enough.

The commandant was standing on the front stoop of the headquarters, arms crossed, as the jeep with Kenneth and four guards pulled up. They climbed out of the vehicle and pushed him toward their leader. Seeing the man's slitted eyes and tense mouth, Kenneth could have sworn the man had steam coming out of his ears. What would he do to Kenneth this time? Put him in front of a firing squad?

"Lieutenant Bordelon, you have a bad habit. I suppose you jumped over the fence again?" the commandant said, his voice tense and nostrils flaring.

Kenneth shrugged. "Yes, sir. That's right."

The commandant's mouth twisted as he glared at Kenneth. "If there is a tunnel, we will find it, then rations will be reduced for the whole camp. And you—you may get transferred to the castle where there is no escape!" He turned to the guards. "The cooler, three weeks."

A tunnel? Maybe next time. And much as he liked sightseeing, the idea of being sent to a castle stirred images of dungeons where prisoners were chained to the wall and tortured. Should he tell the commandant that he'd be a good boy from now on? Nah. On the other hand, perhaps he should hurry up and get out of this camp again before that happened. As he was led back through the gates, the German gate guard said the only English words he knew. "For you, the var is over."

"You need to learn a new line, pal," Kenneth said to the guard. "That one doesn't work."

On the way to the cooler, he spied Angus and James standing by the barracks to his right. He grinned and gave a faux salute. "See you soon, boys," he said.

Once in the cell, he stripped off his jacket, then pulled the wrench from the back of his waistband where he'd moved it in transit, amazed that it hadn't been found. Scanning the room, he tried to decide what to work on. "Time to get to work. This should make a pretty good shovel," he said, walking to the outside wall. Since he'd been measuring distances from various buildings to fences, he knew how far one would have to dig to get outside the fence from the cooler. How he would hide a tunnel, he had no idea, but at least he had something to do for the next three weeks.

He proceeded to dig at the base of the wall with the wrench. Each time he heard the guard's key in his door, he threw his jacket over the hole so the guard wouldn't see it. Sometimes he'd jump up and grab the bars at the window just to catch some fresh air and get a glimpse of the outside. He seldom saw guards nearby. Maybe this would be a good place to get through the fence undetected.

Sweat poured down his face as he dug through the sandy ground of the prison yard, even though it was easy to penetrate. Unfortunately, the sand also fell back into the hole just as easily. He needed to get rid of the sand, so when he accumulated piles of it, he stood and tossed it through the window, making sure no one saw him. How could a tunnel be dug without sand constantly falling in? He'd heard tunnels were being dug under some of the barracks. How were they shoring them up? And with ferrets constantly searching the barracks, how did they hide the sand they'd dug out?

So, what had he learned from this escape? What needed to be done to make it successful?

He needed identification papers so he could pass for a local and have access to transportation. If he could just get ahold of some real papers, he could copy them. One thing he'd learned in art class was how to copy the skills of master artists. Bet his instructor never thought his student would be using his talent to counterfeit documents.

They also badly needed maps and compasses, because so far, he could only guess at where he was and what direction to go. But how could they get those items? Would it be possible to bribe a guard for them?

Kenneth kept track of the days he spent in the cooler by scratching lines on the wall. One night after marking his fifteenth day, he heard shouts outside and a scuffle. Roused from a semi-sleep, he jumped up and ran to the window, pulling himself up to see out.

The searchlight was fixed on three guards wrestling with a man. Kenneth strained to see who it was. A shot rang out, its sound reverberating through the walls of Kenneth's cell. The man dropped to the ground, and as the guards dragged him away, Kenneth's breath caught when he recognized Scott McIntosh. Kenneth turned away, his gut wrenching. Slumping against the wall, he slid to the floor. What had McIntosh done? Kenneth covered his face with his hands. That could've been him. He'd certainly put himself in their sights enough times. What had the man done? Kenneth hung his head. That could have been him. He'd certainly put himself in their sights enough times.

But even though he heard they would, Kenneth never thought they'd just shoot an unarmed man. Why had he been so lucky? Maybe Mom's prayers were working. Was there a limit to how far they'd go? If he tried to escape again, would he meet the same fate?

# ❚ CHAPTER 19 ❚

*Leeds, England*
*August 1941*

Beryl took the tram to see Mrs. Dowd every day after work. With no one else to look in on the elderly woman, Beryl felt responsible. Mrs. Dowd was more bruised than initially known, and her skin was a kaleidoscope of purples, greens, and yellows. However, she was stronger than her little body looked, and she always greeted Beryl with a smile if not taking a nap.

"Hello, dear." She patted the bed. "Have a seat. Did you work today?"

Beryl complied. "Yes, ma'am."

"What kind of work do you do?" the woman asked for the umpteenth time.

Beryl wasn't sure if it was her poor hearing or equally poor memory that made the woman ask the question each time she saw her.

"I'm a secretary at Waddingtons."

Smiling, the woman said, "I used to do that too. Those students could really test my patience, but I loved teaching and did so for twenty-five years!"

Beryl had given up on trying to tell Mrs. Dowd her position was not a schoolteacher but a secretary, deciding it wasn't worth the bother.

The doctor came by and examined the woman. "You're getting better every day, Mrs. Dowd. Soon you'll be able to go home."

Beryl grimaced. Why did the doctor have to say that? Thinking of her home only made Mrs. Dowd sad. Plus, Beryl still had no idea where the woman would go. She still hadn't found any relatives in the area who could take her in, and Mrs. Dowd couldn't remember the married name of her granddaughter in the States. She only saw one choice available— her home. Mother had been coming around since she got Spitfire, and learning of James' POW status had given her new purpose. Could she take on one more responsibility?

When she reached home later that day, Mum ran to the door to greet her, waving a piece of paper.

"We've a letter from James!"

Beryl's mouth fell open. "A letter? Oh my, let me see it!"

Her mother handed her the single sheet with tiny block handwriting and followed her into the kitchen where she plopped down in a chair, not heeding Spitfire's attempt for attention.

"His handwriting looks different than I remember," Beryl said.

"That's because he didn't write it himself." Mum sat across from her. "A friend did."

Beryl frowned. Was this truly a letter from James?

Holding it up, she noticed some holes where some words had been cut out.

"I wonder what the censors took out."

"Thankfully, not too much." Mum motioned to the letter. "Go ahead. Read it. Out loud, if you please. I want to hear it again."

*"Dear Mum and Beryl, Greetings from a prisoner of war camp in xxxxxx."* She glanced up at Mum. "Wonder where? That part was cut out." Mum shook her head. "Go on."

*I want you to know I am all right. Got a little banged up on the way here but am fine now. However, my right arm is in a cast, so a mutual friend of ours, Kenneth xxxxxx from university, is here as well, so he is doing the writing for me. I certainly was surprised to see him here. We have been catching up and discussing his favorite bird, bald eagles. We should be getting some Red Cross parcels, but if you would not mind, please send me some biscuits, jam, tea, Spam, sardines, and fine chocolates, if you can spare them. Kenneth and I are joining a glee club here because we both enjoy singing. You may be surprised to know there is a*

*small chapel here as well. Kenneth said he would attend*
*with me! Much love from James.*

"Kenneth Bordelon? That can't be right. He's an American, and Americans haven't joined the war." Beryl's heart skipped a beat at the thought of the man she knew in college.

"Perhaps it's another Kenneth."

Beryl shook her head, an image of the handsome dark-haired American with the twinkling hazel eyes in her mind. "No, that's rather unlikely. Kenneth is an American name. I've never known any Brits with that name." Besides, how could an American be in a German POW camp when the United States wasn't in the war? Could this letter really be from James? She didn't want to tell Mum her suspicions.

"James said he knew the man from university. Did you know him?"

Memories of the good-looking, fun-loving guy at Oxford swept through her mind. She certainly did know him. "Yes, James introduced us."

"Did you know his favorite bird was a bald eagle?"

"No, but that's rather strange information for a letter, don't you think?"

Mum shrugged. "Perhaps, but why does it matter? I'm just happy to get the letter. But I wonder what James meant by being 'banged up.' I hope he wasn't hurt too badly."

Beryl scanned the letter again. "He says he's fine now, except for a cast on his arm, which is why he needed someone else to help him write it." But how could she verify it was really Kenneth?

"Isn't it wonderful that he and his friend are going to be in a glee club? James has such a lovely voice."

So did Kenneth, remembering him singing show tunes on their motorcycle ride. "Prison life certainly sounds better than I expected," Beryl said, thinking about the stories she'd heard about Germany's treatment of their enemies.

"And a chapel, Beryl! Isn't that nice?"

Nodding, Beryl said, "Yes. Quite unexpected." Which was another problem with the letter. Kenneth didn't attend church when they attended university. The whole idea of the two of them in a prisoner of war camp together was an unbelievable coincidence, especially when one of them wasn't even supposed to be in the war.

"But look, Beryl. He mentions Red Cross parcels! He might very well get the ones I've been putting together. Wouldn't that be wonderful if he did?" Beryl's heart warmed at the sight of her mum's joy. Who was she to spoil it by casting doubt over the letter?

"Yes, it would. And we can send him things as well. I'll see if I can get some extra items from the grocer when I tell him they're for James."

"The Red Cross might let me use some of their goods as well." Mum sighed. "We still don't know exactly where he is. Everything has to be sent to the same address, and then it will be distributed. I wonder how long it will take."

"I don't know, but we should also send a letter right away and let him know we received his and are sending his requests."

"Yes, of course!" Mum jumped out of her chair to fetch stationery. Spitfire meowed, and Mum grabbed him and kissed the kitten on the head. "We got a letter from James! I can't wait for you to meet him!"

But how long would that be?

Mum returned with the paper, and the two of them constructed a letter back to James. They told him about Spitfire, the neighbors, and the garden, being careful to avoid information about the bombings. The government didn't want the enemy to find out what, if any, effect the raids had had on the citizens of Britain. They mentioned that they had stayed busy with volunteer work, not divulging what the work for the war effort was, just in case that would be cut from their letter. Trying to keep the tone of the letter upbeat and cheerful, they congratulated him on joining the glee club and attending church.

"Be sure to tell him he's in our prayers," Mum said. "His friend too."

Beryl paused. Would Kenneth want to hear that?

"What is it?" Mum asked, frowning.

"Oh, nothing, Mum. Do you think the censors would cut that out?"

"I can't see why they would."

Beryl continued writing, adding a line at the bottom to give her regards to Kenneth, saying her cycle was much slower than his. If he were truly the Kenneth she knew, perhaps he would respond to that clue and include some information that identified him better in the next letter. When she sealed the letter, Beryl said, "I'll drop this off at the post tomorrow."

Mum clapped her hands together. "Good! Let's have some dinner and see what goods we can send to James."

"We can send books too, can't we? James always like to read."

"Yes. And let's send a Bible. Do you think it's allowed?"

Beryl shrugged. "Might as well try."

While they were eating, they made a list of items to send, including shaving items and socks.

"He might need a sewing kit too. I'm sure he'll need to mend his clothes occasionally."

"Does James know how to use a needle and thread?" Beryl asked.

"I'm quite sure he can figure it out. He does have some dress standards. And if he can't manage, perhaps another man who is with him can."

Beryl imagined Kenneth trying to thread a needle and chuckled.

"We could send him a scarf. I'll knit one for him," Mum said.

"Mum, it's the dead of summer. Do you think he'll need it now?"

"Perhaps not. I'll wait until it's winter, but I'm sure he could use another pair of socks. And I'll knit him a scarf in the winter if he's still there."

*If* he was still there? Wouldn't he be there for the duration of the war? Mum believed the war would be over early, so James would be home soon. Beryl wasn't so sure, especially after the recent bombings. But Beryl kept those thoughts to herself. She wouldn't steal Mum's hope.

Mrs. Findlay knocked on the door and came inside.

"We received a letter from James!" Mum exclaimed.

Their neighbor's eyes lit up. "You have! Oh my, whatever did he say?"

Mum filled her in on the details, showing her the letter.

"You've only got two holes in yours. I've seen some that look like doilies, they're so cut up," Mrs. Findlay said.

"I supposed James knew what he should or shouldn't include."

"You say a friend wrote the letter?"

Beryl explained that the letter claimed it was written by Kenneth.

"He's an American?"

"The only Kenneth I knew at university was an American," Beryl said. Even though she questioned the veracity of the scribe being that Kenneth, she harbored hope that it was indeed.

"Eagles?"

"Bald eagles," Beryl said.

"Then he must be American."

"Why?"

"Because we don't have bald eagles in the British Isles. They're native to America."

"So perhaps that was a clue that he was indeed the same Kenneth. But why was that important to know?"

"Why would an American be there, I wonder?" Mrs. Findlay picked up Spitfire and set him in her lap where she proceeded to stroke his fur. "I have heard that there are some Americans who volunteered to fly with the RAF called the Royal Eagle Squadron. Maybe your Kenneth is one of them."

Was that what the letter meant? The Kenneth she knew was certainly the type of person who would do something so adventurous. *Your* Kenneth? She blushed at the thought. She couldn't claim him, but the idea sounded appealing.

"We're collecting supplies to ship to him." Mum pointed to the list. "Can you think of anything else?"

Mrs. Findlay perused the list of items. "A comb? Chewing gum?"

"Good idea. Those will fit well."

Glancing at Beryl, Mrs. Findlay asked, "How is the elderly lady you rescued getting along, Beryl?"

"She's doing amazingly well, actually," Beryl said. "In fact, the doctor said she will be released soon."

"Where will she go? Where is her family?"

"I don't know. The only family she has mentioned is a granddaughter who lives in the States. But the granddaughter is married, and Mrs. Dowd can't remember her married name."

"Poor dear. Does she know what state she lives in?"

Beryl shook her head. "I went back to her town house to see if I could find any correspondence, but it had all been destroyed."

"So where is she going?" Mum asked.

Beryl hesitated to ask the next question. What if Mum didn't agree? "I wanted to ask you if we could bring her here. We do have the room. Would that be too much of a burden for you?"

"No, of course not. I was going to suggest it myself," Mum said. "You just tell her she's going home with you. I'll get James' bedroom ready. When he gets home, we can arrange something else. Can she manage stairs?"

Beryl's shoulders relaxed. Thank God, Mum had returned to her old self.

"I'm not sure. She has been up and around a little at the hospital."

"Well, if she can't, we'll make a place for her in the sitting room."

"That would be splendid, Mum. I've been so worried about her."

"I know you have, dear, and it makes me happy to see you care so much for the woman."

"Well, soon you'll have a houseful of women!" Mrs. Findlay said.

"Except for Spitfire. He'll be the 'man' of the house for now," Beryl said.

Mrs. Findlay looked down at the cat purring contentedly in her lap. "I think he's already in charge."

# ⯮ CHAPTER 20 ⯬

*Stalag Luft I, Barth, Germany*
*August 1941*

"Kenneth! We received a letter from home!" James said, waving the letter in his hand as Kenneth entered the barracks after his stay in the cooler.

"Well now, that's the best news I've heard in three weeks!" He rubbed his beard, appreciating the plural possessive his friend had used in "we." "Let me wash up a little before I take a look at it. I can hardly stand myself in this condition."

Kenneth retrieved his piece of soap and razor and went to the latrine, where he shaved and washed off the stink of the cooler. What he wouldn't give for a nice bath. The dip in the sea he'd taken during his last escape was worth the escape itself. Even though he was ready to stretch out on his cot, he hurried to finish cleaning so he could see James' letter. Who wrote it, Beryl or her mother?

Once back in the room, he sat on the bed beside James and read the letter.

Some holes had been cut into it, but they managed to figure out what the letter said.

"Beryl said to tell you hello and mentioned the time she rode your motorbike."

"She remembered." At least she hadn't completely forgotten him. That gave him some confidence.

"It says they found a kitten, but the name is cut out. Why on earth would they do that?"

Kenneth shrugged. Since when did anything about this war make sense?

"They're happy we're in the glee club and going to church. They say they're praying for us too."

A twinge of guilt pinched Kenneth since he'd been avoiding that activity. James had gone without him anyway and talked about the unique combination of a Protestant and Catholic service led by a minister and also a priest. Kenneth didn't really know the difference, but now he felt obligated to attend so they wouldn't be telling Beryl and her mother a lie.

"They're doing volunteer work but don't say what," James said. "I'm sure Beryl is still in the ARP though. I wonder how badly they've had it."

"What have you heard from the wireless?" Kenneth asked, knowing the men listened to the British Broadcasting Company when they rigged up the makeshift radio.

"Nothing about Britain. Only that Germany is still penetrating into Russia. Oh, and Churchill and Roosevelt met in Newfoundland for some kind of alliance called the Atlantic Charter."

"The US is in the war?"

James shook his head. "No, not really. Seems like the two men discussed how things would be run *after* the war, no economic sanctions like those imposed on Germany after the last war."

"As if they'd have a say in the matter if Germany won."

"No doubt. I think it was more of a message to those who oppose Germany but are afraid to admit it. The BBC said Britain dropped millions of fliers over Germany to tell them about it. Besides, Germany isn't going to win the war."

Kenneth crossed his arms. "I don't get it. Roosevelt already signed the Lend-Lease Act to sell supplies to Britain, now this agreement. But still, my country's not officially in the war."

James shrugged and returned his attention to the letter. "They're sending us a box. I wonder how long it'll take to get here."

"At least we know they got our request. I still don't know if my mother did."

"Chin up, I'm sure you'll hear from her."

Kenneth wondered what Mom knew or thought about where he was. Would she know he was alive in a POW camp? What if he met the same fate as Scott McIntosh?

"James, do you know why the guards killed that NCO a few days ago?" Kenneth hadn't been able to get the scene out of his mind.

James looked down and shook his head. "We were shocked to hear about it. Seems he was out past curfew and was near the wire. He refused to answer them when they asked him to stop. I assume he was trying to escape—at least that's what they want us to think."

"From what I saw, he wasn't close enough to the wire to escape. There must have been something else that got them riled."

"Maybe the guard was trigger-happy."

"Or maybe they wanted to set an example. Did you know the guy was one of the ones who escaped with me on the logging work detail?"

James' eyes widened. "No, I didn't. How did you know?"

"I saw from the cooler window. The searchlight was shining right on him." The image still made Kenneth sick.

"So maybe they'd been watching him."

"That's what I think."

"So no doubt they're watching you too, Kenneth."

"All the time. I can feel their beady little eyes crawling on my back." He squirmed at the uncomfortable feeling.

"You must be careful, then. Don't give them a reason to shoot."

Kenneth managed a grin. "I'll be good as gold." He held up his fingers in a scout salute.

"Besides, I'm looking forward to eating good food again. I must've lost ten more pounds from the slop they gave me in the cooler."

"I'm looking forward to seeing Mum and Beryl again," James said.

James' words struck a chord with Kenneth. He'd like to see Beryl again too, sooner rather than later. And on his own schedule, not on Hitler's.

"Let's write her back right now," Kenneth said.

"Sure, if you're up to it, but I thought you'd be tired."

"I am, but sending a letter to Beryl has energized me."

James lifted a brow. "Sounds like you're sweet on my sister."

"Could be—and getting sweeter every day. It gives me satisfaction being able to communicate with the outside world. And I can't communicate with my folks. Or they can't communicate with me, whichever."

"Sorry about that, Kenneth." He patted Kenneth's shoulder. "Meanwhile, I'm thankful you can write for me."

"I don't know what news we can give her since not much has changed here, but we can say we'll see her soon."

"Will we?"

"We can hope, can't we?"

"What else can we do?"

"She said they were sending a package. Wish I knew what was in it before we write back. I guess we can still thank them and assure them we're all right."

"Now, that's a good idea. Let's get it done so we can go outside." Kenneth stood and stretched. "It's hot in here."

The two of them wrote another letter to Beryl and James' mother, and Kenneth made sure to sign it, "penned by Kenneth Bordelon for James Clarke." He wanted to add a more personal note but didn't know how Beryl would receive it, plus the space was limited.

"I'm surprised you don't want to get some rest," James said when they sealed the envelope.

"I feel fine now. I just want to take care of the letter and then go outside. After being cooped up for three weeks, even the limited freedom of the yard is desirable."

When they stepped outside, Kenneth spotted Colonel Gilmore. "Excuse me, James. I need to speak to the colonel."

James nodded and walked away while Kenneth approached the colonel. The other people who were speaking with the man stepped away as if they didn't want to be associated with Kenneth as he neared, and perhaps be labeled a troublemaker too.

"Lieutenant Bordelon, are you ready for your debriefing?"

"I am." Kenneth went on to give his superior the details of his escape.

"So, what kind of information did you gain that can help our future attempts?"

"We need civilian clothes and identification papers, also passes for traveling."

"Right. We've started on the clothes already."

"But we need the papers too. I'm a pretty good artist, and I can probably copy a real one if we can get our hands on one."

The colonel paused and rubbed his chin. "I believe we have someone who can help us. He's pretty fluent in German and has made friends with one of the guards named Klaus."

"Who's the POW, sir?"

"Habersham. He can invite Klein to join him to share a cup of wine."

"Wine, sir?" Since when did the prisoners get wine?

Colonel Gilmore smiled. "He received a parcel with a cleverly disguised bottle of wine. He's very frugal with it, but he understands its importance to the cause."

"So you think he can get the guard drunk enough to get his papers from him?"

"No, that's not necessary. The guard will remove his coat because it's hot inside, and the Fox can relieve him of his papers when he's not looking."

"The Fox?"

"Sly like a fox, you know."

"Oh, I see. But won't that get Habersham in trouble?"

"Do you think the guard will report that his papers went missing when he was having wine with a prisoner?"

Kenneth laughed. "You've got a point there." He looked around them. "Once we have the papers, I'll need some ink nibs and ink."

"Supposedly, we aren't allowed to have ink nibs." At Kenneth's curious expression, he added, "Silly, isn't it? Perhaps they qualify as weapons. Nevertheless, we can probably scrounge those things up. Several of the men get drawing supplies from home, especially the artistic ones."

"Sketch pad paper! That would be good sturdy stock to work with. I know where to get that, and hopefully my mother will send me some too."

"We'll have to cover you while you work too. Once you find a good working space, we'll have one of our men posted nearby to keep an eye on things. If a ferret or guard gets near you, he can send out a signal."

"Sounds good." Lowering his voice, Kenneth said, "Sir, are we working on any tunnels?"

The colonel nodded, glancing around. "Yes, several. Why?"

"I started digging one in the cooler."

At Gilmore's raised eyebrows, Kenneth continued. "Of course, I didn't get far, but it could be done if anyone was in there long enough."

"I doubt that would happen." Gilmore gave a crooked grin. "It could take months, and I wouldn't expect the commandant to keep even you in confinement that long."

"I wouldn't be that lucky." So the colonel had a sense of humor. "The problem with the tunnels is the sand. It keeps falling back in."

"We've found that to be true as well, so we're working to avoid that."

"Shoring up the space?"

Gilmore nodded. "Exactly. More than one man has had the unpleasant experience of being covered in sand."

"What do you do with the sand that's removed?"

"Right now we're putting it in our pockets and scattering it out on the ground. If you have any other suggestions, please let me know."

"Have you considered digging deeper?"

Gilmore glanced around before answering. "So far we hit water if we dig below four feet, but we're hoping to find an area where we can dig deeper. But if we do, we need even more shoring."

"That's true." What could be used to shore the walls better? But getting out was only part of the problem. Back to the documents. "When do you think Habersham will invite the guard over?"

"After I speak with him, he'll invite the guard as soon as it's feasible. What we need to do is borrow the papers for a few days, make a facsimile, then return them to him in good conscience so he knows we don't mean him any harm." Gilmore paused to glance around. "We need to keep him on our side so he can be useful."

They stopped walking beside the athletic field to watch a game of cricket. "Why don't you join in?" the colonel asked.

"I'm not sure I've got the hang of it yet, but I will eventually."

"If they think you're enjoying yourself here, they might think you've given up escaping."

"Maybe." Kenneth watched as what he thought was the pitcher threw the ball toward the man with the bat. He turned to the colonel. "Sir, I must ask you about the shooting of the NCO McIntosh. Did the commandant give anyone an explanation?"

"Nothing besides saying that McIntosh made an unwise decision."

"But what exactly did he do? What was their reason for shooting him?" Whatever it was, Kenneth wanted to make sure he didn't do it too.

Gilmore fixed him with a stare. "Lieutenant, the Germans here are in charge. They do not have to give us their reasons. The Geneva Convention is supposed to serve as guidelines, but who's to hold them responsible?"

Kenneth stared back. Who indeed?

"Please excuse me, Lieutenant. I need to go to rehearsal."

"Rehearsal? Are you in a play?"

Colonel Gilmore's lips curved up. "I am. We'll be performing *A Midsummer Night's Dream.*"

So that's where Angus was. Kenneth was at a loss for words as Gilmore walked away.

---

Kenneth got busy collecting all he would need to make copies of the papers. A counterfeiter. What would Dad say about that occupation? Asking around, he discovered who else in the barracks liked to draw, and assembled ink, ink nibs, and paper. Angus helped him set up a makeshift desk by a window where he would have good light. The colonel assigned a German-speaking lookout to position himself near the window and give an alarm when a ferret or nosy guard got too close. The alarm would be three quick knocks on the window, after which the lookout would engage the German in very loud conversation.

The day arrived when Fox swiped the papers from the guard's jacket and quickly got them to Kenneth. He studied the details, committing them to memory. But the work would take a long time to replicate. He needed a copy, a way to trace the information. An idea struck him, and he called out to James, who was watching from outside the doorway.

"Yes?"

"Quick! Get me some sheets of toilet paper, the Lyles brand they send from Britain."

James raised his eyebrows but asked no questions and scurried away. He returned a moment later with several sheets of the paper in hand.

As Kenneth suspected, the paper made for excellent tracing. The Fox had also procured some typing paper from the commandant's office that would be a good weight for the identification cards. Kenneth traced every detail by pencil, as an ink nib would pierce through. Two days later, the "borrowed" papers were returned to the embarrassed guard who was both thankful and afraid of repercussions.

The project took Kenneth two weeks to complete, having to hand-letter every word, line after line, in a Gothic-style print. Whenever a warning was issued, he quickly hid his supplies in a small box in a place that had been cut in the wall. At night his hands cramped, but he was determined to make the work look authentic. The colonel realized how painstaking and long it took for the work to be done, so he recruited a team of counterfeiters to help. After all, one man would need at least two pieces of identification—an identification card and a traveling pass.

To add to their authenticity, Kenneth used his knife to carve the Nazi stamp with the eagle and swastika out of rubber boot heels, then painted them with ink and stamped the cards. Only an expert could tell the difference.

By mid-September, the cards were ready to be tested.

# ⚎ CHAPTER 21 ⚎

*Leeds, England*
*August 1941*

Freddie approached Beryl at work, smoking and glancing around as if he was afraid of being watched. He appeared more nervous than usual as he fidgeted with his cigarette.

"Hello, Beryl," he muttered, looking over his shoulder.

"Freddie, what's the matter?" Had he gotten in trouble at work?

His hands trembled as he nervously pushed up his glasses. "I can't talk here, but I want to tell you something you need to know. But you must swear not to tell anyone." He coughed as if choking on his words.

What was the poor man talking about now?

"When do you plan to talk to me, if not here?" She pointed to the place beside her on the bench, an invitation she had never offered him before.

But he shook his head and continued standing before her. "This weekend. Will you go to the cinema with me?"

So that was it. A ruse to get her to go out with him. Would he never quit?

"Freddie, I. . ." Should she make up another excuse or just bluntly tell him to stop asking her because her answer would always be no?

"I know what you're thinking. But trust me, I did not make this up. There's something very important I think you'd like to know."

She rolled her eyes. What could he possibly know that she needed to know too?

He leaned over and whispered in her ear. "Your brother might like to know this information."

She drew back and stared at him. Freddie knew James was in a POW camp. What did Freddie's information have to do with James? And if it were that important, how was she supposed to tell James? She had to find out.

"All right, Freddie. I'll go with you on that condition. You sound serious." She frowned at him. "I hope you are."

"I promise. Cross my heart." He made a cross motion across his chest and pointed upward.

"I'll meet you at the cinema Saturday. What time?" There was no need for him to come to her house and collect her as if they were going on a real date.

"Fine. Two o'clock?"

"All right. But if this is such a secret, don't tell anyone I'm going to meet you. Okay?" Since the bombs had started falling at night, the cinemas showed their movies earlier in the day so people could go to the shelters at night.

How was she going to explain to Margaret that she was going out with Freddie? But if Freddie didn't tell anyone, they wouldn't know. Hopefully he'd keep his word.

Mum was delighted to know Beryl was going to the cinema with Freddie.

"Why, it's about time you spent some time with a young man!"

"Mum, it's only Freddie. It's nothing to get excited about. We're just friends, so don't think there's anything more to it."

Mum smiled with a knowing spark in her eyes. "Of course, Beryl. I understand. You're just friends." She resumed her knitting, then said without looking up, "You know your father and I were friends before we fell in love."

"Mum!"

Her mother chuckled. "Oh, all right." She leaned over to retrieve her yarn from Spitfire. "You can't have that, Spitfire. Here, play with this one." Mum tossed the kitten a little ball of assorted yarn pieces and watched the animal pounce on it. Smiling, she looked up at Beryl. "What are you going to wear?"

"Wear? Nothing special. I won't need to wear my ARP uniform

because we'll be out of the cinema before my shift begins." Eager to change the subject, Beryl said, "I wonder if James has received the letter and package we sent him."

"I certainly hope so. I was thinking about his American friend and wondered if his family knows where he is."

"Hmm. If the Americans aren't officially in the war, wouldn't that be a secret?" There were so many secrets in this war.

"Well, I imagine his mum wants to know where he is, poor woman. At least I knew James was in the RAF."

Beryl had even more reason to doubt it was really the Kenneth she knew, but she wanted to believe it. Ever since they'd gone their separate ways, she'd wondered what happened to him. She knew he'd gone back to the States and certainly didn't expect him to be in England during the war. Perhaps the next letter would give her more information.

When Mrs. Findlay dropped by later, her face widened into a big grin when she heard Beryl had a date.

"Good for you! Who's this lucky guy?" Mrs. Findlay set her purse down on the table and glanced around, no doubt looking for tea.

Beryl rolled her eyes. "He's just a friend from work." Beryl put the teapot on as expected.

"Is he the same young man who's been asking you out ever since you started working there?"

Beryl nodded. "The same." She handed Mrs. Findlay a cup and saucer.

"So you like him better now, I see."

"I like him the same, actually. Really, we're just friends, nothing more."

The teapot whistled, and Beryl poured the hot water into their cups as Mum joined them.

"It's no use trying to get more out of her," Mum said. "She insists they're just friends."

"Then I hope you have a good time!" Mrs. Findlay lifted her cup and blew on the tea. "What movie are you going to see?"

Beryl paused. She hadn't even given it a second thought, as focused as she was on the real reason behind the date. "I'm not sure. I didn't ask."

"I believe *They Knew What They Wanted* is playing in town," Mum said. "I heard one of the ladies at the Red Cross talking about it. It's an American film with Carole Lombard and Charles Laughton."

"I suppose we should be glad we still have a cinema in Leeds. So many were bombed in London, I hear."

"Yes, you're right. We should count our blessings." Mum sipped her tea.

"Beryl, you'll have to tell us what it's about," Mrs. Findlay said. "It's been ages since I've seen a film."

Beryl tried to calm her nerves as she got ready to leave to meet Freddie. She wasn't nervous about being with him. No, she couldn't call it that, but she was unsettled about Freddie's cryptic comment to her. She didn't want to appear anxious to see him, but she couldn't fiddle around the house anymore, so she left early.

Freddie waited outside the theater, leaning on the building with the usual cigarette unfurling smoke from his fingers. The building was lined with sandbags, and the glass doors were taped to keep them from shattering in a bomb attack. As she walked up, Freddie threw the cigarette down and stomped on it.

"You came!" A grin broke across his face.

"Of course. I told you I would." She glanced around to see if there was anyone she knew. How could she explain being with him? Everyone would assume the situation was more than it was.

"Yes, well. I'm glad you did." Beryl noticed he'd used extra pomade to comb his hair back.

"When can we talk?" She didn't want to waste any time getting to the main purpose of their "date."

"When we're alone, but not now. Let's get in line for our tickets, shall we?"

She was about to protest until she heard a familiar voice.

"Hello, Beryl. Hello, Freddie!" Beryl turned toward the greeting to see June hanging on the arm of a man Beryl had never seen before as the two headed toward the entrance. "So you're going to see the same film we are! Maybe we can sit together!"

Beryl stifled a groan. Not only was she here with a man she didn't want to be with, but now she was invited to sit with someone else she didn't care to be around. Could this get any worse?

"You two go ahead. We haven't gotten our tickets yet," Beryl said.

"We'll wait, won't we, sweetie?" June said, batting her eyelashes at her escort.

He smiled back, apparently under her spell like most men she was around.

When the ticket agent handed Freddie the tickets, he and Beryl walked toward the entrance where June and her date were standing.

"This is Gerald," June said. "We met at the last dance, didn't we?" She smiled up at him.

He nodded and shook hands with Freddie, who stuttered out his name.

June locked arms with Beryl and led her into the theater as the men followed. "I didn't want Gerald to think I wanted to neck in the theater. I really want to watch this movie. I'm a huge Carole Lombard fan!"

Beryl forced a smile, thinking that June must model herself after Miss Lombard, with the same hair color and style. June steered Beryl and their escorts to seats, making sure the two women were next to each other. Now it would be impossible for Freddie to tell her the big secret he was holding.

She allowed herself to follow the story in the movie about a man who pursued a woman through letters, pretending to be someone else. The thought crossed her mind that there could be a corollary between the letters from James supposedly written by Kenneth, but she pushed that notion aside. James wouldn't lie to her, and even if she didn't understand why Kenneth was with him, she had to believe it. To her left, June cuddled up with Gerald. She cut a glance at Freddie sitting stiff and focused. Too bad he wasn't someone like Kenneth, or even Kenneth himself. *Beryl, you silly girl! Why would you have a thought like that?* The man was in an enemy prison camp, and he certainly wasn't thinking about seeing a movie with her.

In one of the movie scenes, a man reached into a bowl and grabbed an apple. When he took a big bite of it, a moan sounded throughout the theater audience, as the very ability to savor an apple had become a desirable experience from the past. Beryl's taste buds yearned for the fruit she hadn't seen, much less eaten, in so long.

When the cinema was over, June asked if they wanted to join them for a walk through the park, but thankfully Gerald directed her in the opposite direction, saying they had dinner plans.

Beryl breathed a sigh of relief as they walked away. June, clinging to her date, waved over her shoulder. "Toodles!"

"Can we talk now, Freddie?"

He looked around. "I think it'll be safe to sit on a bench in the park.

No one will be very close to us there."

Safe? Weren't they already safe?

They walked around the block to the city park where barrage balloons flew overhead. The blimp-like balloons must be working, since the park or the cinema hadn't been bombed yet. Of course that wasn't always the case, especially in London. Finding an empty park bench, they sat down, and Freddie lit a cigarette.

"All right, Freddie. No one's around now, so you can tell me this secret you've been hinting at. Why all the mystery?"

Freddie's gaze scanned the park, and then he looked down and lowered his voice. "You know I've been assigned to fill Richard Davies' position, right?"

"Yes. And. . ."

"Richard was working on a top-secret project at Waddingtons."

"What on earth would Waddingtons be doing that's top secret?"

Two children ran through the park, followed by a harried mother, and Freddie put his hand out as if to quiet Beryl.

"We're making escape kits for POWs."

Time froze as she absorbed his comment. "What did you say? Waddingtons is making escape kits for POWs?"

Glancing around again, he said, "Shhh. Remember those men who came to see Mr. Watson a few weeks ago? They were MI5, and they asked him to make these special Monopoly games for our POWs in Germany."

"Monopoly games?" Her mind flashed back to seeing the game on Mr. Watson's desk when the men were there. Was it possible?

"Yes, you see, there are certain things hidden in these games that POWs can use to escape."

"What kinds of things?" She envisioned guns, rope, shovels. In a Monopoly game?

"For one, there's a silk map showing routes out of Germany from the POW camps. The maps are hidden inside the board."

"Are you telling me the truth?" Or was this another ruse to impress her?

"Yes, I'm being completely honest. But that's not all. There's real money, German and French, hidden in the play money."

"I can't believe it."

"It's true. Plus, there's a compass and a file hidden in the board as well. When our POWs get these Monopoly games, they will have tools to help them escape."

"But how can they get the games without the Germans knowing about them?"

"The Geneva Convention allows the Red Cross and other charitable organizations to include games in the packages they deliver to the camps."

"So, our men know about these kits?"

"That's the rub. You see, ever since Waddingtons started making them, the RAF has informed all their pilots to look for these specially marked games if they're captured."

"So, James knows about them?" Beryl's heart quickened.

"Probably not. You see, we've only been making them a month, and anyone who was captured before that wouldn't know about them."

"James was captured about three months ago."

"And the games weren't being made then."

"So he doesn't know." Her heart sank as the surge of hope dissolved. "But he needs to be told."

"Yes, somehow, but I don't know how. You can't give away the secret." He laid his hand on her arm. "I swore to secrecy, Beryl. In fact, the pilots have been told that once they use the items in the game, they are to destroy them to keep the game secret. I shouldn't be telling you about it, but I know your brother is a POW. The only way he'll find out is if another Brit gets captured and put in the same place as he is. I just wanted you to know that our company is making something to help the POWs."

She had to tell James. Somehow, she had to let him know but without compromising the whole program.

"You said they are specially marked. How?"

"There's a red dot on the Free Parking space."

How could Beryl put that information in a letter? There had to be a way. She had to help James escape. And Kenneth too.

# ▤ CHAPTER 22 ▤

*Stalag Luft I, Barth, Germany*
*August 1941*

"We hit the jackpot!" James said, as he and Kenneth carried in packages that had arrived at the camp. They each had a Red Cross package, but they also had received one from James' mother.

"Let's see what we got this time!" Kenneth said as he cut the string around his box and pulled open the flaps.

James perused the contents. "They sent all I asked for, plus more. Care for a chocolate?"

"Not this time. Let's save it for dessert when we can savor it. Or better yet, use it for a bribe." Kenneth grabbed a pair of homemade gray socks from James' box from home. "Aren't these nice?"

James snatched them away. "Mum is an excellent knitter. Maybe she'll knit you a pair too."

"I could use a new pair." His Red Cross parcel wasn't nearly as interesting as seeing what James had gotten from home. Kenneth leaned over and picked up a leather-bound book. "Some reading material for you." He handed the book to James.

James flipped open the book and showed Kenneth the title page. "It's a Bible, Kenneth. You ever see one before?"

"Of course. My mom had one, and so did the preacher at the little country church we went to when I was a boy." He smiled at James. "Never thought about just reading one for fun, though."

James cocked a brow. "You'd be surprised what you can find in this book, my friend." He set the Bible on his bed.

"Hey, here's a sewing kit."

"That'll go to Angus," James said, placing it to the side.

Kenneth shrugged, then glanced back inside the box. He picked up a pair of handkerchiefs. "You can always use one of these." He held one to his nose and sniffed. A sweet fragrance lingered, reminding him of Beryl.

"There's two, so take one for yourself," James said.

"Thanks, I think I will." He tucked the handkerchief in his shirt pocket. "Too bad Beryl didn't send a picture of herself."

James shook his head. "Beryl's not vain enough to do that. After all, I know what she looks like."

"Then ask her in your next letter to her if she will send one for me." Kenneth grinned.

James picked up a pack of chewing gum and opened it, offering it to Kenneth.

"Don't mind if I do!" Kenneth said, taking a stick.

Removing the toiletries, James ran the comb through his hair.

"You look much better now." Kenneth grinned.

"Would you like to borrow it? You don't have lice, do you? I heard some of the others have a problem with the little buggers."

"Not that I know of. I scrub my head hard when I wash my hair." He took the comb. "Can't have you looking better than me." He wiped the comb on his pants, then combed his hair, parting it down the side as he looked at his reflection in the window. As he did, he noticed a German looking in. He waved, and James glanced over at the window. "What's that ferret looking for?" The ferret moved away.

"Whatever he can find, I'm sure," James said. He looked back at Kenneth and lowered his voice. "How's your work coming?"

"Good, I think. We'll need to test it. But we need more ink and ink nibs. Why don't we ask Beryl to send you some in the next letter?"

"Of course. Let's write it now so we can get it in the mail soon."

"Sure. Got some more paper?"

James reached into his supplies and withdrew a sheet and a pencil, handing them to Kenneth. "You're not planning another adventure any-time soon, are you?"

Kenneth shook his head. "Not me. Colonel said we need to try someone they're not watching as much."

"Do you know how they're going to get out?"

"No. He hasn't told me, but I know they're working on a tunnel under one of the barracks."

"Hope they don't find that one. I heard the goons found the last two that were started."

"Let's take the rest of the food to the pantry, and then we'll write the letter." They carried the Red Cross boxes to the storage area and unloaded the food contents to be shared with everyone else.

"I'd like to keep the box," Kenneth said. "I noticed some of the guys use them to store their stuff under the beds."

"Good idea." James said. "These can be our footlockers. I'll keep the letters from home in mine."

They took the boxes back to their room to put their things in. Kenneth didn't have much to keep in his. He had used most of his art supplies for counterfeiting and hadn't gotten anything from home and doubted he ever would. He wasn't planning on staying around long enough to collect much anyway. Right now he was just biding his time until the colonel gave him further orders, much as he hated waiting. But so far his efforts had shown more of what was needed to successfully escape.

He took the writing supplies and sat down next to James so they could compose the letter together, but the sound of German jackboots stomping through the barracks door made them look up.

"Everyone out!" the guttural voice of Gooseneck shouted.

Kenneth and James jumped up, ready to leave, but James grabbed the Bible and stuffed it inside his shirt while Kenneth snatched the chewing gum lying on the bed. German guards hustled them outside and forced the POWs to stand away from the barracks.

"What's going on?" Kenneth asked Angus, who arrived by his side.

"One of the ferrets noticed a prisoner spilling dirt from his pockets, so they're searching for a tunnel."

"There's not one in our barracks, is there?" James asked.

"No, but they don't know where it is, so they'll search them all."

"And ransack the place too, no doubt."

"Great. What perfect timing, right after we receive our Red Cross rations. No doubt they'll pilfer some of our goods."

"Blasted goons!" Kenneth hated the way the Germans invaded their quarters but had to remind himself he wasn't planning on staying there very long. This was not his home after all. He just needed to wait a little longer until everything was ready.

"I hope they don't find your work," James said.

"Me too," Kenneth said, hoping the special section of the wall behind which he hid all his supplies wouldn't look suspicious to the guards. "I'd hate to start over from scratch."

The POWs waited outside, watching and talking among themselves for two hours while the Germans ransacked the barracks, looking for a tunnel, making the prisoners miss their midday meal. While the guards searched the barracks in one section, word was spread to the prisoners in the other sections to hide anything that would give away clues to an escape.

When Kenneth's group was allowed back into their barracks, it was a mess. Everyone grumbled, and many cursed the Germans as they tried to put their rooms and belongings back in order. With a beet-red face, Thomas surveyed the disarray of the larder, using some choice Scottish expletives to convey his ire. "The rotten goons stuffed their pockets with our food, the sorry thugs." He set to work rearranging the shelves back into the alignment he required, huffing and puffing in the process.

Kenneth hurried to the room where he'd been counterfeiting and exhaled a sigh of relief to discover the secret storage area in the wall had not been disturbed. He could continue his work now without setback. Colonel Gilmore stepped to the door of the room, hands on hips, worry lines creasing his brow.

"Everything safe in here?"

"Yes, sir. No sign of intrusion."

"Good." He turned to go.

"Sir, was anything found?"

"Not here, thank God. But they're still searching the rest of the barracks and might find something in one of them."

Kenneth raised his eyebrows. The colonel definitely knew more about possible escape attempts than he did.

"A tunnel?"

The colonel nodded. "They found the trapdoor under a bed. Hopefully they'll only find one tunnel, if any."

So there was more than one tunnel being dug. But in which barracks? Much as he wanted to know, Kenneth was rather glad he didn't know everything because he wouldn't be able to reveal or lie about something if questioned. Colonel Gilmore, on the other hand, must have a brain full of dynamite in his head.

At the next roll call when all the camp prisoners were lined up, they learned that a tunnel had been found in Barracks 23, an NCO barracks. The penalty for their "crime" would be to have their rations halved for a month and their Red Cross parcels withheld from them. As if they had so much to eat already. Everyone had lost weight since they'd been POWs due to the lack of food.

While they stood in line, two heavy horse-drawn wagons were pulled into the prison yard and driven around the compound several times.

"They use the weight of the wagons to collapse any tunnels in existence," Angus said as they watched the vehicles roll past.

"Does it work?" Kenneth said, hoping no one was in a tunnel when the wagons rolled over it.

"Yes and no. It's hard enough to shore up this sand, so sometimes part of a tunnel will collapse but part of it doesn't. However, the commandant doesn't expect anyone to go back down the same tunnel afterward. Many times, the tunnel can just be re-shored, but for the most part, we need to abandon the tunnel and let them think they won."

After they were dismissed, everyone returned to what they'd been doing before, except for the poor guy singled out for transporting dirt. He went to the cooler for ten days. For Kenneth, a return to normal at this point meant resuming his counterfeiting. For Angus, it meant continuing to work on making civilian clothing, and for James, it meant being assigned to another tunnel to help with the lighting and air supply. For several others, it meant resuming their digging but in a different location. This time there would be a new way of disposing of the extracted dirt, one that wouldn't attract the goons' or ferrets' attention. Angus was the genius who came up with the idea to conceal the dirt under the benches in the theater.

Prisoners from each of the other barracks sneaked food to number 23 to keep the men from starving. Kenneth was amazed at the brotherhood of guys in the camp. Here they were, an assortment of Allied prisoners from all over the world—Poland, France, the Netherlands, Scotland, England, Canada, New Zealand, Australia, and South Africa—but they were all united in their cause—to fight against the Germans and try to escape. He swallowed the lump in his throat, remembering his own brother, Kevin. When they were kids, they used to talk about flying, the adventures they'd have, and the exotic places they'd visit. But Kevin never had a chance to fly or have an adventure. Kevin was born with a defective heart and died when he was ten, so Kenneth had to experience life for both of them.

The colonel met with the prisoners in his barracks privately and in groups of two or three as they walked the yard and told them the word *tunnel* was not to be used in conversation. Instead, the tunnels would be given personal names. The current tunnel was named Nick, so any talk related to that tunnel was a conversation about Nick and his welfare. More POWs were appointed as guards, now called "stooges" since their job was to loiter, watch, and warn the barracks when a ferret or guard was too close to an area where escape business was being conducted.

# ≡ CHAPTER 23 ≡

*Leeds, England*
*August 1941*

Beryl poised the pencil on the letter she was writing to James and Kenneth. She'd been thinking about how to word the missive ever since Freddie had confided in her about the escape game. How much could she reveal without jeopardizing her company's involvement, much less the secrecy of the plan? What would the censors cut out?

Mum would want to know what she wrote in the letter, but she couldn't tell Mum the secret. She'd just read it to Mum and skip the sensitive parts.

> *Dear James and Kenneth,*
> *How good that you are together, although I'm sure you'd prefer to be back at school instead of where you are. I hope you received the box we sent. Please let me know what else you would like us to send you.*
> *Our kitten, Spitfire, is keeping us entertained, although he does like to get into Mum's yarn.*
> *Is it hot there or cold? We can send you warm clothes if it's cold.*
> *We are going to take in an elderly lady who can't live in her home anymore. She's a sweet lady with no family here now.*
> *What are you doing to pass the time? Are you reading? I'm sending a book James has always liked. Do you*

*play cards or board games? I miss the three of us playing Monopoly together. Perhaps a charitable organization will bring you one of the games and you can play it together. It can be a very exciting game.*

*My job has kept me busy as usual, but sometimes it's hard to find a parking place, especially when someone else takes my spot.*

*Mum and I send our love and keep you in our prayers for your safe return home.*

Beryl sat back and reread the letter. Did she say enough or too much? Would they understand the clues she was trying to convey? In her mind, she saw Kenneth reading her letter. He would have that half smile, holding back his familiar laugh, his green eyes twinkling as if he was thinking of a joke. She smiled, and her heart did a happy dance from the vision.

Would he picture her too when he read it? Did he even remember what she looked like? She could send him a picture, but it might be vain of her to do so. If only she had a picture of herself and Mum holding Spitfire. That would be more appropriate. But it would take too long to get a picture for this letter, and she needed to get it in the mail quickly. Maybe she would have one taken before the next letter.

What else should she say? That she'd seen a movie? That Mrs. Findlay asked about him?

Mum would probably include those items. She returned to the letter and added those tidbits of information. Everything else she could tell him related to the war or the bombings or the way things were because of them, but those subjects were taboo, according to the government. They'd probably be cut out by censors anyway. She folded the letter and addressed the envelope, then took it downstairs to see if Mum wanted to add anything to it before she posted it.

"Mum, I'm sending a letter to James," she said, not mentioning Kenneth.

"Have we gotten a letter back from them?" Mum stirred a pot of lentil soup on the stove, its aroma filling the room.

"Not yet, but since it takes so long going back and forth, I thought I'd just send one now anyway."

"All right. I'm sure they would like to hear from home more often. What did you say?"

Beryl read the contents of the letter, leaving out the part about the Monopoly game. "I can't think of anything else to say. Shall we send another box now or wait to see if they have more requests? I've been thinking it might be getting cold there since it's approaching October. Maybe we should send some more knitted items like caps and scarves."

"I was just thinking about that the other day. I've started on a scarf. Perhaps I should make one for his friend too. What's his name?"

"Kenneth. Yes, I think that would be a splendid idea. Whatever you make for James, make for Kenneth too."

"I wish I could find some yarn in prettier colors. All the yarn is either gray or brown," Mum said. "Hmm. I have an idea. Some of my knitting friends have taken the government's 'make do and mend' to heart and are unraveling old sweaters so they can reuse the yarn to make something else. I'm sure we have some pullovers we can do that with."

"That's a good idea, especially when the jumpers aren't being worn anymore." Beryl's throat caught thinking of Dad's cardigans upstairs that he wouldn't be around to wear this winter. Would Mum be willing or able to take them apart? "I'm sure the men will be happy to get anything you make them, especially if it keeps them warm."

"So, are you going to wait for me to finish knitting the hat and scarves before you mail the letter?"

"No, I'm going to post this today. We'll send the package when we have the items we need to go into it. The next package might reach them by Christmas, so we can make it more festive."

"Wonderful idea. I'll be thinking about what special treat we can add." Mum poured soup into two bowls, then turned and took two spoons from the kitchen drawer before placing them in the bowls and setting the bowls on the table. Glancing at the gray weather outside, she asked, "Are you going to get Mrs. Dowd today?"

"Yes, I'm taking the tram to the hospital, then we'll take a taxi back here."

"The room's all ready for her. Too bad the weather is so rainy." Mum bowed her head and clasped her hands. "Lord, please help us to help Mrs. Dowd recover, and please protect James and his friends. Amen."

"Amen," Beryl said, her mind going back to James and Kenneth.

How were they being treated?

Beryl mailed the letter on her way to catch the tram to the hospital. Her thoughts turned to the lady she was about to collect. Would Mrs. Dowd still be willing to come with her? Beryl wasn't sure how much the woman understood from one day to the next. Did she remember that her husband was dead, killed in the bombing? Did she realize her home was uninhabitable? Beryl had gone by the house a few days after the attack to see if there was anything worth retrieving, but all she found was a photo, the glass broken in the frame. Beryl tucked it in her handbag, saving the only personal effect she could find. She couldn't even go upstairs where the woman's clothes had been.

In addition to the bomb damage, there was water damage from the hoses the firemen had used to keep the fires from spreading through the neighborhood. Since then, the house had been knocked down, leaving a pile of rubble. The poor lady didn't even have clothes to change into until Beryl brought the dress she'd worn to the hospital home so Mum and Mrs. Findlay could copy its measurements. From those they'd made a pattern and two more dresses.

They'd cleaned Mrs. Dowd's old dress, and Beryl returned it to her so she could leave the hospital in it. In addition, Mum had given Beryl a small hat for the lady to wear home. When Beryl reached Mrs. Dowd's ward, she found her sitting on her bed, wearing her old dress and her ever-present pearls.

Beryl offered a warm smile and greeted her cheerily. "How are you today, Mrs. Dowd?"

"I can't find my handbag. I've looked all over for it. The nurses said they don't know where it is either." Mrs. Dowd glanced from side to side and lowered her voice. "I think they took it."

Beryl bit back a smile. "Oh, remember? You lost it on your way to the hospital. We'll have to buy you a new one."

Her brows creased with worry. "But my ration cards were in it."

"That won't be a problem. We'll just inform the authorities, and they'll present you a new book." She held out the hat she carried. "Let me help you put this on."

Mrs. Dowd frowned at the hat. "I don't remember that one."

"It's new, a gift from my mum." Beryl pinned the hat on the woman's cottony hair. "There."

"Is there a mirror?" Mrs. Dowd looked around her.

"I'm afraid not, but don't worry. You look perfect." Beryl extended her hand. "Are you ready to go?"

Mrs. Dowd slowly put her hand in Beryl's, and Beryl put her other arm around the lady's back to help lift her to her feet.

The nurse approached. "Your taxi is downstairs."

She and Beryl helped Mrs. Dowd as she took halting steps out of the room, down the hall to the elevator, and into the waiting cab. Beryl climbed in beside her, and they rode to Beryl's town house. When Beryl helped her climb out of the cab, Mrs. Dowd's eyes widened as she scanned the area.

"This doesn't look like my neighborhood," she said.

"No, it doesn't. It's my neighborhood, and this is my house." Beryl motioned to the front door. "You're going to be staying with me and my mum for a while."

Mrs. Dowd's confused expression revealed her lack of understanding, but Beryl hoped she wouldn't be frightened. The door opened, and Mum came outside, arms outstretched to Mrs. Dowd.

"Hello! I've been so eager to meet you!" She took both of Mrs. Dowd's hands. "I'm Sheila, Beryl's mum. Come on in, Mrs. Dowd, and I'll make us some tea."

"Thank you, that would be lovely," Mrs. Dowd answered and let Mum lead her in with an arm behind her back.

Mum glanced back over her shoulder at Beryl and smiled.

Beryl smiled back, relaxing from the worry she'd been carrying about how Mrs. Dowd would react to her new surroundings. Beryl paid the taxi driver, then followed the other women inside. Mum had seated Mrs. Dowd on the sofa.

"I'll be right back. Just got to put the kettle on," Mum said and dashed to the kitchen, nodding at Beryl to stay with their new guest.

Spitfire strolled in with a meow and sniffed Mrs. Dowd's legs, then rubbed against them.

Mrs. Dowd had apparently not heard the cat and was startled by the feel of the animal. Beryl prayed she wasn't allergic to cats.

"Oh! It's my Minnie!"

She leaned down and lifted the cat to her lap. After sniffing the woman's clothes, Spitfire began kneading her claws and purring.

"Minnie?" Beryl said.

"Yes, I lost her, but she's here." She lifted Spitfire to her face and held her close. "I've missed you, Minnie."

When had she lost her cat? Was it during the bombing or before? Funny that she'd never mentioned the cat before.

"So, Minnie was black and white?"

Mrs. Dowd frowned. "Why of course she is. See?"

Beryl bit back a laugh, knowing Spitfire wasn't a "she," but Mrs. Dowd didn't need to know, being perfectly content with what she thought to be true.

Mum came in carrying a tray with a teapot, cups, saucers, and spoons. She gave a questioning look at Beryl before setting the tray down on the coffee table.

"I see Spitfire has introduced himself," Mum said.

Beryl gave a strong shake of her head, and Mum's eyebrows lifted.

"She likes Minnie and is happy to be reunited with her," Beryl said.

It took Mum a minute to comprehend the message, but then understanding crossed her face and she nodded.

"I'm so happy to hear that," Mum said, pouring a cup of tea. "Would you like a lump?" She held a sugar cube in the silver tongs, and Mrs. Dowd nodded. "Yes, please."

Where on earth did Mum find sugar cubes? They'd been scarce for a year. Had she begged someone for them, or had she been hiding them for a special occasion?

Mum dropped the sugar lump into the cup and stirred it, then handed the cup on a saucer to Mrs. Dowd, who set the cat back down in her lap and took the beverage. Spitfire curled up and purred, content with her new, old friend.

"Mrs. Dowd, where does your family live?" Mum asked as she handed Beryl a cup of tea, then took one herself. Beryl had already told her that there was no family nearby but knew Mum was searching for more information anyway.

"America. Penelope married an American and moved there a long time ago. She had a daughter. I only got to see her a few times before Penelope died."

"I'm sorry."

"It was cancer, they said."

"And what happened to her daughter? Did she stay in contact with you?"

"Yes, she sometimes sends a letter." Mum and Beryl exchanged glances.

"I see. And what is her name?"

Mrs. Dowd frowned. "I can't remember."

They'd reached a dead end again.

"Do you know how old she would be now?"

Mrs. Dowd studied Mum. "About your age, I think."

Well, that was some progress.

"I see. Do you know if she had any children?"

Mrs. Dowd nodded as she sipped her tea. "Yes, but I can't remember how many."

Beryl knew what Mum was thinking. If Mrs. Dowd had great-grandchildren, they'd be around Beryl's age.

"Mrs. Dowd. . ." Mum began, but the woman raised her hand as if to stop her.

"Elinor," she said.

Beryl felt the excitement Mum was feeling.

"Your granddaughter's name is Elinor?"

"No, dear. Elinor is my name. You need to call me Elinor if we're to be friends."

Mum smiled. "Why of course we're going to be friends, Elinor!"

Elinor nodded. "And your name is. . .?"

"Sheila. My name is Sheila, and this is my daughter, Beryl."

"Sheila and Beryl. Nice to meet you."

Beryl and Mum grinned at each other. This was going to be an interesting experience. They had a new friend, and apparently a new cat named Minnie too.

# ⸬CHAPTER 24⸬

*Stalag Luft I, Barth, Germany*
*September 1941*

Erik Hanson was the next one to escape. The Norwegian was tall and thin with a hooked nose. His size was similar to one of the local chimney sweeps who came to the camp each week to clean out the chimneys. Erik had been studying the mannerisms and dress of the sweeps long enough to memorize their habits and apparel. He also determined how often they came into the camp. To prepare, he made a tall top hat like the sweeps wore out of cardboard and painted it black with shoe polish.

He added a row of buttons on his coat to look double-breasted like the coats of the sweeps, then completely covered his clothes with black soot. He also created a cleaning broom similar to the sweeps' tool. The next time a sweep arrived at the camp, Erik covered his face and hair with soot, donned the clothes and hat, grabbed the broom, and after waiting an appropriate length of time, walked out of the camp undeterred by the gate guard.

Kenneth applauded Erik for his boldness and creativity and hoped he'd make it back to Britain since his country had been overrun by the Germans. The only problem was his accent. Even though he had learned some German words, he spoke with a Norwegian accent. However, the escape was also an experiment to see if the papers Kenneth had created would pass for authentic. Erik was supposed to bury the clothes in the woods once he was safely away from the camp, having worn his civilian-like clothes underneath. Obviously, he'd have to clean off the soot as well.

When Erik was recaptured and returned to the camp three days later, Kenneth and the others learned that he had gotten as far as the nearest river and was crossing the bridge when a guard on the bridge recognized him and arrested him. Erik never had to show his papers because he didn't board any trains, so Kenneth didn't know if they would have passed inspection or not. Erik disposed of them before he could be searched. Otherwise, the penalty upon his return would have been a longer time in the cooler and would have jeopardized their escape plans.

As the days wore on, the weather turned cooler, and the lack of food showed its effect on all the men. Kenneth estimated he had lost twenty pounds already, and those who had been there longer had lost even more. If one needed a reason to escape besides one's desire to return home, having enough food to eat gave extra motivation.

It took two months to get a letter from his mother, but he was elated just the same. Despite the missing pieces of the letter, he could tell his mother was worried about him and prayed for him all the time. In fact, everyone in their little country church was praying for him. He chuckled at the thought of several of those people who had more than likely prayed for him many years. He figured they had given up on him by now and probably only told Mom they were praying for him to make her happy.

The letter had been inside a package she had sent that included all the items he'd asked for, except for the pocketknife. Not that he thought he'd get it. Mom had probably put one in but it was removed before it got to him, since prisoners weren't allowed to have weapons. However, receiving the writing supplies was worth their weight in gold, since they were his ticket home. Too bad she couldn't send some home cooking though. He was tired of always being hungry.

He sighed as a wave of sadness swept over him. He hadn't meant to put Mom through such anguish. She'd been through so much with Kevin dying, then Dad last year. Good thing they lived in a small town where she was part of the community. Although she had been an only child, Dad had plenty of siblings and cousins to keep her from being alone. And of course, she had her church ladies to keep her company too.

James walked into the room holding an envelope. "A letter from Beryl, Kenneth."

He glanced at the paper in Kenneth's hand. "You get a letter too?"

"I sure did!"

"Was your mum upset about where you are?"

"I think so. She said she worried and prayed for me every day, but then she always has."

"But this time you're in a POW camp, Kenneth. That must concern her."

"Sure it does." Kenneth took the envelope James offered him and removed the letter within it.

Kenneth read through Beryl's letter, then looked up at James. "You've read this, I assume."

James nodded. "Yes, I did."

"Why is she talking about Monopoly?"

"I don't know, but I found that odd too. Maybe she needed to say something related to her job. I'll bet she mentioned it because Waddingtons makes the game."

"But James, when did the three of us sit down and play Monopoly together? I don't remember that at all."

"Maybe she's just confused. But something else bothers me about her letter. She says she has a hard time finding a parking place at work. She rides a bike, Kenneth, for Pete's sake! Since when did Waddingtons assign parking spaces for bikes?" Worry lines creased James' forehead.

"But maybe they did and it's crowded."

James shook his head. "I don't know. It just doesn't sound right to me."

"Do you think she really wrote it? Maybe it could be someone else, like your mother."

"I don't think so. It must be Beryl. You see here where she mentions taking in a lady that can't go back to her home? I bet the reason she couldn't go back to her home was because it was bombed, but the British censors don't want the Germans to have the pleasure of knowing that."

"Hmm. You may be right. Well, that's nice of them to do that."

"It is. Beryl and Mum both have kind hearts. And this might be good for Mum. She's been rather lost since Dad was killed. She and Beryl share the desire to be of service to others."

"Which is probably why she's with the ARP."

James nodded. "That, and a sense of duty."

"So, let's write them back. You still want me to do it for you?" Kenneth said.

James still had the sling on his arm, but he wiggled his fingers. "Yes, please. My fingers are stiff. I don't think I can grasp a pencil."

Kenneth took a piece of writing paper and a pencil and looked at James.

"Dear Mum and Beryl," *What else?* "We were happy to get your letter and the box you sent. However, the German guards stole some of the contents." Kenneth twisted his lips.

"I don't think that will make it past the censors. Besides that, we don't want to upset the women," James said.

"Yeah, I know. Should we ask for more things?"

"Why not? At the rate it takes to receive packages, we'll need new things by the time the next box arrives."

"True. So I'll ask for more of the same, plus more writing supplies. And also some black shoe polish."

"Ask them for a copy of *The Problem of Pain* by C. S. Lewis."

"You mean Professor Lewis at Oxford?"

"The same. Have you read any of his books?"

Kenneth shook his head. "Literature was not my forte, remember?"

"I believe I did know that. What exactly was your principal interest?"

"Art."

"Of course. How could I forget?"

"Indeed, how could you? My artistic ability might get you home, you know." Kenneth wrote what had been discussed so far. "Should I mention anything about the Monopoly game?"

"Maybe you should. Tell Beryl we're both confused about playing Monopoly with her."

"I will. I'll also tell her Kenneth wants a photo of her."

James laughed, shrugging. "You're the author."

Roommates Clyde and Chester came in looking as though they'd just washed their faces and hair. They hung up their wet long johns on the edges of their beds, sank down on their mattresses, and heaved a sigh. The men appeared to be frustrated and tired. Angus came in behind them, hands on his hips.

"What's the matter?" Kenneth said, looking at Angus.

"We hit water again. Nick is flooded," Angus said.

"Blast! Now what?" Kenneth glanced at Clyde and Chester who had been two of the diggers. That explained the wet long johns, because the men took off their outer clothes to dig so they wouldn't look dirty when they came out.

"We start another somewhere else," Angus said. "Problem with where we are is that we're so close to the sea that we can't dig very far down before hitting water. That's about the twentieth one since I got here."

"Twenty? I had no idea," Kenneth said, being careful not to use the forbidden word, tunnel.

"Unfortunately, it's true. We've wasted a lot of time and labor trying."

"Not really," Kenneth said. "You ever hear of Thomas Edison, the inventor? I studied him in school and liked his attitude. One of the things he said was 'I have not failed. I've just found ten thousand ways that won't work.'"

"I hate to tell you, old chap, but I don't think we'll try ten thousand times."

"No, but he also said many people give up because they think they've failed when they didn't know how close to success they were."

"You tell these blokes and the others that have been working so hard on Nick," Angus said. "Maybe you can convince them."

"I'm sure old Gooseneck would be happy," Clyde said, referring to the commandant's chief lieutenant, always sticking his head in the barracks and looking to catch the prisoners in the act of trying to escape. His guttural voice could be heard fifty feet away, and his brown eyes gleamed with satisfaction when he thought he was on to something.

"He'd be happier if he'd found Nick himself," Chester said.

"No doubt," Angus said.

Later that day, word got around that indeed a new tunnel named Roy had been started. Kenneth was happy to see that the prisoners had not given up on an escape plan. However, not all the prisoners seemed interested in escaping, and Kenneth didn't understand them. In fact, some of them had decided prison was an opportunity to take a class and learn something. He feared the possibility that he could become one of those complacent men if he was in the camp too long more than he feared getting caught trying to escape. He couldn't become one of those who had given up. Right now the only thing he wanted to learn was how to make a successful escape.

An idea planted itself in his mind. Maybe there was something he could study while he was there.

"You know, James, maybe I should ask for a book too."

"A book about art?"

"No. A book about architecture or building design."

"Funny you should say that," James said. "Dad was a construction engineer. I think he had a couple of books at home on the subject."

"What a coincidence. So I'll ask Beryl to get one of your dad's books and send it."

"Yes, tell her to look at his bookshelves and find one about building construction or something similar. I'm sure she can find one that's appropriate."

"Beryl to the rescue," Kenneth said with a smile. "I sure am glad she's on the other end of this letter. It's quite comforting to know she's there to help us as much as she can."

"Tell her. It'll make her happy to know her efforts are appreciated," James said.

"I'll do just that. And someday I hope to show her my appreciation in person."

# ⧉ CHAPTER 25 ⧉

*Leeds, England*
*September 1941*

"Let's have a picnic! Shall we?" Mum's question startled Beryl, since she normally helped her mother with chores and laundry on Saturdays.

"A picnic? Where?"

"I was thinking about the four of us taking the bus to Temple Newsam."

"Four of us? You, me, Mrs. Dowd, and Mrs. Findlay?"

"Yes. We need to get outside of the city, and it's always been lovely there."

Beryl glanced toward the ceiling where Mrs. Dowd's room was as she stirred her tea. "Do you think Elinor is up to such an outing?"

"Yes, I think so. She seems to be getting stronger, and we'll go slow."

"Do you mind if I ask Veronica to go with us? She hasn't had a restful day away from the city either. She could certainly use one."

"Why, of course not. I'd love to see Veronica again. Is she still driving ambulances?"

"Yes, she is. A terribly brave volunteer job in my opinion." Beryl put her cup down. "What time would you like to go? I'll ring Veronica and see if she can join us."

"Hello? Is anyone there?" Mrs. Dowd's high-pitched wavering voice came from the stairs.

Beryl hurried to the foot of the stairs to see the woman coming down. "We're here, Elinor," she said in a loud voice so she would be heard.

"Oh, there you are. Have you seen Minnie?"

Beryl nodded. "He's. . .I mean she's in the kitchen eating breakfast."

Elinor took each step gingerly, gripping the banister. Beryl helped her navigate the last step, then led her to the kitchen.

"Good morning, Elinor!" Mum said in her cheeriest voice. She poured their guest a cup of tea and set it on the table, motioning for the woman to sit down. "We have a lovely day planned. We're going to Temple Newsam. Have you been there before?"

"Yes, I believe I have, a long time ago."

Mum set a piece of bread with jam on a plate, putting it in front of Elinor.

"We're going to pack a picnic and take it there to eat on the grounds. It's a beautiful day to enjoy the fresh air in the country." She looked at Beryl. "Tell Veronica to come here half-nine, and we'll take the ten o'clock bus."

Beryl was thrilled to hear Veronica could go with them and so excited to see her friend again. She couldn't wait to catch Veronica up on the news from James. She was dying to tell Veronica about the secret Monopoly game too, but she'd promised Freddie she wouldn't tell another soul.

When Veronica came over, she was surprised to see Mrs. Dowd. "She's living with you now?" she whispered to Beryl.

"Yes. We can't find any other relatives. Seems like her one daughter moved to the States many years ago, and it's been just Mrs. Dowd and her husband here ever since."

"Does she know what happened to her husband?"

"I told her, and she seems to be taking it well, but then she's a little forgetful and might not remember. I don't want to delve too hard and upset her."

"Just as well. What can she do about it? Well, it's good of you and your mum to take her in."

Beryl brought Veronica into the kitchen. "Mrs. Dowd, this is my friend Veronica."

"Oh, I didn't know you were friends with a movie star!" Mrs. Dowd said.

Beryl and Veronica exchanged glances, and then Veronica extended her hand to the older woman. "It's very nice to meet you, Mrs. Dowd."

"Oh, you must call me Elinor!"

"Hello, Veronica," Mum said. "How are you and your family getting on?"

"Hello, Mrs. Clarke. We're fine, thank you." Spitfire meowed and rubbed against Veronica's legs. "So, how are you?" As everyone did, Veronica leaned over and picked up the cat.

"That's Minnie. She's my cat," Mrs. Dowd said.

Veronica frowned and glanced at Beryl, who shrugged. "Mum and I used to call him 'Spitfire.'"

"I see. Well, he's a sweetie!"

"She," corrected Mrs. Dowd.

Mrs. Findlay arrived and greeted everyone, smiling. "I'm so looking forward to this outing! How nice to have a girls' trip!"

"We're all here now. Shall we go?" Beryl said.

"Yes. Come, Elinor." Mum helped Mrs. Dowd out of her chair. "Let's get our hats and gloves from the hall tree and put on our coats. Beryl, will you please pick up our lunch basket?"

While walking to the tram stop, Veronica leaned toward Beryl. "Do you think this might be too much for her?"

"I hope not. We'll take it easy and let her rest often. Mum is convinced the outing will do her good."

As they rode the tram, Beryl sat beside her friend while Mum and Mrs. Findlay sat on either side of Mrs. Dowd.

"We got a letter from James," Beryl said to Veronica.

Veronica's head jerked around. "You did? Oh my. What did he say?"

"He said he got banged up a little, but he's okay now except for an arm that hasn't healed yet."

"So he's allowed to write you, then?"

"Yes, he's allowed. However, since it was his right arm that was injured, his friend is penning the letters for him."

"Then it's a good thing he's made friends."

"Well, actually, you won't believe this because I have a hard time believing it myself, but I know his friend too. He's an American who attended Oxford when James and I were there."

"An American? How did he end up in a prison camp?"

"From what I've been told, there are American volunteers who have come over to join us in the fight against Hitler."

"Wait. I've heard of the Eagle Squadron. Do you think that's the group he's with?"

"He must be. James dropped a hint in his letter about a favorite bird being a bald eagle."

"Sly of them. So what's this guy's name?"

"Kenneth. Kenneth Bordelon."

Veronica studied Beryl's face. "You're sweet on him, aren't you?"

"What are you talking about? Why would you say that?"

"Beryl, you're talking to me, your best friend. You have a little spark in your eye and your face lights up when you mention this guy. Hey, I think I remember you talking about him a couple of years ago. Is it the same guy?"

Beryl shrugged and looked away. "I'm not sure who I talked about two years ago."

Veronica tapped her red lips with her fingertip. "Let's see, something about a motorcycle ride in a sidecar?"

Beryl's face warmed. "I suppose that could be the same one."

"Aha! I knew it. And now he's writing to you. How romantic."

"Veronica. How can being in a prison camp be romantic? I doubt he's given me a second thought. Besides, he's not actually the one who is writing to me. James is."

"Sure. But that doesn't mean he hasn't thought of you. I hope you get to see him again."

Beryl lowered her gaze. "I hope I get to see my brother too."

"When the war is over, we'll all see our loved ones again. We must believe that."

She hated to ask but had to. "Any news of Rodney?"

"Yes and no. I heard his ship is still somewhere off the coast of Africa. But I'm praying he'll be safe and that I'll hear from him soon."

Beryl hoped her friend was right. "And I'm praying for him too."

Veronica squeezed her hand, her eyes moist. "Thank you, friend. And I too will pray for James. And his friend Kenneth."

The two turned to look out the windows of the bus as they left the outskirts of Leeds and entered the western Yorkshire countryside where the golds and reds of autumn were painting the leaves. The road became more hilly as they entered the dales, and forest bordered each side. Turning down a brick road, the tram passed between two stone columns topped by sphinxes and into the thousand-acre property of the historic estate of Temple Newsam. At the top of a hill, the

Tudor-Jacobean manor house came into view in the distance, creating a stir of muttering among the tram passengers. As they descended the hill, the trees gave way to a vast lawn of green grass that stretched as far as they could see.

Finally, the bus pulled into a circular drive in front of the impressive house and stopped. The women disembarked and walked to the entrance. Taking Mrs. Dowd by the elbow, they went up the six low stone steps to the door. Before they entered, Mrs. Dowd looked up at the coat of arms above the door. "That's Lord Darcy's coat of arms. He was the first owner of the house."

The other four women glanced at each other with surprise. That was only the beginning of their surprises. As it turned out, Mrs. Dowd was quite familiar with the house, remarking as they moved from room to room with some fact about the room's history.

"Mrs. Dowd. . .I mean Elinor. . .how do you know so much about the history of the house? Have you been a frequent visitor?" Beryl asked.

The woman nodded. "Oh yes, I've been here many times."

Apparently her memory had returned.

"Harry was a docent here for several years after he retired, so I've heard the story repeated quite a bit."

Beryl glanced at Veronica and said in a low voice, "I had no idea."

"Mrs. Dowd is turning out to be an interesting person," Veronica said.

In fact, the older woman appeared to regain energy as she gave a personal tour of the house to the others. They strolled through the immense picture gallery in the north wing, where valuable pieces of art were displayed all over the walls, and Mrs. Dowd was familiar with each one, pointing with her bony finger as she described each painting and its artist. "Mr. Hendy, the new museum director, is responsible for bringing much of the art here. Harry was quite pleased with his effort." In the same wing, they visited the chapel where centuries of family worshippers had gathered. The south wing contained Mr. Woods', the former owner's, impressive library.

When they visited the west wing, seeing bedrooms, boudoirs, the blue-striped dressing room, and the blue damask dressing rooms, Mrs. Dowd's crackling high voice told about each of the famous people who had occupied the lavish rooms, adding historical details to the explanation, including royal complexities and political intrigue. Slowly taking each step of the grand staircase to the second floor and surrounded by the other women ready to help her up or catch her if she fell, the diminutive snow-haired woman continued her descriptions of the paintings on the wall, many of which were portraits of the manor's former residents.

From the second floor, Beryl looked out through windows down to the fountain and formal gardens behind the house, catching a glimpse of the surrounding property. Surprised to see evidence of coal mining beyond the tree line, she nudged Veronica to take a look.

"What a pity they have to tear up the landscape so near the house," Beryl said.

"It's gotten even worse because of the war. Now the mines are supplying coal to wartime factories," Veronica said, gazing out the window.

"Wouldn't Capability Brown, the landscape designer who created these beautiful grounds, roll over in his grave if he knew the land was being torn up so rudely?"

"Wouldn't he now?"

Mrs. Dowd pointed to one wing of the house. "This is the south wing, which was used as a hospital in the Great War. Everyone did their part, you know. While the owner of the estate, Edward Wood, Earl of Halifax, fought in the army, his wife, Dorothy, oversaw the hospital."

*Everyone did their part,* Beryl mused. Weren't they doing the same thing now? But it was James and Kenneth who were doing the hardest part.

Mrs. Dowd ceased speaking, and Beryl glanced at her to see why, noting the woman's pale face was even whiter. She must have gotten tired, and Beryl hoped the outing hadn't been too much for her. From Mum's expression as she looked at the elderly woman, she must have been thinking the same thing.

"Let's go outside and find a place to have our lunch," Mum said. She took Mrs. Dowd's elbow and, with Beryl on the other side, helped her back down the stairs. They found their way out to the garden and sat down on a stone bench. Mum opened the lunch basket and removed the thermos. She poured a cup of tea into one of the cups she'd packed and handed it to the elderly woman.

"Here. A cuppa is just what we need now, isn't it, Elinor?"

Elinor took the cup and sipped, then gulped the rest of the tea down. "Thank you," she said and gave the cup back to Mum.

Mum cut an amused glance at Beryl, then poured them each a cup while Beryl took out the wrapped jam sandwiches and gave one to each of the women.

"The air is so fresh out here," Veronica said. "Thank you for inviting me. I needed to get away from town and see something lovely for a change."

"I know what you mean," Beryl said, although she didn't elaborate since she knew her friend was talking about the war damage they saw every day in town. Mrs. Dowd didn't need to hear about it.

"I hope this place survives unscathed," Veronica said, "after all it's seen through the years."

Mrs. Findlay spoke up. "Apparently the town council thinks it's safe. They sent some of the Leeds' City Art Gallery pieces here for safekeeping since the bombing back in March when Town Hall and the city museum were hit. Funny that when war was first declared, they closed this place a few months. But people protested, and the city leaders decided the citizens needed something of beauty to keep their spirits up."

"Thank God, they did," Mum said. "We need something beautiful to see, especially such a symbol of survival."

"You know this property was once owned by the Knights Templar?" Mrs. Dowd said, breaking her silence, perhaps a sign she was regaining her energy.

"Imagine that," Mum said. "Why, that was at least a thousand years ago."

"Elinor, what did Mr. Dowd do before he was a docent here?" Beryl asked, raising her voice to be heard.

"What did she say?" Mrs. Dowd said to Mum, who repeated Beryl's question.

"He was a professor at the university," she answered with a tone that sounded like everyone should know that fact.

"I see. A professor of what field of study?" Mum asked.

"Art, of course."

Of course. How would she know that? It must've been years before she was born. Dare she ask what university? She didn't have to ask, however, as Mrs. Dowd volunteered the information.

"He was a Slade professor at Oxford. He retired in 1915 and became the museum director for the Leeds Museum."

"And that's why you know so much about art," Mum said.

"Yes, I suppose so. He passed that interest on to our daughter too."

A gust of cool air swept through the garden, and Mrs. Dowd shivered.

Mum pulled Mrs. Dowd's collar up and made sure the buttons on her coat were fastened. "We best be getting back home," Mum said. "I could use a little nap."

Beryl cut her eyes to Mum, knowing she made the suggestion for Mrs. Dowd's benefit. The rest of the women caught on and nodded in agreement.

"You know, I could use one myself," Mrs. Findlay said.

They collected their things and stood, then walked back to the area where they could catch the next bus. On the ride back to town, Veronica said, "Do keep me informed about your letters from Kenneth. Since I haven't any letters from Rodney, let me enjoy yours."

"I will. I just wish it didn't take so long to hear from them."

"You should send them a picture from home. Rodney has one of mine."

"But brothers don't normally carry pictures of their sisters."

Veronica pursed her lips. "You know what I mean. I bet James would love anything from home, but you need to let his roommate remember what you look like."

"Veronica, that's awfully pretentious, isn't it? Besides, I don't have any recent pictures of me."

Veronica's eyes lit up, and she snapped her fingers. "I know what you can do! I have a good picture of you and me from last Christmas. I'll give it to you, and you can send it to them. James would like to see it, and that way you won't seem so vain."

"That's not a bad idea. Thank you, I'll do that."

Veronica smiled, then sobered. "I wonder how long it'll be before this war is over and we can see our guys again."

Maybe they wouldn't have to wait until the war was over. Beryl fought with herself to keep from telling Veronica about the Monopoly game and how it could help the guys get home sooner, but she just couldn't give in. James and Kenneth were the only ones who needed to know about it right now.

# ≡CHAPTER 26≡

*Stalag Luft I, Barth, Germany*
*November 1941*

Kenneth pulled his collar up around his neck. "Gets cold here early, doesn't it?" James walked alongside as they made their regular circuit around the compound.

"Reminds me of England. Since it's November, the weather will be getting chilly there too, no doubt."

"I forgot. Guess I'm thinking of home in Louisiana. This feels like winter to me."

"Good thing Mum knitted these mufflers for us."

"Yeah, that was really nice of her. If the sun would come out, it'd feel warmer, but this damp air cuts right through."

"Courtesy of being near the sea."

Angus walked up and joined them. "Have you heard the latest?"

"What? Germany's surrendered?" Kenneth said with a note of sarcasm.

"Not yet. In fact, they're going hard into Russia."

"Is that the truth or just bragging?" Kenneth said.

"I believe it's true. But that's not the worst of it," Angus said, lowering his voice. "A British aircraft carrier was hit by a U-boat and sunk off the coast of Gibraltar."

"Oh no," James said, shaking his head. "I hope Veronica's fiancé wasn't on that ship."

"Who's Veronica?" Kenneth asked.

"She's Beryl's best friend. Her beau is in the navy."

"How did you find out?" James said.

"Habersham's friend told him. He said things weren't looking good for our side and we should just surrender."

"Well, I say we're only getting one side of the story, the wrong side," Kenneth said.

"Habersham's friend did reveal some real news, though. After a few drinks, he told Habersham that the ferrets had installed sound-detecting microphones in the ground around the huts. Guards with headphones, sitting in the administration compound, listen to them day and night. Now they can pick up any noise underground."

"Blast! What now?" Kenneth asked. How would they affect the new tunnels being worked on? Hugh, Jack, or Jude was going to be his path to freedom.

"The colonel said we'd just have to dig deeper to get below the microphones, plus there can be no talking underground."

Kenneth exhaled a sigh of relief that the tunnel plan wouldn't be abandoned. His stomach growled, reminding him of how little he'd eaten. The Germans weren't giving them the required amount of food, and lately they received sauerkraut all the time. He was so sick of the stuff, he never wanted to eat it again. But like everyone else here, he was hungry all the time, so he ate what was available. The kriegies tried not to think about being hungry, but that was like trying not to see the elephant in the room. Meanwhile, visions of his mom's delicious cooking kept invading his mind. Right now he craved some of her jambalaya. When he got out of this place, he would definitely pig out and make up for lost time.

Kenneth shook his hands, then clenched and unclenched his fists. He had spent so much time gripping the ink pen while writing intensely and carefully that his hands cramped. His documents were getting better and better with practice, though, so he couldn't quit. He walked away from the others and strolled over to the cricket field where he asked to join the game. He had recently learned how to play, and the exercise helped to relieve stress. Besides, the exertion helped warm him up when it was cold. Angus told him the cold was just beginning, having experienced winter in the camp before.

"Just wait until snow is on the ground and they make you stand for roll call. Your fingers, toes, and nose freeze," he said.

Thank God—rather, thank Mrs. Clarke, for her knitting. At least he had something to cover his fingers, toes, and nose. He couldn't wait to thank her in person. But the colonel said the winter was the worst time to escape. Once you got out in the weather without shelter, you would be susceptible to frostbite. One of the guys who had escaped the previous winter lost some toes as a result of being in the elements three days in subzero temperature before he was caught. And the cooler wasn't heated either, which made solitary confinement painfully worse.

After Kenneth had played cricket for over an hour, the loudspeakers summoned the prisoners for mail call. The guys dropped their equipment and headed to their barracks. Kenneth entered his barracks just as James' name was being called. A letter from Beryl! He hurried over to James, who had the letter in hand. When Kenneth's name wasn't called, he stuffed the hints of depression and followed James to their room to read Beryl's letter.

When the envelope was opened and the letter unfolded, a photograph fell out. Kenneth snatched it before it hit the ground. His heart pumped a little faster when he took a look at the picture. "Now there's a couple of beauties! I know that's your lovely sister, Beryl, on the right, but who's the gorgeous girl with the black hair standing next to her?" He turned the photo for James to see it.

"That's Veronica, the friend of Beryl's I spoke about, the one with the fiancé in the navy. Remember?"

"So that's Veronica. She's a doll."

"And she's engaged."

"That's okay, pal. She still doesn't hold a candle to Beryl. I'd take Beryl over her friend any day."

"You assume Beryl would give you a chance?"

Kenneth grinned. "With my charm, of course! Besides, I think she likes me."

"Actually, I believe she did like you back in college, but I don't know how much."

"Do you know if she's seeing anyone now?"

James shook his head. "Not that I'm aware of."

"So, what did she say this time?"

James leaned against the bunk bed as he scrutinized the letter. Kenneth crossed his arms and stood beside him, listening.

"Let's see. She said five of them went together—Mum, Mum's friend and our neighbor Mrs. Findlay, the lady that's moved in with them, and Veronica—on an outing, a picnic she says, at Temple Newsam."

"What's that?" Kenneth said. "A church?"

James shook his head. "No. It's a huge Tudor mansion in Yorkshire, outside of Leeds. It dates back to the sixteenth century. It's been converted into a museum now with scores of valuable art pieces."

"Hmm. Sounds like it's right up my alley. I'd like to see it someday."

"I'll take you when we get back. It's worth seeing."

"Sounds good, but I'd rather Beryl take me."

James rolled his eyes, then returned his attention to the letter. "Let's see what else she says. Veronica is still hoping to hear from Rodney and asked if he was here with us."

"You said he was in the navy, right? Then he's not going to be in a Luftwaffe camp. It's just for airmen. What else did she say?" Kenneth tilted his head to see the letter better.

"Weather's getting cooler, autumn colors are pretty in the Dales, Mum's still knitting and will be sending us more warm accessories."

"Cooler here too, but our colors are the same every day, no matter what season it is. However, I'm looking forward to more warm things from your mum. It's nice of her to make things for us."

"She loves to knit, especially for others. One thing our family never ran out of was jumpers and caps."

"I wish Beryl could tell us the real scoop about what's happening outside this place. Are the Germans really doing so well, or is that only what they want us to believe?" Kenneth crossed his arms. He didn't trust anything the Germans told them, even the so-called "good" Germans.

"You know she can't write anything about the war. Oh, but look. She says something about a Monopoly game again."

"She's a little obsessed with the game, isn't she?" Kenneth said. "Must be pretty bored."

"Actually, she never liked playing it that much before, come to think of it. She thought the game took too long to play. Listen. She says we should brush up on our game because she's getting very good and will beat us at it when we get home. In fact, she says she's gotten very lucky about landing on the Free Parking Space with the red dot."

"What a strange thing to say. I don't remember red dots on the Free Parking Space, or on any other space, honestly. But it's been a while since I've seen a game. Maybe the game is different now," Kenneth said. "Too bad I didn't get to play it with my brother. He would've been good at it."

"You have a brother? You haven't mentioned him before."

"*Had* a brother. Kevin died when he was ten. Had a bad heart." The familiar sting of grief pierced him as he mentioned Kevin.

"I'm sorry, Kenneth," James said.

Kenneth shrugged. "Thanks. Like I said, it was a long time ago." He refocused the subject of the conversation. "Maybe we'll get a Monopoly game in our next package, and then we can see what she's talking about."

"Yes, and practice playing so she won't beat us when we get home."

"I like the sound of that—'when we get home.'" Kenneth wasn't sure if he meant back to England or home in Louisiana, but right now either one would be welcome.

"I do too."

"Did you notice she didn't say 'when the war is over'? She said when we get home."

"Which is one and the same to her," James said.

"Maybe so. But it's not to me." Kenneth would not lose hope, no matter how bad things were in camp. In fact, the worse camp was, the more inspired he was to leave it.

Angus came into the room, his cheeks cherry red from the cold air. He placed his hands on his hips and faced them. "So, guys, we just listened to the BBC. They mentioned that the *Ark Royal* was hit by a U-boat."

"The *Ark Royal* was the ship they hit? So it's true. That's quite a loss. But I'm surprised the BBC mentioned it on the radio, knowing the Germans would be listening."

"Right, but here's the clincher. They said only one life was lost. The destroyer *Legion* was in the convoy and came alongside, rescuing all but one of the over fourteen hundred survivors. I believe the BBC announcement was meant for the Nazis to know it wasn't as bad a blow as they thought it was," Angus said.

"Wow. That's amazing. No doubt we lost a lot of valuable equipment, but our men were rescued, thank God," James said. "That's a miracle."

Kenneth arched an eyebrow. A miracle? He wasn't sure he would call it that. But maybe that's how James explained amazing events. As far as Kenneth was concerned, if he wanted a miracle, he'd have to create it himself. And if God wanted to help, He was welcome. He could start with a hot dish of jambalaya.

# ⟩CHAPTER 27⟨

*Leeds, England*
*November 1941*

Beryl watched for the mail every day, her heart racing each time the mail carrier arrived. Had Kenneth and James gotten her last letter? Did they understand the clues she'd sent, or were they censored? The more she thought about them, the more she wanted to see them, but her desire to see Kenneth had grown even greater than she'd expected. When they'd parted at the outbreak of war, she never thought she'd see him again. But now that there was a possibility of him coming back to England, memories of their time together had resurfaced, reigniting the attraction she'd had for him before.

Was there a way to add something more personal in her next letter without being too forward? What would James think? He knew she was interested in Kenneth in college, but that was two years ago.

On the spur of the moment, she purchased a Monopoly game, suggesting she could play with Mum, Mrs. Findlay, or Veronica. She doubted Mrs. Dowd would understand the game, but she might like to watch. Her main purpose, however, was to familiarize herself with the parts of the game so she could figure out how to post better clues.

She also realized the normal flow of letters back and forth between her and the prison was not to be expected. Not knowing when she'd receive a letter from the guys, she couldn't wait for normal protocol to send one to them. There had to be some way to hurry up the process and help them escape. What difference would it make if they got several of her letters close together? That would be even better, as they could piece the clues together more quickly.

She carried the game into the kitchen where Mum sat at the table sipping tea and listening to the BBC cooking program, *Kitchen Front*.

"You want us to play a game?" Mum said. "When did you take an interest in board games?"

"We make these, Mum, so I thought I should support the company." She opened the box and viewed the contents. "Besides, we send these to the POWs too."

"Is that right? I knew about the playing cards but not the board game."

"Yes, I recently found out about that myself, so I was thinking about Kenneth and James playing one of our games and thought it would be sort of like playing together with them if we played one too."

"That's a thought. I like the idea. Let's do it!"

"We need four players, and I don't know about Mrs. Dowd's ability to play."

Mum frowned. "I would be surprised if she could."

Beryl laid out the game board, noting the places on it and looking at the thickness. Did they really put a map inside the boards? Of course, there was no red dot on the free parking space of this one. Freddie had told her the "special" games were shipped directly to the charitable organizations that would pack them and deliver them to the prisoners. She picked up the stack of money and rifled through it, imagining their reaction when the guys found real money in their stack.

Removing the tokens from the box, she set each one of the six metal pieces in the center of the board facing her. The race car reminded her of Kenneth, not that he owned one like it, but because it represented speed, reminding her of the motorbike he'd had. Unfortunately, there was no motorbike token. Beside the car was the iron, boot, thimble, battleship, and rich Uncle Pennybags' top hat. She picked up each piece and turned it over to look at the bottom, trying to figure out how tools could be hidden in them.

"What are you doing, Beryl?" Mum asked, watching her.

"Oh, I just wanted to see the detail of these. I've never really looked that closely at them."

"What piece would you like to use?" Mum said. "I'll take the thimble."

No surprise there. "I like the race car," Beryl said, picturing Kenneth using the same token. "Which token do you think James would use?"

Mum put her hand under her chin. "Hmm. The boot or the battleship."

"The battleship makes me think of Rodney, Veronica's fiancé."

"I heard one of our big ships was hit by a torpedo. I hope it wasn't the one he was on."

"Me too. That would be terrible."

"Why don't you call her and see if she wants to come over today and play the game with us? I'll go next door and ask Mrs. Findlay."

"Where is Elinor?"

"Taking a nap on the sofa with Spitfire curled up beside her."

"Good thing he answers to both of his names."

"When it comes to attention, he's not particular," Mum said, smiling. "As long as he and Elinor are happy, I'm happy too."

"Did you inquire of anyone at Temple Newsam about Mr. Dowd?"

"Yes, they knew who he was but didn't know anything about his family besides his wife. But his health had gotten poor in the last two years, so he didn't go as regularly to docent as he had before." Mum shook her head. "Did you check the post office to see if they'd gotten any mail?"

"Yes, but nothing has shown up."

The telephone rang, and Beryl ran to the foyer to answer it. When she lifted the receiver, she barely got the word "hello" out before Veronica's excited voice interrupted.

"Beryl! I've got the most wonderful news! Rodney's ship is going to be in port for repairs, and he wants to get married while he's in the country!"

"Oh my goodness, Veronica! How exciting! When?"

"He said he can only get leave for two days, so he plans to come next weekend."

"Next weekend? So soon?"

"Yes! Mum is in a state worrying about how to prepare for the wedding in such a short time. Can you please help?"

"Of course I can. Shall I come over there, or do you want to come here to set up plans?"

"I'll come over there. It will be better if we can make some decisions without Mum going into a flurry."

"All right. Are you coming now?"

"Be right over."

Beryl hurried to the kitchen to tell Mum Veronica's news. She picked up the parts of the Monopoly game and put it away. Playing the game would be the least of Veronica's interests right now. Beryl was eager to share her friend's excitement. It wasn't the first time they'd talked about their future weddings, sharing dreams about that perfect day when they'd marry the perfect man. But Veronica got engaged first, and her wedding had been delayed by the war.

Veronica showed up at the house in record time, carrying magazines and a notebook. Beryl embraced her in a big hug.

"I'm so happy for you, Veronica!"

Mum greeted her with a big smile and gave her a hug too.

"So, you're getting married next weekend? My, that's not much time to get ready for a wedding. What is your mum doing? I'll help any way I can."

"Thank you." Veronica blew out a breath. "I left her arguing with Dad about what to wear. He's going to call the church today and arrange the time for the ceremony."

The women headed to the kitchen, but their excited chatter apparently woke Mrs. Dowd. She stood at the door of the sitting room holding Spitfire.

"What's all this about?" she said as they walked past her.

"Veronica's wedding!" Beryl shouted her words.

Mrs. Dowd followed them into the kitchen. "A wedding, did you say? Who's getting married?"

Mum and Beryl both looked at her and said, "Veronica!"

Veronica waved her hand. "*I* am."

"Oh, why didn't you say so?" Mrs. Dowd said.

Mum put the kettle on, then sat at the table with the other women. Veronica opened the magazines, which had articles about wartime brides. She spread them out on the table, pointing to various pictures of brides and weddings.

"I'd love to have this," she said, pointing to a picture filled with white flowers. "But we can't get those flowers this time of year, especially this quickly."

Beryl pointed to a bride. "What kind of dress are you going to wear?"

"Mum wants me to wear her old wedding dress, but I was thinking of something newer, like this knee-length cocktail dress with a matching coat. It's rather chilly weather now, and I can wear the coat for our going away."

"Where are you going to get one so quickly? You can't make the outfit by this weekend, can you?" Beryl said.

"I can't make the whole thing myself, but I can make the dress. It's a basic shift. Can you help me make the coat?"

"I can do that," Mum said. "But won't your mum be disappointed if you don't wear her dress?"

"Maybe, but I'll tell her to save it for Nancy's wedding."

"Have you seen any material anywhere? You don't want it made out of blackout curtain fabric."

"I certainly don't. I saw some pale pink cashmere at Fitzgerald's."

"Then we'd better grab it. It'll take a lot of fabric for a dress and coat," Mum said. "We'll give you our clothing coupons to use."

Veronica turned to Beryl. "You should wear a dress like mine but in a different color since you're going to be my maid of honor. You will be, won't you?"

"Why, of course. We planned that years ago when we were little girls—I'd be your maid of honor and you'd be mine."

"But now I'll be a matron of honor instead," Veronica said.

"No sense talking about my wedding when I don't even have a boyfriend," Beryl said.

"Ooh, look at this cake! Isn't it beautiful?" Veronica said.

"You know sugar is rationed, and now bakeries are restricted from making iced cakes, referring to it as the wanton waste of sugar," Mum said.

"Look," Beryl said, peering at the picture. "That isn't a real cake. It's a fake one made from cardboard, the kind bakeries put in the windows."

"What it says here is you make a small cake, then set the fake one over it so it looks good," Beryl said.

"Do you think Mr. Stewart will let us borrow his cardboard model?" Veronica asked.

"Veronica, if you ask him sweetly and bat those long eyelashes of yours at him, I'm sure he will," Mum said.

"Don't forget, chocolate covering is still allowed, and who doesn't like chocolate?" Beryl said.

"I do love chocolate too, but shouldn't a wedding cake be white?" Veronica said.

"What if we make a chocolate cake and cover it with the fake white cover? It'll still look the part and taste good too," Beryl suggested.

"I like that idea!" Mum said. "We can even make a cherry cake with chocolate icing."

"That sounds wonderful," Veronica said. "Yes, let's do it."

"What do you plan to wear on your head? A veil? Hat?" Beryl asked.

"Both. A smart little hat with a shoulder-length veil that just covers my head." Veronica said. "I was thinking about asking Mrs. Findlay if she could make a hat for me to match my dress. She makes such nice hats."

"I'm sure she would be happy to do that for you," Mum said.

"You're not buying new shoes, are you?" Beryl asked.

"No, my church shoes will be fine. I'll wear my white gloves as well."

"So you'll have something old—your shoes and gloves. Something new—your dress and hat. . . What do you have that is blue?" Mum counted each item on her fingers.

"Rodney will be wearing his uniform, which is dark blue. Does that count?" Veronica asked.

"I assume it could, but it should be something the bride is wearing."

"I wonder if there are any blue flowers blooming," Beryl said.

"There aren't many flowers blooming this time of year, but come to think of it, Mr. Cuthbert's family farm had a beautiful garden," Mum said. "They probably have dahlias blooming now. Would you like some for your bouquet? I remember seeing some very pretty pink ones when I was there."

"They sound lovely. I do hope they have some," Veronica said wistfully.

Beryl had a sudden thought. "I know what we could do—put some blue ribbon around the bouquet."

"Perfect," Mum said.

"So, what will you do for something borrowed?" Beryl asked. "I don't think I have anything suitable for a wedding, and I doubt you'd like to borrow my nylons."

Veronica responded with a fake grimace.

Mrs. Dowd had been sitting quietly. Beryl assumed she was trying to take everything in.

"You can wear these for 'something borrowed.'" At the sound of her small, wobbly voice, the women looked at her.

Her fingers fidgeted with the pearl necklace she always wore.

"I used to have more things you could use. I had hats and purses and jewelry. But all of that is gone now. I have this because I never take it off. Harry gave it to me as an engagement gift. These pearls, my wedding ring, and my memories are all I have left of him."

"Oh, I couldn't possibly take them," Veronica said. "They're too valuable."

"You're just borrowing them," Elinor said. "You'll return them to me after your wedding."

Beryl's eyes misted at the woman's offer. Elinor was amazing. Just when Beryl thought Elinor didn't understand what was going on around her, Elinor surprised her, contributing in unexpected ways. And now she was offering her only possession that survived the bombing, and that only because she was wearing the necklace at the time.

Veronica placed her hand over Elinor's. "In that case, I'd be honored to wear them."

# CHAPTER 28

*Stalag Luft I, Barth, Germany*
*November 1941*

Snow had a way of making everything look cleaner and more picturesque, even a prison compound. But that was the only good thing about the frozen stuff. Once the boots of prisoners walked through it, the beauty turned to ugly brown slush. Kenneth double-timed around the yard with other kriegies in a mock formation, the sole purpose to generate body heat and get warm. Talk was limited as each man puffed out clouds of vapor in rhythm with their footfalls. Kenneth's lips were already chapped from being outside in the cold, not that he had to go outside to be cold.

The small coal stoves in the hut barely generated enough warmth for one room, much less the whole building. Kenneth's air vapor could have been steam if his temper had a chance of creating that much warmth. He'd never expected to still be here in prison since his capture five months ago. James kept telling him to pray for patience, but Kenneth guffawed, saying there were a lot of other things he'd rather pray for, that is, if he were a praying man. Patience had never been one of his attributes.

Kenneth had taken on the role of calisthenics leader, and each day he led the men in runs, push-ups, jumping jacks, and stretching exercises. Push-ups couldn't be done outside when snow was on the ground, but he had enlisted the help of a safe goon to petition the commandant for enough wood and a strong bar to make a couple of pull-up bars. The exercise routine was voluntary, but barracks leaders encouraged the men to participate. Kenneth's motives weren't entirely unselfish. He did want to stay in shape, and becoming the leader enforced his commitment. But his other motive, and one Colonel Gilmore strongly supported, was keeping the other men in shape. Not only did the exercise keep them busy, it prepared their bodies for the eventual escape.

When new prisoner Paul Wilson arrived in the camp, he came with a reputation for being somewhat of an expert at escaping. The first time he was a prisoner was in 1939, when his plane had been shot down over France. After multiple attempts, he had escaped his captors and previous camps and made it back to England. He returned to flying, only to have the bad luck to be shot down again a year later during the Dunkirk battle. He spent a year at Dulag Luft, escaping several times only to be recaptured, so the Germans decided to send him to Stalag Luft I. En route, he had escaped his captors twice and might have been sent instead to Colditz Castle, the so-called inescapable prison, had it not been for a last-minute change of plans by the men in charge.

The colonel welcomed him to the camp with great respect for his escape prowess. The two met together at length before word spread that Wilson had been put in charge of the escape committee. A new surge of hope ran through the prisoners, many of whom were on the verge of giving up completely. Kenneth was convinced the biggest motivation for getting out now was food. Wilson did a good job of tantalizing the prisoners' taste buds as he spoke of the food he ate while free.

He was a stocky, muscular man with thick, wavy black hair, bushy black eyebrows that met in the middle when he frowned, and ice-blue eyes. He had been a wrestler in college before becoming a barrister in England, a profession that made him more eloquent than most fliers. As a result, it took him a short time to impress the commandant with his smooth talk, despite his escape record. When he met with Kenneth to look over his counterfeiting work, Wilson seemed pleased. "Good job, chap! We'll need quite a few of these—travel permits, gate passes, letters of authorization, and identification cards. We may need to produce some payment books as well."

"How many men are you planning to break out at once?"

"Twenty or thirty, at least. We'll organize them to go in pairs in separate directions and in different ways once they're out."

"That's quite a lot." Kenneth calculated how long it would take to produce so many forgeries. "It'll take a while unless I can find a few more forgers to help."

"I understand. It's better to take the time to get them as authentic as possible. Right now we can take advantage of the bad weather to do the work because it's a nasty time to escape."

"I'd like to volunteer myself and my pal James to be in the group that escapes." Kenneth said. "Do you have a map of the country and know the best routes out?"

"Not from here. We're much farther east than I've been before and nearer to the Baltic coast of Germany. It's a long way from the French border from here." Wilson put his hands on his hips. "So, you're with the Eagle Squadron. I hear you've made a few escapes also."

Kenneth nodded. "Got as far as the train station and the sea, but no farther."

"But that's a start and shows possibilities. Glad to have you on the team, Yank."

"Thanks. I just want to get out of here as soon as possible and stay out next time. I learned what doesn't work. Do you have any idea where there are safe houses?"

"Not exactly, but I know there are some. When I was back in England, I learned that MI5 is working on some escape routes, and they'll try to get some maps to the prison camps somehow. I'd never hope for someone to become a prisoner, but perhaps the next one will have more information to help us. It's been a year since I've been out, and I'm sure there's more organized help outside, if we just know where to find it."

Organization was one of Wilson's strengths, and soon the escape committee had become more structured with additional people assigned to specific teams, or "factories," as he called them. The men were told not to react or question anything they saw one of their fellow kriegies do that might appear curious, because it was part of the scheme.

One of the teams was assigned to lookout, and an alarm system was arranged so that whenever a goon was in an area near a work site, there would be certain types of signals, silent physical actions, used to relay the information. The goons and guards were assigned to two different categories—safe and dangerous. The safe ones were friendly and often helpful by being bribable. The dangerous ones were always looking for prisoner attempts to escape. These were the ones who made sudden searches of the huts. Gooseneck was one of the dangerous ones.

A lookout would send a warning signal as soon as one of the dangerous people was heading toward a particular hut. Often the men working in those huts had less than a minute to hide anything they didn't want the goon to find.

Another way the security team provided help was by having a German-speaking kriegie follow any dangerous goons around and listen to their conversations. Another method they used was to create a diversion if the goons were too near a tunnel site or work area. They might stage a fight between two kriegies to create a distraction. The fights needed to look authentic, so the guys who engaged in them often received a black eye or knuckles to their cheeks. Another diversionary tactic was to "accidentally" throw a ball over the wire, then call up to the goon box to get the guards' attention and permission to retrieve the ball without getting shot.

Angus now had a team of costume makers working with him to provide realistic-looking copies of German uniforms as well as everyday street clothes, ranging from peasant wear to businessman attire. The outfits were kept in the theater with other costumes, but the uniforms were hidden in a box that was part of a bench in the audience. James worked with other electricians and engineers to provide light for the diggers. He was also working on a system to provide air to the tunnelers doing such claustrophobic work.

Progress on the tunnels moved rather slowly, sometimes only a few feet a day, as falling sand and cave-ins were a constant problem. More than one digger had received a mouthful of sand and been partially buried alive. Thankfully, the diggers worked one behind the other so that if one got buried, the other could quickly pull him out. In those cases, the work had to start over. And of course, sand disbursal was an ongoing issue. Wilson set up a disbursal committee who retrieved sand from the diggers and sprinkled it on the ground through their pants legs, mixing it in with the other compound dirt. The least suspicious time to do so was while they walked or, even better, participated in games like volleyball and so avoided notice from any goons watching.

Disappointment in the slow progress was a feeling Kenneth fought daily. He tried to distract himself with other thoughts, and often those thoughts went to Beryl. But thinking of her made him even more disappointed that he hadn't made it out yet. Wilson told them that winter was the worst time to try to escape because not only would they expose themselves to the elements but snow would show tracks.

The only thing Kenneth looked forward to besides escaping was getting a letter from Beryl. Although she was writing to her brother, she addressed the letter to both of them. Several times a day, he pulled her photo out of his pocket and stared at it, which made him feel more and more familiar with her. "I'll see you soon, Beryl," he said to the photo, then kissed it before dropping it back into his pocket.

The next letter they received was as confusing as the last.

"Is that another letter from Beryl?" he asked, seeing the envelope in James' hand.

"It is. Let's see what she has to say."

He opened the envelope, and his eyes scanned the letter.

"Veronica's fiancé is safe. He sent a telegram to her and said his ship was going to be in port for repairs and he could get a short leave so they could get married. Beryl said they're busy getting things ready for the wedding in a very limited period of time."

"Good for her friend. And her soon-to-be husband, lucky guy."

"Are you saying you want to get married?" James asked, smiling.

"I'd just like to have the chance to go home like he did. Of course, having a girl would be nice too."

"Look, Kenneth. Here she goes again, talking about the Mono-poly game."

"Are you kidding me?" Maybe she wasn't as interesting as he thought she was. Is that all she'd want to do if he saw her again?

"Listen, this time she's talking about the playing pieces. She says, *'My favorite token is the race car. I think of you, Kenneth, when I see it, not that you have one, but I can imagine you driving one. I bet that would be your favorite token too. And, James, I was thinking you'd like the battleship, but then you're not in the navy. So I think you'd like the top hat the best. It's really a magnificent copy of a real top hat. I'd love to hear if you find those pieces just as interesting when you get your game. I really do hope you get one soon, and then we can communicate even better, both in letters and someday in person. I look forward to seeing you pass Go and getting home.'*

"She continues, *'Kenneth, I bet the British version of Monopoly looks much different to you than the American version. I wonder if you'll recognize the names of the places on the British board. We've changed it a lot. Maybe our tokens will meet on the same street, like perhaps Piccadilly Circus. You might need help finding your way around.'"*

Kenneth glanced at James. "I think she's trying to tell us something, and it's not about playing Monopoly."

"I agree. Why else would she talk about the game so much?"

"But what is she saying? A race car is fast, like a quick getaway, maybe."

"And since when is a token magnificent?" James said, shaking his head.

"Let's think about this awhile. Do you think there's some reason she mentions the streets on the board, like maybe using a code?"

"There could be. As far as I remember, they are streets in London. But how could she know a code, much less expect us to know it as well?"

"Hmm. I haven't been in London since we were in college and went there on the weekend," Kenneth said, rubbing his forehead. "Meeting on Piccadilly Circus? Is she suggesting that happening in reality or only on the board? How and when could we meet otherwise?"

"One thing is for certain," James said. "We need to get our hands on a Monopoly game and see if we can figure out what she means. Let's hope one of us gets the game in our next Red Cross package."

"I'd like that, but I'd also like to see any kind of package pretty soon, whether it has a game in it or not. Seems like it's been a while since we last got one, and the pantry is practically bare. I sure could use some kind of addition to our diet, even if it's Spam."

Later that day, the camp speaker announced the arrival of a charitable organization that had brought gift boxes for the men, and the prisoners hurried to get in line for their boxes. Kenneth and James each received a box. As they entered the barracks, the colonel said, "Make your rations last. We don't know when we'll receive more boxes."

Kenneth groaned but understood the reality of their situation.

"Did you get a box, sir?" he asked the colonel.

He nodded. "I gave mine to Wilson. He didn't get one."

As he and James entered their room, he said, "The colonel sure is a noble man. I can't believe he turned his box over to Wilson. I'm sure he's as hungry as the rest of us."

James nodded. "He's a fine Christian man for certain."

"What does being a Christian have to do with what he did?"

"The Bible says to treat others the way you'd like to be treated and to think of others before you think of yourself."

Kenneth shook his head. "Another reason I couldn't be a Christian—I'm not that unselfish."

They set their boxes on the floor and opened them. Kenneth resisted the urge to stuff his mouth with the candy bar inside before he looked at the other items. He dug through the box, which was full of the usual things, but he didn't take them for granted, treasuring each item as if it was worth its weight in gold. The box was almost empty when he noticed something at the very bottom.

It was a Monopoly game.

# ⫸CHAPTER 29⫷

*Leeds, England*
*November 1941*

Beryl's house was a beehive of busyness as the women worked to get things ready for the wedding. They met each day at her house to sew and create the wedding outfit. Beryl couldn't remember the last time she'd felt the current of excitement that surged from one woman to the next. Veronica's mum had joined them, and they had all contributed to planning the menu for the reception. Even though they had to contend with a scarcity of available products, they became extra creative to invent items from what they could find. Friends and neighbors offered some of their rations and coupons so there would be plenty of food.

It turned out that Rodney had been assigned to the HMS *Nelson*, a battleship that escorted other ships in convoys through the Mediterranean that were delivering troops and supplies. While in one of those convoys, they were attacked by the Italian Air Force, and a torpedo bomber dropped a torpedo that blew a hole in the bow. The ship had made it back to Gibraltar for emergency repairs and was then sent back to Rosyth Navy Dockyard in Fife, Scotland, where it was docked now for more permanent repairs.

Rodney was able to secure a two-day leave so he and Veronica could get married and have two nights together before he had to return to the ship. The minister had committed to perform the ceremony, having become accustomed to quick marriages during the war. Veronica's parents had reserved a room for them at the Leeds Hotel for their brief honeymoon.

Everything was coming together nicely, and Beryl was happy for her friend. Every now and then a streak of sadness trickled down her spine in a spell of self-pity. Those nagging questions—*Will I fall in love? Get married? Or will I and my future husband get killed in a bomb attack?* She wanted to kick herself for such desperate thoughts. She couldn't allow herself to be morose and spoil Veronica's happiness.

No, she would do everything in her power to make sure her friend's wedding was the most perfect wedding possible. The government had banned the practice of throwing rice on the newly married couple due to the food shortage. Margaret at work had suggested they use the circles from punching holes in paper to throw on the couple. The idea was good to Beryl, so she recruited every person in the building who used a hole punch to save the holes for her.

Beryl requisitioned Margaret to help throw a hen do, a party for Veronica the night before the wedding. Veronica said that Rodney's fellow sailors were going to throw him a stag party as well.

"Then we must do an even better hen do and a much more civilized one, to boot," Margaret said, smiling. "I do love throwing parties!"

Time flew by, which kept Beryl from focusing so much on whether or not Kenneth and James had received her last letter. And if they had, did they understand the clues she'd sent?

On the day of the wedding, everything was ready. All they needed now was the groom. Rodney was supposed to take the train from Scotland to Leeds, a five-hour trip if there were no delays. The wedding was scheduled for three o'clock in the afternoon to take advantage of daylight and have the reception afterward in the garden of Veronica's house. The weather turned out to be perfect, crisp but sunny, and the atmosphere at Beryl's house was exhilarating.

Even Elinor shared the enthusiasm, asking over and over when the wedding would be and where. Mum helped the woman dress and style her hair. The absence of the pearls on her neck reminded Beryl of Mrs. Dowd's selfless act. Beryl and Mum packed up the food that had been made at their house, and Mr. Findlay drove it over to Veronica's house.

At two o'clock, they all headed over to the church to make sure it was ready and to be there to greet guests. Forty people had been invited, just enough to fill the church appropriately and plenty to provide refreshments for afterward. The church was decorated with ribbons collected from the ladies at the Red Cross who wanted to contribute to the wedding. Mum seated Elinor in a pew while she scurried about attending to last-minute touches. Veronica's little sister, Nancy, was dressed in her Sunday best and sat beside Elinor, chatting nonstop about Veronica and Rodney, the wedding, and who knew what else. Beryl smiled at the pair and hoped Elinor was entertained. She appeared to be giving Nancy her attention, whether she understood all the girl said or not.

Beryl's heart warmed at the sight of Mum in her heather green suit and matching felt hat. Father had loved that suit on her mother and claimed it brought out the "emerald green in her lovely eyes." Mum hadn't worn the suit since his death, and for her to wear it now meant she'd come to terms with his absence. The wedding had certainly given them all something to look forward to.

"Beryl, you look lovely," Mum said, smiling admiringly at her. "Almost as pretty as the bride."

Beryl's face warmed. "Thank you, Mum." She knew Mum looked forward to the day her daughter would get married as well and hoped she'd be able to see that same happiness on Mum's face. It would be sad not to have her father give her away. The thought made her feel the absence of James from today's event. Strangely, she missed Kenneth today too. He didn't even know Veronica, yet Beryl would have loved for him to be there. By her side.

"Let's go check on Veronica," Beryl said, and she and Mum went to the dressing room where Veronica's mum was adjusting Veronica's veil.

"You look stunning," Beryl said, admiring the way her friend perfectly fit the pastel pink dress. Veronica's black hair and beautiful face were barely concealed by the veil.

"Thank you." She glanced nervously around. "What time is it?"

"Two fifteen."

"Oh my. Rodney should be here now."

Beryl placed her hand on Veronica's arm. "Don't worry. He'll be here soon."

But he wasn't. The women chatted, trying to make small talk to defuse the tension as they waited for the groom to appear. Veronica's father went to the front door of the church to stand guard and greet the guests who entered the sanctuary and waited as well.

"He's not coming. I know something terrible has happened. Or he changed his mind," Veronica said, her voice trembling. She picked up a tissue and wiped her eyes with her gloved hand.

"Yes, he is. He's just been delayed," Beryl said, and the other women echoed her comment.

Nancy came in and asked when the wedding was going to start and said that she and the lady were getting hungry.

"Why don't you introduce her to some of our friends?"

"I did. She can't hear anything, but she's talking to them anyway. She thinks she knows them."

Beryl wondered if she really did. If so, maybe the people she talked to could give Beryl more information about the woman.

The afternoon dragged on as they waited. The minister came to the door and checked on them a couple of times, probably wondering if the wedding should be called off. Had it not been wartime, the ceremony might have been canceled. But these days, normal events and schedules were often disrupted by unexpected delays. The minister returned to the sanctuary and told the guests the groom had been delayed and suggested they use the time to stretch their legs or avail themselves of the facilities while they waited. Beryl wished they had some tea or something to offer the guests. She left the dressing room to check on Elinor and found her engaged in conversation. In fact, she had acquired an audience of sorts, so Beryl didn't want to interrupt.

The sky was getting dark when a harried sailor rushed into the nave, apologizing for his tardiness. Mr. Holmes greeted him and calmed him down while Beryl rushed to the dressing room to let Veronica know Rodney had arrived.

It was dark by the time the ceremony began, and the church was unable to turn on the lights due to blackout requirements. As a result, candles were lit all over the sanctuary, giving an ethereal glow to the building. The pianist began the wedding march while a handsome sailor stood beside the minister, his eyes locked on the back entrance. Nancy skipped down the aisle, tossing dahlia petals. Beryl followed and took her place on the other side of the minister. The audience smiled in admiration as Veronica floated down the aisle on the arm of her father, who gave her hand to Rodney, standing with a radiant face at the sight of his bride.

As Beryl took in the candlelight glow of the room and the love reflected on Veronica's and Rodney's faces, she sensed the sanctity of the ceremony and how perfect it was. Despite the fact that the wedding was late, the candles added a special atmosphere that couldn't have been better planned. She listened as her friend pledged her love to Rodney and promised a lifelong commitment to their marriage. Beryl's heart swelled with joy as Veronica and Rodney were pronounced "man and wife."

When Rodney was finally given permission to kiss his bride, the audience oohed and aahed and applauded. As the piano began to play the recessional, the sound of sirens began to penetrate the music, rising in tone above the piano.

Everyone exchanged glances as realization set in. Beryl jumped into her ARP role and assumed a position in front of the audience.

"Everyone must go to the church basement for shelter. Follow Reverend Parker, and he will lead you there. Quickly but carefully, please proceed."

She glanced at Mum, who took Mrs. Dowd by the arm and ushered her in the direction of the basement.

Rodney and Veronica clung to each other as they joined the queue. "Mum?" Veronica said, looking over the heads of the crowd.

"Your mum is fine, Veronica. Not to worry, your dad has her." Beryl glanced around and spotted Nancy assisting Mum on Mrs. Dowd's other side. "And Nancy's fine too. You two go on down to the basement now."

Beryl waited until everyone else had proceeded in front of her, then followed along, grabbing a couple of candles on the way. In the distance, bombs piercing the earth could be heard, followed by the rattle of anti-aircraft guns. Once all the people were inside the basement and the door was closed, the minister prayed, thanking God for a safe place and for the wedding that had just taken place.

Mum and Nancy were keeping Mrs. Dowd company, so she didn't appear to be frightened. As she listened to the sound of war outside, Beryl was thankful that tonight the bombs stayed farther away. In fact, the atmosphere inside the church basement was peaceful.

"It's a shame this had to happen now and spoil their wedding," a lady near her said to her husband.

Beryl couldn't help herself. "On the contrary, the wedding was perfect, and everything happened just in time."

# ☰ CHAPTER 30 ☰

*Stalag Luft I, Barth, Germany*
*December 1941*

Kenneth carefully unwrapped the Monopoly game and removed the lid. He opened the board and laid it on the bed. James sat on the opposite side of the board and assembled the Chance cards and Community Chest cards. Kenneth picked up the playing tokens and set them on the board.

"So, here's the pieces she referred to. Guess I'll take the race car like she suggested. Which do you want?"

"Hmm. I'll take the top hat like she said," James said.

"Let's see. There's a red dot on the free parking space that she mentioned. But I don't understand the meaning of it. Is it in the directions?" Kenneth picked up the sheet of directions in the game and scanned it. "Nope. No mention of it here."

"You can see the streets are places in London." James pointed to several.

James sorted through the houses and hotels, and Kenneth riffled through the money. Some of the bills looked different from the money on top of the stack. He paused and went back through the stack for a closer look. He choked back a whoop. Glancing around, he leaned toward James and lowered his voice. "James, there's real money in here."

James' eyes widened. "What? What kind of money? British pounds?"

Kenneth handed James one of the bills. "See for yourself. What do you think it is? German?"

Kenneth nodded. "And look, here's some francs. These would come in handy when we get out."

"So, you think this is intentional?" James asked, looking around to see if anyone else heard.

"Has to be. This stuff doesn't appear by accident."

"Could this be an escape kit?"

"Maybe that's exactly what it is. Maybe that's why Beryl's been writing about Monopoly so much."

"Right. Waddingtons makes the games, so she would know if they made escape games."

"Maybe there's something else in here then."

James looked at the top hat token, examining it as he turned it around in his hand. "Could there be something hidden in this?" He continued to play with the token, but nothing appeared unusual.

"I wonder if the race car is hiding something." He flipped it over and scrutinized it. "Nothing here."

"What else did she say that might be a clue?"

"I don't know, maybe something about the streets," Kenneth said, frowning at the board.

"Right. She said something about finding the places. How hard can it be to find the streets on the board? They're right there in plain sight," James said.

Kenneth stared at the board. Was there a hidden word on the street names? He picked up the board and angled it toward the light. Nothing showed up. "What exactly did she say?"

James retrieved Beryl's last letter. *"You might need help finding your way around."*

"Hey, if I need help finding my way around, I need a map. There must be a map in here somewhere!"

James and Kenneth turned over every playing piece and every card in the game, searching for something that looked like a map. Not finding anything, they stopped and crossed their arms, gazing at the game.

"We've looked at everything," James said. "Maybe that's all there is."

"No, I don't think so. She mentioned the places for a reason." He paused, and then he picked up the board and ran his fingernail along the edge until the printed side of the game began to separate from the cardboard underneath. He carefully worked his way all the way around. Then he gently lifted the paper, and it came away from the cardboard.

Lying underneath was a silk map.

"Bingo!" He retrieved the map and held it up to the light. "Well, I'll be a monkey's uncle!" He laid it down so James could see it.

"Is that Germany?" James asked, peering at the map.

"Yes, and the countries around it, France, Switzerland, Poland, Sweden. . ."

"What do you think are these little red dots?" James used the magnifying glass to look.

"Could they be safe houses?" Kenneth blew out a breath. "James, this is just what we need! Man, this map is worth more than gold!"

"And it's an answer to our prayers, Kenneth."

Kenneth hated to take credit for praying, but he appreciated James' effort. "Well, look at this," he said, running his fingers over the exposed inside of the cardboard. Barely visible were indentations where a magnifying glass and a file were placed. "How ingenious!"

"We're going to have to share this with Wilson and Gilmore," James said. "Everyone needs to know about this."

"You're right, of course," Kenneth said, despite wanting to keep the treasure to himself. His hands shook slightly as he folded the treasured map and laid it back onto the cardboard. Then they carefully put the paper playing surface back on the board and placed it and the other parts of the game in the box before closing it up. "And we'll probably have to copy that map a few times so others will have it."

"You're the man for the job, then."

"You know, James, I didn't think this Christmas was going to be a very good one, but I think we just got the best Christmas gift ever!" Kenneth said, grinning.

"I have to agree, the timing is fortuitous. We'll have to write Beryl and thank her for her Christmas gift, so to speak."

"Your arm seems to be healed up fine now, so I guess you don't need me to write it for you. But if you don't mind, I'd like to send her a letter from myself anyway."

"You go right ahead. I believe she'll be very happy to hear from you directly and not just from me."

"I can't wait to tell her 'thank you' in person!" Kenneth envisioned what that reunion would be like, putting his arms around her and pulling her close, then giving her a great big kiss. His heart pounded at the thought, and that reunion couldn't come quickly enough, as far as he was concerned. But they still had more work to do before they'd be ready to escape. He tucked the box under his arm. "Shall we go find Wilson and Gilmore and see if they'd like to play a game of Monopoly?"

"Absolutely, let's go."

Fortunately, both men were in Wilson's room when they knocked on the door.

"Enter," the colonel's voice answered.

Kenneth and James went inside and closed the door behind them.

"Gentlemen, we'd like to discuss something with you privately, please." Kenneth laid the game down on a small table in the room. "We just received a package from one of the humanitarian organizations, and this game was in it."

Wilson and Gilmore stood with their arms crossed, eyeing the game. "And just why is this important?" Gilmore asked.

"First, I want to tell you that we've been corresponding with James' sister in Leeds, England, who works for the company that makes these games. She kept mentioning the Monopoly game in her letters, and we couldn't understand why. But today when we opened this one, we realized she was trying to give us clues that they were making escape kits in some of the games. This is one of those games." At that, Kenneth opened the box and revealed the escape items they'd found.

Wilson and Gilmore leaned over to look. Wilson surveyed the stack of money. "This would have come in handy when I was out."

"But look here," Kenneth said. "This is what we've been needing." He lifted the stack of Monopoly money and retrieved the silk map.

Wilson set down the money and took the map from Kenneth. Gilmore eased over beside Wilson as they studied the map. Wilson gave a low whistle.

James pointed to the dots. "We think those are safe houses."

"I think you're right. So this is what MI5 was working on," Wilson said.

"We need to see if anyone else in camp has received one of these games, or at least let the other POWs know to be on the lookout for them. We'll need more than one of these," Gilmore said.

"I believe the clue is the red dot on the Free Parking place, because that's what she mentioned in the letter," James said.

"Meanwhile, we can't wait around until another one of these kits shows up," Wilson said. "We need to start copying this map and make enough for our big escape."

"I'm on it, sir. Will start right away," Kenneth said. "Do you think Habersham can get some onionskin typing paper from his friend? Or maybe there's another guard who will cooperate."

"We can find someone," Wilson said. "There are now several safe goons who have become more cooperative. We have to be careful not to get them in trouble though, or they'll be no use to us anymore. I heard that yesterday one of them was thrown in the cooler for being too friendly with kriegies. In addition, the commandant threatens to send them to the Russian front if they are caught collaborating with us. And trust me, no one wants to be sent to Russia during the winter."

Kenneth almost felt sorry for the nice guards, the safe ones. These guys just wanted to get home to their families too. James told him they needed to pray for the guards. If he was a praying man, he might consider praying for the safe ones. But the others, like Gooseneck? No way. He'd prefer they meet less pleasant ends.

Someone pounded on the door, and Kenneth quickly put away the Monopoly game.

"Who is it?" the colonel demanded.

"Sir, we just received some important news!" A familiar voice on the other side of the door said. "Permission to enter."

"Come in."

The door opened, and one of the radio guys who monitored the BBC broadcasts entered. He glanced around, then his eyes rested on Kenneth.

"What's so important?"

"The Japanese have bombed the American navy base at Pearl Harbor."

Kenneth's mouth dropped open. "Is this a fact or a trick?"

"No sir, it was a real BBC broadcast. Apparently, there were several ships sunk and a lot of men killed."

Kenneth sank down on the nearest bunk and put his face in his hands. He had friends from Louisiana who had joined the navy. He thought they had an easy assignment, being sent to Hawaii and away from the war in Europe. But he didn't think so anymore.

"President Roosevelt has declared war."

Kenneth scanned the sympathetic faces looking at him. They all knew what he was feeling. Their country had been going through this for two years now.

"Well, it's about time," he said.

# ⧮ CHAPTER 31 ⧮

*Leeds, England*
*December 1941*

The radio played in the background while Beryl tried to make the house more festive for Christmas, decorating the hall tree with sprigs of holly she'd dipped in Epsom salts to make them look frosty. "When is Mr. Cuthbert bringing us the tree from the farm?"

"Any day now. I told him we don't need a big one, just something to put our ornaments on." Mum sat on the couch knitting, and Elinor dangled a piece of yarn for Spitfire to play with, chuckling and smiling at the kitten's antics.

The music on the radio stopped, and a stern voice came through. "We have to interrupt this program for this special news bulletin. The Japanese have bombed the American naval base in Hawaii. Much damage and loss of life has been reported. President Roosevelt has declared war."

The holly fell from Beryl's hand. "Mum! Did you hear that?" She hurried to the radio and turned it up louder. The announcer was describing the incident and its repercussions. "Listen. It says Britain will also declare war on Japan."

Mum dropped her knitting in her lap. "Dear God. Just when we were hoping for an end of the war in this part of the world, the war gets bigger."

"I wonder what this means. What about Hitler? Are we going to take our men out of Europe and send them to the Pacific Ocean?"

"I think we may send some ships over there," Mum said, her brow creased.

"Oh dear. So Rodney might be sent over there?"

"I'm sure he could be."

"Well, thank God, his ship is still at the shipyard being repaired. At least he's been able to see Veronica another time since they got married." They'd been married a month now, and Beryl had almost been jealous that her friend was able to see her husband when so many other women were still waiting for theirs. But he might be sent even farther away this time.

"I wonder how this will affect our men who are prisoners in Germany," Mum said.

"Surely they won't be treated more harshly," Beryl replied. She hoped not.

Someone knocked at the door, and Beryl went to get it. Mr. Cuthbert stood with a little fir tree under his arm. "Where shall I put this?"

Beryl stepped back and let him enter. "In there." She pointed to the sitting room. They placed the tree opposite the window in case its lights peeked through the blackout curtains.

"Thank you," she said, gazing at the sparse, undecorated tree. "It seems rather odd to be festive at a time like this."

Mr. Cuthbert nodded. "Aye. But we mustn't let that devil steal our Christmas spirit."

Elinor walked over to the tree and gave it a once-over. "What a pretty tree. You are very kind to give it to us," she said, peering up at Mr. Cuthbert. "Wouldn't you like to join us for a decorating party?"

Beryl and her mum exchanged surprised glances.

"A decorating party?" Beryl said.

"Why, of course. Harry and I always had a decorating party for Christmas. We'd invite all the neighborhood children to help us. And we'd give them treats and play with Christmas crackers."

Where would they get treats? And Beryl only knew one child, Nancy, Veronica's sister.

"Thank you, ma'am, but I don't believe I can make it to your party," Mr. Cuthbert said.

"What a pity." Elinor looked so crestfallen, Beryl thought she might cry.

"We can still have a party, though," Beryl said. "I'll ask Nancy if she'd like to bring some friends." She glanced at Mum, who shrugged her shoulders.

"I'll be taking my leave now. Happy Christmas to you." Mr. Cuthbert tipped his cap and left.

Elinor clasped her hands with a broad smile on her face. "We can make Christmas custard! I love custard, don't you?"

Mum nodded. "Yes, I do. You can help me make it."

This should be interesting. So far the woman had only been able to make her own tea. Sometimes Beryl believed Mrs. Dowd thought that Beryl and Mum were servants. On the other hand, how capable was she of cooking?

After she closed the door behind Mr. Cuthbert, she went to the telephone to call Veronica.

"I'm sure Nancy would like to come over. By the way, she wants to ask Elinor to come to her Christmas play at school. Of course, you and your mum are welcome too, but she especially wanted to ask Elinor."

"I'd put her on the phone, but you know she probably wouldn't be able to hear Nancy."

"That's fine. The play is Friday afternoon at the school. Do you think you can get off work?"

"I think Mr. Watson will let me. He's a family man too." She paused, afraid to ask her friend about the latest news.

"Will you be able to see Rodney again before Christmas?"

"I think so. But I don't know how much I'll be able to see him afterward. He called today and said he might have to ship out right after Boxing Day. His ship isn't ready yet, but I think he's going to be assigned to another ship in the meantime." Veronica sniffed, and Beryl was pretty sure her friend was about to cry.

Beryl cringed, certain that Rodney was going to be sent to the Pacific. "Well, thank God, he came home long enough for you to be married."

Veronica sniffed again, then exhaled. "You're right. I need to count my blessings. God brought him back to me once, so I must trust Him to bring him back again."

"That's right," Beryl said. "So, I'll see you Friday at Nancy's school. And tell Nancy that Elinor wants to have a Christmas tree decorating party and would like her to come. If she has any friends she'd like to bring, that's fine too."

"A Christmas tree decorating party?"

"Yes, Mr. Cuthbert just delivered our tree, and Elinor suggested the party. I guess we'll humor her and have it."

"Well, that's special. Nancy would love that. She can invite her Brownie friends."

"And tell her we'll have some Christmas cake and punch for them too."

"I will. See you at the school Friday."

Beryl said goodbye and hung up the phone as the mail slid through the slot in the door.

She went over and picked it up, her heart leaping when she saw a letter from Kenneth.

The letter was addressed to her from him, not to her mum and not from James. Was something wrong? Had something happened to James?

"I'll go get the baubles and tinsel," she said, wanting to read her letter privately. She dropped the other envelopes on the telephone chair in the hallway and went upstairs to her room. Her hand shook as she slid a nail file under the edge of the envelope and opened it, removing the letter.

> *Dear Beryl,*
>
> *Since James no longer needs my help to write you, I'm out of business as his secretary. However, I still wanted to send you a letter from me, so here it is. We received a wonderful Christmas present through one of the charity organizations this week, and in it was a Monopoly game! Now we can play the game as you suggested and think of you all the time. Although I think of you often anyway. I look at the picture of you every day and can't wait to see you in person. I'm hoping that day will be very soon and am working on those plans. Maybe we can meet at Piccadilly Circus. I want to take a spin in a car like the one in the game. Will you go with me? Happy Christmas and see you soon.*
>
> > *Yours truly,*
> > *Kenneth*

Beryl unclenched her fingers, loosening her grip on the paper to let her fingers relax. She read the letter three more times, then lowered it and reflected on its meaning. So they had received the special Monopoly game with the escape tools. Thank God. Hopefully the kit would help them. See you soon? How soon would be soon, according to Kenneth? Her pulse quickened at the notion of him looking at her photo. He truly thought of her all the time? She smiled at the idea of riding with him in a car like the one in the game, enjoying fresh air and having so much fun together.

He was working on those plans, plans to escape. A shudder raced through her, realizing the danger they'd be in. Did she really want them to risk their lives to escape? Wouldn't they be safer if they stayed where they were? And if they escaped, how would they get back to England since Germany occupied almost all of Europe? She needed to get a copy of a map and see where they might go. Rumors of Nazi barbarism came to her mind, bringing horror and fear. Had she just encouraged Kenneth and James to put themselves in a more dangerous situation than they were already in? She would never forgive herself if they got killed trying to escape, all because she encouraged them.

*God, please keep them safe if they try to escape, and lead them back here.*

# ☰ CHAPTER 32 ☰

*Stalag Luft I, Barth, Germany*
*Christmas Day 1941*

Kenneth's hands cramped and his eyes burned. He'd spent hours every day copying the map, in addition to his counterfeiting. One good thing about his repetitive job was that now he was completely familiar with the map, so in case he had to destroy it to keep it out of Nazi hands, he would still know where to go and where the safe houses were. Wilson had in fact told the others who were planning to escape that they too needed to memorize the map. It was imperative that the map be destroyed once they got out so the safe houses wouldn't be compromised.

He shivered from the cold. Even though he was inside, the uninsulated wood huts barely kept out the wind, much less made the temperature any warmer inside than out. He figured it must be at the most freezing because it was below freezing outside. Wilson told them they would escape when it was warmer, probably in March, and only the prospect of being colder and in the snow gave him enough patience to wait. He opened and closed his fists, noticing how red and bony his hands were. He must look terrible, much like his compatriots—skinny and sallow. Some of the guys were even losing their hair due to their poor diet.

The commandant had patted himself on the back for being extra generous to the prisoners today for Christmas. Their rations had been doubled, which meant they were close to what they should have been all along. Today they had received some horse meat and potato soup with their brown bread, an almost hearty meal. But it wasn't enough to fill their empty bodies. James and Kenneth had received a package from home that contained a fruit cake, which they shared and savored. The package also contained some extra hats and mittens, so they'd given them to Angus and Wilson, who were most appreciative of the gifts. Kenneth felt a little like Santa Claus when he saw the gratitude on the men's faces. Sharing might have its benefits, especially when it made another person's life a little better.

A knock on the door made him quickly put away his work. He had gotten very good at hiding it so quickly, less than a minute now. James opened it to one of the guys in the chorus. "We're going caroling. Put your warm things on."

"In this cold?" Kenneth was ready to withdraw his participation from the group.

"Yes, quickly. Let's go. I hear some of the other barracks have some hot brew to share."

"Well, in that case, I'm in." Kenneth and James grabbed every warm thing they owned and headed outside, where they met with the other chorus members. They went from barracks to barracks, going inside instead of singing outside as carolers would normally do. A couple of the barracks greeted them with hot chocolate, thin but warm and enough to keep the group motivated and persistent. At each hut, the men inside sang along, and all were in good spirits.

Kenneth glanced at James' red cheeks and wide grin. "You look downright jolly, James!"

"As do you, my friend. As we should be to celebrate Christ's birth."

He had a point there. Christmas should be a joyous occasion, even in such a miserable place as this. Kenneth scanned the face of every man, seeing the glimmer of hope on most of them. He pitied those who didn't have that hope, because it was hope that kept them going. How could one live without it? Truth was, they couldn't. Without hope, they were empty shells of men. He considered James' words and wondered if his hope was in escaping or seeing his family again, or did it have to do with his faith? Something told Kenneth that James' faith was what propelled him to pursue the rest of what he did, and he envied James for that kind of faith.

As they left each hut, calls of "Happy Christmas" rang out between the men. Happy indeed. This was nothing like the Christmases he'd remembered back home, especially when Kevin had been alive. His eyes moistened, and he tried to wipe them before they froze. Kevin had that kind of faith—faith in his older brother and faith in God. He had the joy that James had too. Kevin and James were different than he was, and he'd never be like them.

When they'd been to all the barracks in their compound, a bell rang, echoing throughout the cold.

"Let's go to the Christmas service in the chapel," James said.

"Is there a heater in there?" Kenneth asked the question, knowing the answer was no.

"Come on, Kenneth. There should be enough warmth in there with so many crowded together."

Kenneth shrugged. He might as well go to church on Christmas Day. Inside the chapel, he was surprised to see so many men, probably more than he'd ever seen there before. "Are they giving away steak?"

James shook his head and shot him a glance. "These men are here to receive something, but not steak."

Kenneth listened to the minister, who read from the verses in the Bible that told the Christmas story. His mind flashed back to his childhood when he performed in a Christmas play at school. He'd played a wise man. Kenneth suppressed a chuckle. He was wise all right. Some had called him a wiseacre, which wasn't meant to be a compliment. His wise man gift was supposed to be gold. He wouldn't mind having some of that now. But if he did, would he give it away? It was one thing to give someone an extra knit cap that cost him nothing, but gold was another matter. Besides, what did God need with gold anyway?

At the end of the service, the minister prayed for them and for everyone in the world, even the Germans, that they would know Christ and that there would be peace on earth. Is that what it would take? The minister certainly didn't mean to include Hitler in that prayer, did he? Who would pray for that monster? Why didn't he pray for God to wipe him out? That would solve a lot of problems.

The men exited the chapel to a light snow falling.

"We didn't need more snow," Kenneth grumbled.

"Hey, Kenneth, it's a white Christmas. Isn't that the way Christmas should look?"

"Not in Louisiana," Kenneth said. "Not unless it's white rice with gumbo or crawfish étouffée poured over it."

James laughed. "Someday you'll have to take me to Louisiana and let me try all that strange food you talk about."

"James, that's one thing I would absolutely love doing!" The thought crossed his mind that maybe Beryl would like to go too. Wouldn't that be nice? And she could meet his mom, and whoa! Where was he going with those thoughts?

As they re-entered their barracks, the other guys were sitting around the radio and motioned for them to be quiet.

"King George is about to give the Christmas speech," one of the men said.

Kenneth and James found a spot on the floor and sat cross-legged, listening as the radio operator tuned in to the BBC frequency. Soon a British male voice came over the airwaves.

> *I am glad to think that millions of my people in all parts of the world are listening to me now. From my own home, with the Queen and my children beside me, I send to all a Christmas greeting.*
>
> *Christmas is the festival at home, and it is right that we should remember those who this year must spend it away from home. I am thinking, as I speak, of the men who have come from afar, standing ready to defend the old homeland, of the men who in every part of the world are serving the Empire and its cause with such valor and devotion by sea, land, and in the air.*
>
> *I am thinking of all those, women and girls as well as men, who at the call of duty have left their homes to join the services, or to work in factory, hospital, or field. To each one of you, wherever your duty may be, I send you my remembrance and my sincere good wishes for you and for yours.*
>
> *I do not forget what others have done and are doing so bravely in civil defense. My heart is also with those who are suffering—the wounded, the bereaved, the anxious, the prisoners of war. I think you know how deeply the Queen and I feel for them. May God give them comfort,*

courage, and hope.

All these separations are part of the hard sacrifice which this war demands. It may well be that it will call for even greater sacrifices. If this is to be, let us face them cheerfully together. I think of you, my peoples, as one great family, for it is how we are learning to live. We all belong to each other. We all need each other. It is in serving each other and in sacrificing for our common good that we are finding our true life.

In that spirit we shall win the war, and in that same spirit we shall win for the world after the war a true and lasting peace. The greatness of any nation is in the spirit of its people. So it has always been since history began; so it shall be with us.

The range of the tremendous conflict is ever widening. It now extends to the Pacific. Truly it is a stern and solemn time. But as the war widens, so surely our conviction depends at the greatness of our cause.

We who belong to the present generation must bear the brunt of the struggle, and I would say to the coming generation, the boys and girls of today, the men and women of tomorrow—train yourselves in body, mind, and spirit so as to be ready for whatever part you may be called to play, and for the tasks which will await you as citizens of the Empire when the war is over.

We must all, older and younger, resolve that having been entrusted with so great a cause, then, at whatever cost, God helping us, we will not falter or fail. Make yourselves ready—in your home and school to give and to offer your very best.

We are coming to the end of another hard-fought year. During these months our people have been through many trials, and in that true humanity which goes hand in hand with valor, have learnt once again to look for strength to God alone.

So I bid you all be strong and of a good courage. Go forward into this coming year with a good heart. Lift up *your hearts with thankfulness for deliverance from dangers in the past. Lift up your hearts in confident hope that strength will be given us to overcome whatever perils may lie ahead until the victory is won.*

*If the skies before us are still dark and threatening, there are stars to guide us on our way. Never did heroism shine more brightly than it does now, nor fortitude, nor sacrifice, nor sympathy, nor neighborly kindness, and with them—brightest of all stars—is our faith in God. These stars will we follow with His help until the light shall shine and the darkness shall collapse.*

*God bless you, every one.*

# CHAPTER 33

*Leeds, England*
*January 1942*

"I can't believe Christmas is already behind us," Mum said. "What a different kind of celebration we had this year." The night before had been Twelfth Night, so it was time to take down the decorations. She handed Beryl another ornament to wrap and place in the storage box.

"I know. Who would've thought a year ago what changes there would be?" Beryl didn't want to mention the missing people—Dad, James, and even Elinor's husband.

"Elinor fit right in. I'm glad we were able to have her here."

"And it seems Nancy's Brownie unit has adopted her as their mascot. Since they like pixies, Elinor reminds them of one," Beryl said. "Nancy and her friends have been so enamored of the Brownies ever since Princess Margaret became one. Now they feel even more special that they have their own mascot."

"Well, she certainly has a way of livening things up. I hope I have as much spunk when I'm ninety years old like her."

"Don't we all?" Beryl glanced outside. "It's snowing."

Mum turned to look. "So it is. I've always thought it's lovely to look at."

"I agree, but it's no fun to drive in. And once it turns to slush, it's not pretty at all."

Elinor came downstairs and looked out at the snow. She clasped her hands together. "Oh, I just love snow!"

Spitfire wove between the legs of each woman, meowing.

"I bet he's never seen snow before," Beryl said. "Let's see what he does."

She donned her coat, hat, and gloves and carried the kitten to the back door, then went outside with him and set him down. The kitten's head jerked this way and that, watching the snowflakes fall. Next he tried to catch them, leaping and bouncing after them. Beryl laughed and glanced at the back door where Mum and Elinor stood inside watching and laughing too. Beryl allowed the kitten to frolic in the snow with his newfound toy for a while until she got too cold, and then she picked him up and went back inside. She grabbed a towel and dried the cold, wet kitten off before placing him back on the floor.

"Did you enjoy yourself, Minnie?" Elinor asked. "You need some warm milk now."

"And I need some hot tea!" Beryl removed her outer garments and hung them up. Her mind flashed to Kenneth and James. Were they cold? Did they have a chance to get hot tea? Would they try to escape in this kind of weather?

Mum poured the hot tea as she warmed up the kitten's milk. "How is Veronica doing since Rodney left?"

Beryl shook her head as she sat down at the table and lifted her cup with both hands, embracing the warmth. "She's in a state. Rodney is shipping out this week and can't tell her where he's going. Again. When I talked to her this morning, she was so upset she'd developed a case of nervous stomach."

"Now that she's a navy wife, she'll worry about him all the time, I suppose," Mum said.

"That feeling isn't restricted to wives of men in the navy. It applies to anyone who has people in the military—army and air force too."

"That's right. We just have to keep them in our prayers every day."

———————— ≈ ————————

Three weeks later, Beryl composed another letter to Kenneth and James. She had been nervous ever since she found out they had received the escape kit. Should she send separate letters, one to James and one to Kenneth? Even though he had sent her one, she felt uncertain about sending one to him only. However, she'd love to get another letter from him. Meanwhile, she wrote to them both once a week, never knowing when or if they'd receive the letters. She filled them with mundane news about things at home. Mum said they'd appreciate hearing from home, no matter how boring the communication seemed to Beryl. She didn't want to talk too much about the game in case some censor thought she was revealing too much. Did the censors even know about it? She had no idea who the censors were—MI5 possibly?

At work the buzz was all about the Americans coming to England. The first group of thirty thousand men had arrived in Ireland, and more were coming. Their transit across the Atlantic was not without danger. Hitler had stepped up the U-boat attacks since the United States and Germany had declared war on each other, so ships carrying troops to England had to maneuver past the U-boats and try not to get hit.

Americans had been sent to Ireland where they would be staged before going on to other parts of Europe to join the fight. The Irish had welcomed them with open arms, although there were a few who complained about them. Beryl chalked the negative talk up to jealousy because the Irish women were supposedly smitten with so many young men arriving in their country. Added to that attraction was the fact that the Americans had not suffered as the British Isles had and arrived with plenty of money and food to go around.

"And they have chewing gum!" Margaret said. "My cousin Bridget said the Americans could get anything they want, so why not hang out with them?"

"I'd think the Irish men would be happy to see them too, chewing gum or not," Beryl said.

"Indeed. That's what I said. We need more men to fight for our side. But Bridget said it was quite common for fistfights to break out when the Yanks went to town and ran into a local, especially one that's had his fill of whiskey."

"Well, I'd be happy to welcome the Americans if they were in our area," Beryl said, referring to one American in particular that Margaret didn't know about.

She had just returned home from work when the phone rang. She picked up the receiver. "Hello?"

"Beryl, it's Veronica! I need to see you. I'll be right over." The phone disconnected, and Beryl stood holding the receiver and staring at it.

"Beryl? Who was that?" Mum said from the sitting room.

"Veronica."

"That was a short call. What does she want?"

"She said she needed to come over but didn't say why. I suppose she's on her way."

"How strange. I wonder if something happened to Rodney."

"She didn't sound upset, so I don't know."

Shortly afterward, Veronica appeared at the door. Beryl opened it, and her friend rushed in.

Beryl followed her to the sitting room.

"Good! You're all here!" Veronica scanned the women's faces.

"What is it, Veronica?" Mum asked.

"Do you remember me telling you how sick I felt after Rodney left?"

Beryl nodded.

"Well, I wasn't sick. I'm expecting!"

"Oh my." Beryl hugged her friend. "What wonderful news!"

"I'm tickled to bits!" Mum said, setting her knitting aside to get up and hug Veronica.

Elinor looked from one to the other as if trying to comprehend.

"Veronica's going to have a baby, Elinor! Isn't that grand?"

A smile crept across Elinor's face, and she pushed herself off the couch to go to Veronica, where she took Veronica's hands in hers. "What a blessing. I can't wait to meet your little one. I'm sure you'll have a baby as beautiful as you are."

"Does Rodney know yet?" Beryl asked.

The light in Veronica's face dimmed.

"No. I sent him a letter because I couldn't tell him in person."

"Well, I know he'll be thrilled," Mum said. "And anxious to meet his child."

"I hope he'll be here when the baby comes."

# ᴲ CHAPTER 34 ᴲ

*Stalag Luft I, Barth, Germany*
*February 1942*

The camp was crowded now that more prisoners had been captured. The newest barrack was almost full, and soon the camp would run out of room for new prisoners. Another American had been captured, bringing word of what was actually going on outside their camp. Gary Knight was one of the newer recruits in the Eagle Squadron and had been shot down flying over Germany. The tall, lanky Texan had a country drawl and an easygoing nature.

"Yep, we've got about sixty thousand in Ireland and Scotland now. We're working on a big invasion, but I don't know when it will happen yet. They didn't tell me." He grinned. "These guys better look out."

"They don't act worried yet," Kenneth said.

"Ole Hitler is still trying to get into Russia. He's getting quite a fight over there."

"I think the guards here are scared to death they'll get sent to the Russian front."

"Minding their p's and q's, are they?" Gary said, hands on his hips. "Just tell them they're going to lose anyway, so they might as well make friends with us."

"We've tried, but meanwhile, the other threat is more immediate."

"Just wait until the Americans start bombing Germany. That'll get their minds off Russia."

"So, when are we going to bust out of this place?" Gary said, looking from one man to another.

The other guys gestured to Gary to be quiet. "Feel like going for a walk? We'd like you to meet someone." Kenneth motioned for Gary to follow, grabbing his coat and hat and putting on the knit scarf and mittens Mrs. Clarke had made.

"Nice mittens you got there, Bordelon. Where did you get those?"

Kenneth glanced at James who had similar attire. "A mutual friend sent them."

Once they found Wilson, they introduced him to Gary, and the two went walking together.

"Wonder what he's good at?" James asked.

"Besides talking? My guess is roping steers. He strikes me as a cowboy."

The name stuck, and Gary became Cowboy, a name he was proud to wear. Gary had heard about the Monopoly game.

"They told us about them before we flew. We were supposed to look for the specially marked games, use the information, then dispose of the items so the Germans couldn't find them."

"So these must've been created after we became prisoners," Kenneth said.

"Yep, they started making them last year sometime. I found out about them back in September."

"We were here then. No wonder Beryl wanted to let us know," Kenneth said to James.

A few days later, Wilson met with the men in small groups inside the theater.

"Habersham got some information that'll affect us. The Germans plan to move us to another prison camp."

"Another camp? Why? Because we're crowded now? Why not just move some of us or build more barracks?" Questions rang out from the group.

"I don't know exactly, but the plans are to move all of us."

"Do we know when?" Angus asked.

"April. So we must move our plans to March. Once we're somewhere else, we'll have to start all over again. I was hoping to wait until it was warmer and there'd be no snow, but we have to move sooner now."

March. Next month. Were they ready? Would the tunnels be ready? Good thing they'd gotten the Monopoly game with the map in time to make copies beforehand.

Work sped up as everyone worked longer hours to get ready for the escape. Jude had progressed the farthest, so Wilson had the diggers focus on that tunnel. They still had a problem disposing of sand, so Wilson decided to put it down one of the other tunnels. He appointed Jack as the dispersal tunnel, so now the men in charge of that job had to go from one tunnel to the next to get rid of the sand. Worried that Gooseneck might catch on to them and the constant stream of traffic, he had the men walk in separate directions and take roundabout routes between the two barracks.

All was going along well until one of the men in the dispersal unit tripped and fell in the yard, causing the sand to fall out of his clothes and onto the snow. The nearest ferret saw it and shouted. Soon Gooseneck came running and confronted the poor kriegie.

"You are digging a tunnel! Where is it?"

The kriegie shrugged his shoulders. "I don't know what you're talking about."

He was dragged off to the main headquarters and interrogated but never revealed any information. Of course, he ended up in the cooler, and Wilson made work on the tunnels stop until he could think of another way to dispose of the sand. Meanwhile, Gooseneck brought in two dozen guards to search for the tunnel, wreaking havoc and interfering with the work.

All the documents, maps, and clothes were hidden in walls while the prisoners waited and watched, hoping nothing would be discovered.

"Let's pray they don't find anything," James said, holding his Bible.

If ever Kenneth thought about praying, this might be the time, but God was surely too busy to worry about something so unimportant compared to all the big problems in the world. Still, they were so close to tasting freedom. He just hoped James' prayers worked. After standing outside in the cold for two hours, they were finally allowed to go back in. As usual, the searchers had made a mess, dumping all their belongings out into the middle of the floor. Even the pieces of the Monopoly game had been scattered and thrown up on the pile in the middle of their room.

Kenneth choked back a curse word when he saw the game's condition. They had tried to save all the important parts, not knowing they were supposed to dispose of them until Cowboy told them. In his pocket, he carried the race car token, and in James' pocket was the top hat token. The money and the copied maps were still safe behind the wall. *Well, thank You, God, if You had anything to do with this.*

A thought struck him. Where was the original map? It wasn't with the copies.

"James, I think they found the silk map. I can't find it."

James smiled and opened his Bible. Tucked between the pages was the silk map. "I found it on the floor before we left the room and had already put things away. It's so light, it must've flown off the other papers and you didn't notice in your hurry."

Kenneth blew out a heavy sigh. "Looks like that book is good for something after all."

"It's good for a lot of things, Kenneth. You should look at it some-time. You'd be amazed at what's hidden in it."

James was speaking in code, no doubt, but Kenneth didn't care to question his meaning. To him what was most important was that they hadn't lost anything of significance, at least not in his room. Had Angus been as successful? His grin when he walked into the room later answered his question.

"They never looked in the theater, thank God," he said.

After a couple of days of doing nothing, the prisoners got busy again, this time trying to make up for the time they lost due to the searches and suspicions of Gooseneck. Kenneth couldn't wait to be rid of the guy.

———— ≈ ————

The Ides of March arrived, and the tunnel now reached beyond the fence. One of the diggers had gone the distance and tunneled up outside the line just beyond the tree line. The sky was overcast, which would help hide their movement, and no new snow had fallen in a couple of days. Twenty men were selected to leave in the first shift, and then, after a pause, ten more would leave. They all had memorized the map and locations of the safe houses. Wilson had decided which route each pair would take so they wouldn't all go the same way. Kenneth and James would be together, and the responsibility for James' welfare rested heavily on Kenneth's shoulders. They had to make it—together, or Beryl would never forgive him. Hopefully James' arm was strong enough now to carry his body weight if he had to lift himself up or over something.

Each man had a story and ID papers to back the story up. Kenneth and James were supposed to go to the coast and get onboard a Swedish ship and seek amnesty once in the neutral county of Sweden. However, if they were stopped beforehand, their disguises were as French contractors who had been sent to Germany to work, and they carried work papers to prove it. They also each had some French francs and transportation passes. James had tried to help Kenneth practice his French, but since they were staying together, Kenneth planned on letting James do most of the talking since he was so fluent in the language.

Wilson watched the time, and the men lined up to go down the tunnel. Angus offered to go first. He was brave to expose himself so long and wait until the last man was out before he left himself. Once he was out, he would tie a rope around a tree that reached back to the tunnel. He would signal the others behind him when to come and when to stop if it wasn't safe outside by tugging on the rope. The escapees would have to exit the tunnel when the searchlights on the compound were aimed farthest away. They also had to watch out for the German shepherd dog that Gooseneck walked around the compound a couple of times each night.

To help further distract the goons, there would be a party on the opposite side of the compound from the place where they would exit. The party would get kind of rowdy and perhaps even stage a fake fight. They had thought of everything. Hadn't they?

Kenneth fought his nerves and muttered jokes to break the tension. In reality he hadn't been so nervous since before his first flight in the Spitfire. That had gone well, and he hoped this would too.

"Let's pray for success," James said. Wilson heard him and nodded. "Good idea."

All the men in line silenced, and most bowed their heads as James offered a prayer for safety and protection. He also asked for God's guidance and for the escape to go smoothly, without any obstacles. When James said, "Amen," a chorus of the word echoed down the line.

Slowly each man dropped into the hole in the floor and began scooting on his belly along the length of the tunnel to the end where they had to climb up. Kenneth tapped his shirt pocket, feeling the race car underneath, then dropped down the hole, fighting claustrophobia since he'd never been in such a closed space for so long. It was like a tomb or the catacombs in Rome, a place of death. *Why are you thinking such dire thoughts, man?* He shoved those thoughts away. Just as he was about to reach the ladder, the man in front of him stopped.

"What's going on?" he whispered to the man in front of him.

"Either the dog or the searchlight, I hope."

The rope alongside the ladder jerked, giving the sign to go.

"Wish me luck," the guy said, following his partner out.

Next it was Kenneth's turn. He climbed up the ladder and placed his hand on the rope so he could feel its tug. Then he whispered down to James below him. "We're almost home."

If only that were true. The rope tugged twice, the signal to stay put. So he did. And he waited.

# ⧨CHAPTER 35⧨

*Leeds, England*
*March 1942*

Beryl ducked inside the house and took off her wet raincoat. It had rained for four straight days, made even more miserable by cold temperatures.

She rubbed her arms, shivering. "When is it going to get warmer?" she said as Mum greeted her with a cup of hot tea.

"Not for another month, at least." She motioned toward the fireplace in the sitting room. "Go in there and warm yourself up."

Beryl didn't need an invitation to move her body in front of the warm fire. "Thank God, we have firewood. It would be miserably cold in here without the fire."

"Yes, there's always something to be thankful for if you look for it," Mum said.

"You're right, and another thing is that we haven't had any bombings for some time. I don't know if the Germans have given up on us or if it's the foul weather keeping them away."

"Whatever the reason, I'm thankful for it. As I'm sure London is as well. This time last year, they were in the middle of the Blitz."

"Do you think the American presence in the UK has had an effect on the Germans?" Mum settled back into her knitting chair.

"My granddaughter is American," Elinor said, surprisingly interjecting a comment into the conversation. Beryl didn't know if they had developed a habit of speaking louder for the woman or if the woman's hearing was better. Nevertheless, the remark was unexpected.

Beryl and Mum focused on the older woman sitting with Spitfire on her lap.

"She was born there, isn't that right?" Mum asked.

"Yes, and what did you say her name was?" Beryl tried a tactic she hadn't used before to get information. The fact was, Elinor had never mentioned her granddaughter's name.

"Helen's daughter was named Judith. Pretty little thing she was."

"So, Judith still lives in the States. Do you know which state?"

"No, I'm not sure."

Beryl didn't want this moment of clarity to escape Elinor, so she continued her questions.

"Did Judith get married?"

"Oh yes, I have a photo. . ." Her voice trailed off as she looked around her.

A memory sparked in Beryl's mind. She had found a photo at Elinor's house after it had been bombed, but she'd forgotten about it. Where had she put it? On top of her dresser!

"Wait a minute. I might have that photo." Beryl ran upstairs and found the photo. Sure enough, it was a man and woman holding a baby with a young boy beside them. Until now she thought the woman was Elinor. The photo was scratched from the broken glass, and she hadn't shown it to Elinor before because she was afraid it might be a sad reminder of her loss. Beryl gently wiped the photo with the edge of her skirt, then hurried back downstairs with it and handed it to Elinor. "Is this the photo you mean?"

Elinor scrutinized it. "Yes, that's Judith and her husband and their children. What happened to the frame?"

"It got broken, I'm afraid. I'll get you a new one." Beryl felt remiss for not already doing that. She glanced at her Mum. "Do you remember her husband's name? Or the names of her children, your great-grandsons?"

Beryl shook her head. "No, I can't remember now." She continued to stare at the photo.

"I wonder how old your grandsons are now." Beryl calculated that her granddaughter must be in her mid-forties by now, perhaps the age of her own mother.

Elinor's face clouded with confusion, and Beryl noticed how she tired with so much questioning, so she decided not to press the matter anymore. At least she knew more now than she did before. She reached for the photo. "Let me take that so I can remember to get a frame for it."

Elinor slowly relinquished the picture. Beryl studied it again, then turned it over. There was a date on the back—Christmas 1920. Some words were written below the date: " 'Judith, Robert, and. . .' I can't make out the others." The words were illegible due to a scratch on the back of the photo. So a few pieces of the puzzle were coming together. If only she had a last name and a location where she could find these people.

"Robert was her husband's name. I think they named a child after him too, Robert Junior. I don't know what the other one's name was."

Another piece of the puzzle. When would the rest be discovered, if ever?

"Speaking of babies," Mum said, breaking the tension, "how is Veronica feeling?"

"She's much better now, besides being hungry and sleepy all the time."

Mum chuckled. "Oh, I remember those days. I couldn't eat enough or sleep enough, but it's a good thing she's got the morning sickness behind her."

"Mum, I want to do something special for her. Can we throw her a baby party?"

"Of course we can, but we still have months for that. She's due in September?"

"Yes, September 5, she thinks."

"So, in the meantime, we can make her layette. I'm hoping to find some soft, pretty yarn."

"I wish I knew what I could make her, since I can't knit." Beryl had never mastered the hobby, although Mum had tried to teach her for years. Mum said she didn't have enough patience, which was probably true.

"Right now just being her friend is enough." Mum studied the yarn in her hands.

"I don't think they called the child Robert. I think he had a second name."

Beryl looked at Elinor. She was figuring things out.

"And Robert's last name was?"

Elinor shook her head. "Something strange, not a British name. Seems like it was a name that was more popular where he was from."

"Another country?"

"No, no, another US state."

Maybe she could remember the region. "Perhaps they lived in the northeast, near New York City?"

"No, not there."

"Out west—California perhaps? Or Texas?" Maybe the name was Hispanic.

"No, not there either. Let me see that picture again." Elinor reached for the photo. "Judith used to send me letters, but I haven't gotten any for a long time."

"Do you know how long it has been?" What did Elinor consider a long time?

Elinor sighed and closed her eyes. Mum and Beryl exchanged glances, agreeing silently that they had asked enough questions for now. If only they could get in touch with Judith.

# ≡CHAPTER 36≡

*Stalag Luft I, Barth, Germany*
*March 1942*

It was an eternity before the rope jerked again. "We're back in business, James. Let's go."

Kenneth climbed out of the tunnel and crawled across the ground to the tree, holding his breath to keep from making any noise. He slipped alongside Angus behind the tree. "What was the problem?" he whispered.

Angus put his finger in front of his mouth to signal silence, then pointed toward the compound. Gooseneck walked along the perimeter of the yard with his German shepherd beside him. They had apparently just passed the area nearest the escapees and were going the opposite direction now. Kenneth nodded in understanding. Angus tugged the rope, and soon James was next to them.

"Wait just a minute," Angus whispered. When the goon box lights turned away from them more, he said, "Okay. Go!"

Kenneth clasped him on the shoulder to say thank you, goodbye, and good luck, holding back any more conversation but wanting to convey it all. Would he ever see Angus again? He hoped his fellow kriegie got away safely.

He and James ran through the dark forest as quietly as they could. When the moonlight reached through the trees, he took out his compass and checked to make sure they were heading in the right direction. He nodded to James and pointed, and they adjusted their course. They ran as fast as they could, only taking brief rests to catch their breath. Once the light of dawn revealed their surroundings, Kenneth took out the map and checked their destination.

"We should try to catch some sleep before we go any further. I think we could hide over there." Kenneth pointed to a small hut that housed a goat.

"Do you think the goat would mind?" James asked.

"He looks friendly enough." They slipped over the fence where the hut was, the goat standing at its entrance. "Excuse me, please," Kenneth said as he stooped to crawl into the hut. James followed suit as the goat stared at them, letting out a soft "baaa."

The two of them sat with their knees bent facing each other.

"It stinks in here," Kenneth said.

"I agree," James said with a wry smile. "But the goat won't mind."

They sat that way awhile and tried to take turns sleeping, but it was no use.

"I can't sleep," Kenneth said. "I'm too hyped up."

"Me too. I even tried counting sheep, but it didn't work."

"Maybe you should count goats instead."

"I doubt anything will work right now."

"You're right. We'd better keep going," Kenneth said.

"Do you think they've noticed our absence yet?" James said.

Kenneth shrugged. "I don't know, but as soon as they do, they'll be swarming all over the place."

"Then let's get moving again," James said and crawled out the door.

Kenneth followed him, half-afraid they'd be facing a pistol or an angry farmer when they climbed out. But much to his delight, no one was in sight. He and James climbed back over the fence and took off running again, hiding behind trees or anything else when they heard noise. For two days, traveling mostly at night to avoid being seen, they continued, staying away from roads. They finally got some sleep the second day in the cover of some woods. At dusk during Kenneth's watch, he heard vehicles approaching. He strained his ears to detect where the vehicles were and if they were heading toward them or away. He shook James awake and gestured for him to be quiet.

James nodded, then lay on his stomach beside Kenneth as they peeked through the trees. Four Nazi motorcycles and a car passed by, heading the direction they needed to go.

"I think they miss us now," Kenneth said.

"I think you're right," James said, watching the vehicles go down the road.

"Things could get dicey."

James gave a thumbs-up. "We're ready."

"Then let's go. We can't stop now."

The two of them scanned the horizon before leaving their hiding place and resuming their trek, ducking for cover whenever they heard or saw anything. Several hours later, they saw moonlight glistening off the deep blue water of the Baltic Sea.

"That, my friend, is freedom," Kenneth said.

James smiled. "I'm happy to see it."

They continued until they reached the last edge of tree cover, then paused to survey the area. Dropping to their bellies, they watched the shoreline crawling with Nazis. There was no way they could slip onboard a ship without being seen.

"I believe they've been expecting us," Kenneth said.

"No doubt. What do we do now?"

"We'll have to abandon this plan."

"But where do we go from here?"

"Let's move away from here first, in case they look this direction." He and James scooted backward until they could stand without being seen and moved to the tree line. Kenneth took out the map and opened it. "We need to go west toward the Netherlands."

"That's a long way from here," James said, looking at the map.

"True, but the route that goes south is even farther, and more populated."

"Too bad we can't get to Sweden. That's the closest route to a safe country."

"Which is why the Germans are watching the coast. If we're lucky, we'll get to a safe house on the way," Kenneth said, pointing to the map. "Come on, let's get out of here." He paused. "We have to destroy this map you know. If it got into the Nazi's hands, it would put everyone on our side in danger. We should have it memorized by now anyway."

James nodded, and the two of them studied the map one more time. Then Kenneth tore the map into as many pieces as possible, dug a hole and buried the pieces. He then covered the place with leaves.

Staring at the spot, he said, "I sure hated to do that."

"Thank God, we had it in the first place," James added.

*Thank Beryl,* was more like it in Kenneth's mind.

For the next three days, the two traveled west, mostly at night, using only the compass and their memory as their guides. Kenneth had never been hungrier, even in the POW camp, so they stole what they could find along the way. At one farm, they even took some of the potato peelings that had been thrown out to the pigs. "Reminds me of the story of the prodigal son," James said as they ran off with their stolen food.

" 'Fraid I'm not familiar with that story," Kenneth said, nor did he want to be. But later that night, James told him about it. The story made him uncomfortable, even though he had not taken his father's money and squandered it on wild living. He'd just gone away.

They had several close calls with the Germans who were scouring the countryside looking for escapees. Once they had to jump into a ditch when they heard vehicles coming down the road. They listened and waited for the vehicles to pass, but they stopped a mere ten feet from where the men lay hiding under some bushes that ran alongside the ditch. The Nazis were so close that Kenneth and James could hear their conversations. A couple of the soldiers got out to relieve themselves by the side of the road.

Kenneth held his breath as his pulse pounded, afraid they'd be spotted. But soon the men got back into the vehicles and drove away. Kenneth was satisfied the Germans had gone far enough, they came out from under the bush and looked around.

"Thank God for protecting us," James said. "I was praying with all my might."

It was nice to have a guy with him who apparently had God's favor, if that was the reason for their good luck.

They continued to cross the country, fighting the March cold and occasional snow until they saw a farmhouse with smoke curling from the chimney and a small barn nearby.

"I think that might be a safe house. Do you remember one on the map in this area?" Kenneth said.

"I'm not sure, but it seems like we should be finding one pretty soon," James said. "But what if it's not a safe house?"

"That barn looks pretty inviting, and I'm cold and dead-tired. Right now, I'm willing to take my chances to have a place to rest."

The barn was built on an embankment so that the barn door was around the back and below the level of the front. They sneaked along the stone side of the barn to the rear, sliding the bolt across the opening as quietly as possible. Once inside, the scent of manure hit them as they entered and crept past a cow and two goats, their eyes following them. Kenneth put his finger to his lips as he looked at the animals and said, "Shhh." Finding the ladder to the loft, he and James climbed up and collapsed in the hay, a welcome place to rest their aching legs.

Kenneth woke with a start at the sound of a creaking door hinge. He sat up, listening. Had they been caught?

"*Wer ist da?*" a woman's voice called out.

James sat up, glancing at Kenneth.

"Wer ist da?" the voice repeated, and Kenneth understood the German words for "Who is there?"

The two leaned over the edge of the loft and looked down. Below stood an attractive woman in a typical German dirndl with her black hair covered by a headscarf.

"*Guten tag,*" James said, smiling as if it was perfectly normal for him to be sitting in a hayloft and greeting someone.

The woman put her hands on her hips and cocked her head to the side.

James glanced at Kenneth and muttered under his breath. "Smile. She has an accent that's not German. I think she's French. *Êtes-vous français?*" James said, looking back at the woman.

"*Oui!*" she said, then unleashed a torrent of French that left Kenneth dazed.

James responded in French, telling her who they were.

"She says to come on down; she will not get us in trouble," James said, then began to climb down the ladder.

Kenneth shrugged, then followed him down. The woman continued talking in French, excited to find someone who understood her language. She motioned for them to follow her to the cottage, which they did. Kenneth glanced around. When would the Nazis show up?

Once inside, the woman, whose name was Joelle, told James she was kidnapped from her region in France when the Germans took it over and became the housewife of a German soldier. When she learned that he had been killed in the fighting, she'd turned her home into a safe house, hoping to return to her home in France someday. Joelle fed them a hot meal of hearty potato soup flavored with onion and garlic plus thick bread with real butter. Kenneth's taste buds celebrated the good food, and he ate more than his stomach was accustomed to. Afterward, he was too full to move, so Joelle told them to rest in the house until they felt well enough to leave.

Kenneth marveled at her courage and hospitality and wished he could help her, but she said she believed God would not let Hitler win, and someday she'd be able to get back to France. Wanting the Allies to win, she'd help any way she could. After resting at the cottage for a day and night, Kenneth told James it was time to leave.

"I know. I told her this morning."

Joelle found some of her husband's clothes that they could wear, which were most appreciated after the wear and tear they'd done to the ones they'd been traveling in since they escaped. She also gave them each a loaf of bread wrapped in a cloth and some cheese.

"Thank you," Kenneth said with heartfelt appreciation. *"Merci."*

She smiled and kissed him on the cheek, lighting his cheeks on fire.

"Merci," James said. *"Tu es un don de Dieu."*

Joelle kissed him on the cheek also, then stepped back and pulled a pistol from her apron.

Kenneth's eyes widened and his heart froze. Was this a cruel trick?

But she handed the gun to James, and in a soft, soothing voice said, *"Pour toi. Dieu va avec toi."*

He stuck the gun in his waistband, then took both her hands in his and kissed the back of them. "Merci."

She smiled and withdrew her hands, then stepped outside and pointed the way they should go to avoid running into anyone. As they left, she stood in the doorway and waved goodbye.

Kenneth turned to James as they crossed the field. "She scared the stew out of me when she pulled that gun out. I'm glad you could speak French so well. What did she say to you?"

She said, "This is for you. God go with you."

"What did you tell her?"

"I told her she was a gift from God. She was, Kenneth. Don't you agree?"

He couldn't deny the favorable turn of events they'd had. Maybe God did have something to do with it.

# ⫤ CHAPTER 37 ⫤

*Leeds, England*
*April 1942*

Beryl scanned the letter in her hand. "I'll be seeing you soon. Will you give me a welcome home kiss when I get there?"

Her face heated at the thought of kissing Kenneth, and she yearned to fulfill the desire his comment created. Her imagination ran wild at the image in her mind of being enveloped in his arms the way Rodney had held Veronica the night they got married. How had she grown so fond of him when he was so far away? It had now been over three years since she'd last seen him, but instead of feeling farther away, she felt closer.

But what did he mean by "soon"? Had they escaped? Were they safe? There was no way to know. She glanced at the date on the letter. March 5, a month ago. The next letter would let her know if they were still in the prison. Much as she wanted to hear from him, not receiving a letter from the prison camp would be a good sign. Wouldn't it?

Meanwhile, she occupied her time preparing for Veronica's baby. Veronica's parents were providing the bassinet and stocking up on other baby essentials like bottles and diapers. The christening gown would be the same one Veronica and Nancy wore.

Mum and Mrs. Findlay were knitting baby sweaters, caps, and booties. Even Elinor was working on a baby quilt with pieces of fabric Mum found at the Red Cross store. Beryl was at a loss for what to do for her friend.

What did babies like? Maybe there was something they had that would prompt her for an idea. She climbed up into the attic to look at the old toys she and James had played with when they were small. In one dusty corner, she found a box of wooden toys her father had made for them. Tears filled her eyes as memories of those times came to her, times when her big brother's imagination prompted games that she participated in. Maybe one day these toys would be played with by her own children. Or James' children. Because he would come home and marry and have a normal life, she was sure. But it would be some time before any babies played with these or any like them if she could get some new ones.

In the bottom of the box were a few books. She pulled them out and smiled at her old Beatrix Potter books. She'd loved those characters of Peter Rabbit, Jemima Puddle Duck, and Jeremy Fisher Frog. Every child should have books like these, something to keep forever.

Like a shooting star, an idea raced through her mind. She'd make a keepsake book for the baby. Something with pictures from the Beatrix Potter books with pages where Veronica could fill in important information about the baby. Information about the baby's characteristics—weight, length, eye color, hair color. A page for the christening, a page for firsts, like first tooth, first step, first word. She grabbed her books and hurried downstairs, eager to begin working on Veronica's baby book.

"That's a marvelous idea!" Mum said when Beryl shared it. "Veronica will so appreciate it, and it is truly a book she will treasure more and more as time wears on. I wish I had one for you and James."

"I'm so glad I finally thought of something," Beryl said. "I can't wait to start collecting things for it."

"If you knew if the baby was going to be a boy or girl, you could know what colors to use," Mum said.

"I don't think it matters. Baby things are universal, and the pictures in the Beatrix Potter books are happy colors—yellow, red, and blue."

"Helen liked blue. I tried to dress her in pink, but she liked blue better," Elinor said.

How long ago was that memory? And yet Elinor still remembered. Unfortunately, there was a lot of distance between that memory and more recent ones.

Beryl thought about the picture Elinor had, all she had of her family's past. Wouldn't it be nice if she had more? If she had some way to connect to her family now?

The doorbell rang, and Beryl went to answer it. The mail carrier stood outside.

"Miss Clarke? Does a Mrs. Elinor Dowd live here?"

"Yes, why?"

"We received this letter at the post office a while back and didn't know where to deliver it, seeing as how the Dowd home was demolished in the bombing. But someone recently said they heard Mrs. Dowd was living with you."

"Yes, she's been here for several months, so all her mail should come here. I've been inquiring at the post office ever since, but no mail had come for her."

"Well, here's something. It's postmarked from the United States," he said, handing her the letter.

Her breath caught. The return address was from Mrs. Judith Bordelon from Louisiana.

# ⟩CHAPTER 38⟨

*Somewhere in Germany*
*April 1942*

Kenneth and James spotted a small town in the valley ahead. A man on a bicycle was pedaling toward it.

"Should we go there or go around it?" James asked.

"I don't know about you, but I'm pretty tired of walking. Why don't we borrow a couple of bikes?" Kenneth said, pointing to the man.

"Isn't that risky? I don't want to raise an alarm."

"Well, let's just venture close and see. Just act natural. We don't look like prisoners, do we?"

James looked them over. "I suppose not."

They adapted a more casual walk and sauntered into town. Joelle had even given them some money to use if they needed to. The town was only a couple of streets long, and most of the people were at the market, with a few older men sitting at tables and drinking from steins. Kenneth and James kept their caps pulled low and ordered a couple of drinks from the tavern, sitting outside to watch the activity. They drank their beer pretty quickly since they were very thirsty, then stood and walked away.

Around the side of the tavern were several bicycles. The men at the other tables seemed to be in no hurry to leave, so Kenneth and James each nonchalantly selected a bike, climbed on it, and rode out of town. Once they were out, they looked over their shoulders to see if anyone was watching or chasing, but no one was.

"That was easy," Kenneth said.

"Almost too easy," James said, looking back at the town.

They rode on about five miles until they saw an airfield ahead. Kenneth pulled over and stopped. "This looks interesting."

"There doesn't seem to be much activity. In fact, I think all of the planes are damaged."

"Maybe. But I'd like a closer look," Kenneth said.

"What are you planning to do?" James asked.

"You know, I've always wanted to fly one of those."

"Those are German planes, Focke-Wulf 190s."

"Exactly."

"Kenneth, don't do something stupid."

"Come on, James. Remember we have a gun."

"Right. Just one."

Kenneth hopped back on the bike and pedaled up to one of the planes. He looked it over, then put the bike down and walked to another plane with James following. There were about twenty planes parked along the makeshift runway, all of them with some form of visible damage. Kenneth stopped at one that was bullet-ridden and climbed up on the wing to look inside.

"Full tank of gas."

"Kenneth, don't."

"I have to." He climbed into the cockpit. "James, this is our best way to get home."

"It's a one-seater."

"You know we can both fit. I'm the biggest, so you can sit in my lap and do the flying."

A man shouted at them in German and ran up to the plane. Kenneth's heart raced, and he and James exchanged fearful glances.

"He must be the mechanic. James, show him the pistol. Tell him we won't kill him if he'll just keep quiet and get out of the way."

James pulled out the gun, pointed it at the German and gave him the message. The man glanced at James, the gun, then Kenneth, who lifted his eyebrows in question. Nodding, the German raised his hands and backed away.

"All right, James, get in."

James shook his head. "No, Kenneth. I'll stay here and take my chances on the ground."

"James, come on, man. We've come so far! Please! What will I tell your family?"

James smiled. "It'll be all right. I'll pray we both make it home safely. Go on, and God be with you."

Kenneth knew his friend was serious and would not change his mind. So he gave him a thumbs-up, closed the canopy, opened the throttle full power, and went across the grass field to the runway. Once he got airborne and pulled the landing gear up, the stupidity of what he was doing hit him. He was flying a German airplane without a parachute. The plane had a swastika painted on the side, so his own people might shoot at him. His heart thumped against his chest as fear threatened to claim him. His hands were sweaty on the throttle and the stick as the full gravity of his predicament set in. Fortunately for him, the sky was overcast at about four thousand feet, so he pulled up to the bottom of the overcast so he wouldn't be a target. Flying low should keep him from being spotted by his own side as well.

He didn't know exactly where to go but figured if he kept heading west, he'd see the windmills of Holland. Although the country was still occupied, the Germans would think he was one of them. If only he could convince some sympathetic Dutch to help him evade the Germans whom they hated. While he kept his eyes on the sky and the distance, his mind pummeled him with accusations. Kenneth's gut clenched with regret. Why did he leave his friend behind? Was he so selfish that he put his life first? And if he survived, what kind of welcome would he get from Beryl once she found out he'd left her brother behind? The enormity of his act and love for his friend was more than he could handle alone.

*All right, God. I'm not experienced with praying, but here goes. I know I'm not as good as James is, but please listen to me anyway and save him. Please keep him from getting caught and bring him safely back home. Forgive me for being so selfish, and if You let me live through this, I promise I'll pay more attention to You. Thank You for all You've done for me despite my stubbornness. Amen.*

Did God hear him? Was that prayer good enough? Or was He laughing at Kenneth's meager attempt to pray? He'd find out pretty soon. When he saw the coastline coming into view, he checked the fuel gauge once again. It looked like he was down to less than ten liters, not enough to make it across the channel, even at its closest point to England. Seeing an open field ahead of him and with the engine coughing and sputtering on fumes, he managed to set the plane down. There went the landing gear. When the plane rolled to a stop, Kenneth released a deep breath. Safe. For now.

But as he opened the canopy and climbed out, he found the plane surrounded by a group of local farmers who didn't appear to be happy to see him, based on their frowns. Besides the fact that he landed in someone's field, they thought he was German for obvious reasons. He waved and told them in English that he had escaped from the Germans, hoping someone understood him. A man stepped slowly out of the crowd toward him. Kenneth scanned him for a weapon.

In broken English, the man said, "I have friends in the resistance. We must get you away from here quickly before the Germans come."

From there the man led him to his contacts with the resistance forces that would eventually get him back to England if nothing went wrong.

# ⯮CHAPTER 39⯬

*Leeds, England*
*April 1942*

Beryl was at her desk when Margaret rang through on her phone.

"Beryl, there's a man in the lobby who wants to see Mr. Watson."

"Does he have an appointment?" Beryl checked the calendar.

"No, he said he just wants a few minutes of his time to thank him, but he won't tell me what it's about."

"All right, I'll come see him."

Beryl walked into the lobby and saw a man with broad shoulders and rich, dark hair facing away from her. Something about him looked familiar.

"I'm Mr. Watson's secretary. Can I help you?" she said.

He turned around, and her heart leaped out of her chest. Warm hazel eyes met hers, catching her breath. Was she seeing things? No, it couldn't be.

"Kenneth?"

"Ah, you remember me. I'm looking for the courageous young lady who's responsible for me being here."

Beryl cut a glance at Margaret, whose face registered curiosity.

"I see. Perhaps I can help you with that."

"Actually, you already have. And I promised to give her something in return."

Kenneth stepped toward her and opened his fist to reveal the race car Monopoly piece.

She closed the gap between them and opened her hand as he dropped the piece into it.

"I wanted to give you something else too, if I may." He put his arms around her and leaned his face toward hers.

"You may." Her lips met his as they blended together in a kiss that took her breath away, a kiss even better than the one she had imagined.

When he finally lifted his head, he said, "Wow. Beryl, I've missed you so much."

She smiled up at him, her heart bursting with happiness. "I've been hoping and praying you would get to England. James told me the last time he saw you, you were flying a German plane."

"James is here? Thank God."

"Thank God indeed. I hear you two had quite the adventure."

"We did. Boy, I'm glad to hear James made it. I did a little praying myself."

She cocked her head and focused on his handsome face. "Yes, he's here. Been here about a week. He's at home now until he has to report back to duty."

"I can't wait to see him."

"Oh, and there's someone else you need to see."

"Someone else?"

"Yes. Your great-grandmother Elinor is waiting to meet you."

# ⚏ EPILOGUE ⚏

*United States*
*Present Day*

"So, Grandpa Ken's name was Robert Kenneth Bordelon. He gave you the race car, and the pearls came from Great-Great-Great-Grandma Elinor. Right?"

Beryl nodded. "That's right, Jillian."

"And now I know where Mom got her middle name, Elinor."

"Yes, Kenneth's great-grandma Elinor." Beryl reached up and unclasped her necklace. "And now the necklace is yours." She handed Jillian the necklace.

"Mine? Oh, Grandma Beryl. I can't take these."

"Oh yes you can. It's up to you now to carry on the tradition of strong women in this family."

Jillian studied the necklace in her palm, stroking the car with her opposite hand. Tears filled her eyes as she looked up at Beryl.

"I will, Grandma. With God's help, I will."

# AUTHOR'S NOTES

A work of historical fiction requires a vast amount of research, especially if an author wants to stay as true to actual events as possible. That has been my goal with every historical novel I've written, so I spend hundreds of hours reading and looking up facts about the people, the time, and the places of my books.

The story of the Monopoly escape kit is true—a story that was kept secret for about fifty years after the war. The Watson family who owned Waddingtons affirmed the story about MI5, the British espionage agency, who developed the idea and presented it to Victor Watson in 1941. Waddingtons was chosen because it had perfected creating maps on silk, maps that wouldn't get torn or destroyed when wet, and maps that could be hidden inside a game board. The project was so top secret that most of the employees at Waddingtons were not aware of it, to keep the ruse from being inadvertently discovered by the Germans. I had the opportunity to communicate directly with Amanda Latchmore, the great-granddaughter of Victor Watson, who graciously verified the story and gave me additional information from the book *The Waddingtons Story*, written by Victor Watson.

Thankfully, there are many records detailing the events of World War II and many survivors who wrote about their experiences. I have them all to thank, most of whom are no longer with us.

I owe much of my information to the late Jim Crooke, who was a member of my church and a prisoner of war in Stalag Luft I from 1944 to 1945. Jim was a navigator in a B-17 bomber that was shot down over Berlin, and thankfully, he lived to write a book about his experience.

Jim never tried to escape, that I know of; however, according to Wikipedia, over 140 tunnels were dug at Stalag Luft I, and some of the camp's more famous POWs were among those who were later transferred to Stalag Luft III and participated in the "great escape." There are quite a few books about POW escapes written by the escapees themselves. Although many escapes were attempted, few escapees made it all the way back to England. I have used some of the actual escapes for my fictional characters to perform. Some may seem unbelievable, yet they truly happened as POWs became extremely creative and daring.

I'd like to thank the Imperial War Museum in England for the cooperation and help they provided, including many personal stories of life in England during the war. Special thanks also goes to the Royal Air Force Museum who answered my questions about RAF prisoners and Geneva Convention rules. My research on Temple Newsam was aided by the friendly present curator Adam Toole. Alex Pearson of the West Yorkshire Archive Service provided me with links to photos of Leeds during the war, and the National Library of Scotland provided me with maps of the area at that time.

Very special thanks also goes to my British friend and avid reader Julia Wilson, who patiently withstood my questions about the home front in England during the war when her father was a little boy. Julia also suggested several reference books for me to read.

Of course I owe much thanks to my research assistant and flying expert—my dear, patient husband, who is a retired air force colonel. He advised me on flying operations and lingo, trying to explain technical jargon to my simple little mind.

Thank you to all my friends who have encouraged me to write this book, the most challenging book I've ever written. Thank you to my personal editor Sarah Tipton and also to editor JoAnne Simmons who cleaned up my mess. And thank you to Barbour Publishing and Rebecca Germany for giving me the opportunity to have the story published.

And above all, thanks to God, who guided me through this story and surprised me with plot twists and character development as He always does.

Love and blessings,
Marilyn

Award-winning author Marilyn Turk writes historical fiction flavored with suspense and romance. Marilyn also writes devotions for *Daily Guideposts*. She and her husband are lighthouse enthusiasts, have visited over one hundred lighthouses, and also served as volunteer lighthouse caretakers at Little River Light off the coast of Maine.

When not writing or visiting lighthouses, Marilyn enjoys boating, fishing, gardening, tennis, and playing with her grandkids and her golden retriever, Dolly.

She is a member of American Christian Fiction Writers; Faith, Hope and Love; Advanced Writers and Speakers Association; and Word Weavers International.

Connect with Marilyn at http://pathwayheart.com; https://twitter.com/MarilynTurk; https://www.facebook.com/MarilynTurkAuthor/; https://www.pinterest.com/bluewaterbayou/; Amazon: https://www.amazon.com/Marilyn-Turk/e/B017Y76L9A; Bookbub: https://www.bookbub.com/profile/marilyn-turk. Email her at marilynturkwriter@yahoo.com.